ON THE
BANKS *of*
the MAYYAZHI

ON THE BANKS *of* *the* MAYYAZHI

M. MUKUNDAN

Translated from the Malayalam by
GITA KRISHNANKUTTY

This English edition published in India by arrangement
with DC Books by Harper Perennial 2025
An imprint of HarperCollins Publishers
4th Floor, Tower A, Building No. 10, DLF Cyber City,
DLF Phase II, Gurugram, Haryana – 122002
www.harpercollins.co.in

2 4 6 8 10 9 7 5 3 1

Originally published in Malayalam by DC Books, Kottayam, Kerala, India 1974

Malayalam copyright © M. Mukundan 1974, 2025

English translation copyright © DC Books 2025

P-ISBN: 978-93-6569-279-2
E-ISBN: 978-93-6569-905-0

This is a work of fiction and all characters and incidents described in this book are the product of the author's imagination. Any resemblance to actual persons, living or dead, is entirely coincidental.

M. Mukundan asserts the moral right
to be identified as the author of this work.

All rights reserved. No part of this publication may be reproduced, stored in a retrieval system, or transmitted, in any form or by any means, electronic, mechanical, photocopying, recording or otherwise, without the prior permission of the publishers.

Typeset in 11.5/15 Adobe Garamond at
HarperCollins *Publishers* India

Printed and bound at
Nutech Print Services - India

This book is printed on FSC® certified paper
which ensures responsible forest management.

1

L ONG, LONG AGO, THAT IS, BEFORE DASAN WAS BORN.
Today's jostling Rue de la Rèsidence was a narrow, uneven little street. So were the Rue de la Prison and the Rue du Gouvernement. Neither the white wall of the pier that now separates the sea and the river from the shore nor the row of electric lamps that run along the wall, lighting up the water, were there in those days. Oil lamps burnt sullenly on the widely spaced lamp-posts in certain important streets like the Rue de l'Eglise and the Rue de la Rèsidence. They generally burned themselves out by midnight, plunging Mayyazhi into darkness.

However, in Big Sayiv's house on top of the hill, lanterns continued to blaze even after midnight. The sea lay at the back of the bungalow. On calm nights, the light from the lanterns fell in window shapes on the placid water. If you stood on the beach at sunrise, you could see Big Sayiv's elegant bungalow, surrounded by pine and eucalyptus trees, reflected in the sea.

No one except Big Sayiv had a car in those days. David Sayiv, Notary Leslie Sayiv, Mayor Chekku Moopar and Sergent-en-retraite

Kunhikannan drove horse carriages. They had their own horses, carriages and carriage drivers. Leslie Sayiv, who was part-French, had the finest horse of all. It was white and had a silvery mane.

Kurambi Amma would say, 'Leslie Sayiv's horse, now there's a horse for you! Watch it lift its head and speed away.'

Big Sayiv's car had arrived from France in a ship. The Mayyazhi folk had never seen a car before. A bus went through Mayyazhi twice a day, spitting fire and smoke. It went north to Thalassery in the mornings and south to Vadagara in the evenings. The only other motor vehicle they ever saw was a lorry that sometimes went to the Vadagara shandy and returned through the village.

'Kurambi Amma, aren't you coming to see the car?' Kunhichirutha called out from the road. Dressed in her finest clothes, she was on her way to the beach. A well-known courtesan of Mayyazhi, her fame had spread east to Pondicherry and north to Mangalore. David Sayiv was her most important admirer.

'Kunhichirutha, I want to see the car too.'

'Come with me then, Kurambi Amma.'

Kurambi Amma hesitated. She had been impatient to see the car ever since she knew it had landed. But she had to get permission from Damu, who had gone to work early in the morning. She was waiting anxiously for him.

'Come in for a minute. Damu will be back by the time I make you some tea.'

'Ayyo! I have to be at David Sayiv's by ten.'

'You go along then.'

Kunhichirutha left in a hurry, wafting behind her the heady scent of a perfume some white man had given her.

Disappointed, Kurambi Amma waited for Damu, dreaming of Big Sayiv's limousine.

Damu came back at noon.

'Damu, my son, can I go and see the car?'

'Wait until evening, Amma. All Mayyazhi is at the beach now, looking at it.'

That evening, after the crowd had thinned out, Damu took his mother to the beach. Kurambi Amma feasted her eyes on the car. She longed to touch it but it was guarded by armed French policemen.

Coming back, she called out even before she entered the house: 'Kowsu, it shines like a mirror! You can look into it and put on your pottu. What a pity you didn't see it!' Kowsu, Damu's wife, smiled.

Kurambi Amma sat down on the veranda and stretched her legs out. The car filled her thoughts. People were still on their way home from the beach. Unni Nair was among them.

He asked, 'Did you see it, Kurambi?'

'Yes, I did, Nair. How it shines!'

Kunjakkan, who limped along behind Unni Nair, said, 'There are better cars in France.' Kunjakkan was the municipal lamp-lighter. He lighted the lamps on the tar-covered wooden lamp-posts. He always carried a ladder on his shoulders and an oilcan in his hand.

Kurambi Amma paid him no attention. She could hear the clatter of horses' hooves in the distance. Leslie Sayiv's carriage turned the corner. Its wheels creaked as they spun and the bells on the horses' neck jangled.

The carriage slowed down in front of Kurambi Amma's thatched house. Leslie Sayiv peered out. 'Kurambi, will you give me a pinch of snuff?'

Kurambi Amma had a snuffbox made of ivory.

'Of course, Sayiv. You don't have to ask.'

Kurambi Amma stood up. All she wore was a mundu that came to her knees. She had big thakkas in her ears.

Leslie Sayiv got down from the carriage. He wore a hat and coat and trousers. Leslie Sayiv was the most fashionably dressed man in Mayyazhi in those days.

'Sit down, Sayiv.'

Kurambi wiped the bench clean with the tip of her mundu. Leslie sat down, took off his hat and held it on his lap.

'A tiny pinch will do, Kurambi.'

Kurambi Amma took the ivory snuffbox from her waist and held it out. Leslie Sayiv shook a pinch on to his palm. His palm was as red as blood. Which other person in Mayyazhi who was part-French had such a beautiful complexion? Leslie Sayiv looked like a real white man.

Leslie inserted the snuff in his nose. His face, red as gulmohar flowers, grew redder. He closed his eyes in ecstasy.

'Sayiv, I have a dream.'

'What is it, Kurambi?'

Leslie's eyes were still closed. He always closed them tight to savour the delight of the snuff.

'You must buy a car, Sayiv.'

'A car?'

'Yes, a car like Big Sayiv's. One that shines like a mirror, so you can see your face in it.'

'Why, Kurambi? Isn't my horse carriage enough?'

'How I wish you had a car!' Kurambi Amma's wish had been born the moment she saw Big Sayiv's car. She had been dreaming of Leslie Sayiv in a mirror-bright limousine ever since.

'Won't you buy one, Sayiv?'

More people owned ships in those days, they were easier to buy than cars. Leslie promised to think about it. Kurambi was happy. She moved closer to him and asked affectionately, 'Another pinch?'

'Just a tiny one.'

Kurambi shook another pinch onto his palm and he closed his eyes again.

'Sayiv, will our Vazhayil Koran get better?'

'He has cancer, Kurambi.'
'It can't be cured?'
'How, Kurambi?'
'Oh God! His wife and children will be homeless.'

Vazhayil Koran was a coolie. He had a wife and three very small children. The cancer had struck without warning.

Leslie Sayiv and Kurambi Amma talked of village matters until dusk, helping themselves now and then to a pinch of snuff.

'I'll leave now, Kurambi.' He stood up and put on his hat.
'You have to go?' Kurambi's voice was sad.
'You know I'll come back tomorrow.'

He turned his carriage towards Big Sayiv's bungalow. Drinks and dinner were served there every day. David Sayiv, Chekku Moopar and Sergent-en-retraite Kunhikannan were among those who were regularly invited. While they ate and drank inside the big bungalow illuminated by chandeliers, the carriage drivers dozed in the carriages lined up on the river bank and the horses chewed cud.

At midnight, the carriages followed one another down the Rue de la Rèsidence, carrying Big Sayiv's inebriated guests home.

Next day, and every evening, Leslie Sayiv went to Kurambi Amma's house. She waited for him at sunset, snuffbox in hand. He would stop the carriage on the road, peer out and call, 'Kurambi, will you give me a pinch of snuff?' And she would answer: 'Oh Sayiv, you don't have to ask.' On the days when Leslie Sayiv did not come she could not sleep at night.

LESLIE'S FATHER, CLEMENT SAYIV, was the first person Kurambi could recall who was part-French. He had a wine shop in the Rue de l'Eglise. He made a lot of money selling wine.

Clement Sayiv loved to sit in his wine shop boasting about his family connections. His greatest boast was that he was the descendant of Count Lally who had fought against the English at Pondicherry in the eighteenth century. He imagined the royal blood of France flowed through his veins.

He would sit by the glass-fronted cupboards filled with bottles of wine, twirl his moustache, puff out his chest and declare, 'Moi, descendant du Comte Lally!'

Most of the regulars who came to the wine shop were policemen. Drunk and senseless, they would listen to Clement Sayiv, and nod in the true spirit of an obedient audience. Seated in rows on the long benches, they would gulp down the wine, their red caps on the tables before them.

Clement Sayiv was happy when the policemen nodded in approval. He would order the servers: 'Pour them a little more wine.'

The policemen would raise their glasses and shout: 'A la santè du Comte Lally!'

To the health of Count Lally.

And Clement Sayiv would sit contentedly, his eyes half closed, behind the cash box.

Leslie was Clement Sayiv's eldest son. He was clever and handsome. Clement Sayiv had sent him to France when he was very young to pursue his studies there and the boy had done well.

'How can he not do well? He has to, with Count Lally's blood in his veins,' Clement Sayiv would say to the policemen, who would nod in assent.

The policemen usually stayed very late. They would totter away on unsteady legs, singing Clement Sayiv's praises in French, Tamil and Malayalam.

The Mayyazhi policemen were Tamils from Pondicherry. People had not yet begun to resent the French in those days. The Mayyazhi folk were as meek as lambs. They worked, ate and slept like tame animals. The policemen did not have much work to do. They drank and slept with women, praising the whites and part-whites impartially.

When Leslie Sayiv returned with a degree, Clement Sayiv was at the wharf to receive him. All the policemen who drank his wine were there as well.

Clement Sayiv made sure that wine flowed through the Mayyazhi, streets that day.

Leslie Sayiv began his career as a notary at the court of Mayyazhi. He soon made quite a bit of money and built a bungalow facing the sea and the river in the Rue de la Rèsidence.

The Mayyazhi girls fell in love with the handsome, wealthy, fashionable young man—some secretly and some openly.

'What elegance! What style!'

Kurambi Amma used to stare wide-eyed at Leslie Sayiv when he went to the Palais de Justice in the carriage drawn by the white horse with the silvery mane. She'd been a young woman then.

Leslie finished his studies, found a lucrative position and built a bungalow. All he needed now was a wife. Clement Sayiv wanted him to marry. But ...

He looked at the policemen. 'Will I find a girl in Mayyazhi worthy of my Leslie?'

'Non, non, monsieur,' they replied in chorus.

There were part-French girls who might have suited Leslie. But Clement Sayiv wanted a pure French bride for him. He knew he would not die happy unless he achieved this.

He continued his search for a bride for his son until he found Armand Sayiv's daughter.

Armand Sayiv had come to Malabar to do business in spices. The business had failed and he had moved to Mayyazhi with his family. He had a son in the army and the money he sent kept them from starving.

One day Clement Sayiv came to Armand Sayiv's house in his carriage, the one with the white horse. They talked for a long time. Armand Sayiv was not rich but he was a pure white. And when

Clement Sayiv saw Armand Sayiv's daughter, Missie, he felt as if his eyes had seen the golden sun and grown dazzled.

Clement Sayiv galloped back home through the Rue de la Prison. Dust rose from under the hooves of the white horse.

'She has shining blue eyes!'

'She has curly golden hair!'

He threw up his hands and danced on his long legs.

That was how Armand Sayiv's daughter, Missie, had the good fortune to become Leslie Sayiv's bride.

'Made for each other!' said all the Mayyazhi folk as Leslie Sayiv and Missie walked along the seashore hand in hand.

Wine merchant Clement Sayiv saw and heard and died a contented man.

2

Prominent among the native thiyyas of Mayyazhi were Mayor Chekku Moopar, whose rosewood-black skin had not grown even a shade lighter though he had spent three decades in France, and Sergent-en-retraite Kunhikannan, who had fought wars in Indochina on the French side.

Chekku Moopar had come back to Mayyazhi with a French wife.

'What style he has!' the women remarked, looking at the stately, dark-complexioned Chekku Moopar strolling hand in hand along the street with his French wife.

Only Kurambi Amma, who adored every man in Mayyazhi who wore a coat and trousers, said wistfully: 'If only he had been a little more fair-skinned.'

Unlike Leslie Sayiv, Chekku Moopar never mixed with the poor natives. No matter how many times he walked down the street, he never cast a glance at Kurambi Amma. After all, she would try to reason, he lived in France for so many years and even married a French lady, why should such a great man talk to her, coconut merchant Kelu Achan's woman?

But Leslie Sayiv never kept the natives at a distance as Chekku Moopar did. He dressed more fashionably than Chekku Moopar and had the carriage with the best horse in Mayyazhi. And yet, he put his arm around Kelu Achan when he talked to him. Leslie Sayiv's son, Gaston, and Kurambi Amma's son, Damu, were inseparable companions.

Kurambi Amma's man, Kelu Achan, never wore a coat or trousers. All he wore was a short white mundu that came up to his knees. And once he came home he took off that as well. He hated clothes. Restless by nature, he would rush around the yard, heap manure at the roots of the palms and dig channels in the courtyard so that the rainwater could flow out. He could not sit still for a minute.

Destiny had perversely willed that Kurambi Amma, who worshipped men dressed in coats and trousers, should get the mundu-clad Kelu Achan as her husband.

One night it began to pour. Gusts of wind swirled through the rain-lashed palm trees and brought down the coconuts. Kelu Achan hurried out to pick them up. The pits and furrows in the grove were filled with muddy water. Dead frogs hindered Kelu Achan at every step.

'Oh, Kurambi, something has bitten me.' Kelu Achan hopped in on one leg. Blood dripped from the heel of his left foot.

Kurambi's heart beat fast when she saw the blood. It was during the rainy season that the snakes came out.

'Save my man.' Her eyes turned towards the cross on the steeple of the Church of the Virgin.

She brought Kelu Achan his palm leaf umbrella.

'Don't you want your mundu?'

'In this rain? No.'

He hopped on one leg all the way to Malayan Kadungan's house.

There was no poison that Malayan Kadungan's magical powers could not draw out. Once a snake had bitten a Mapilla boy who lived eight miles east of Kadungan's house. The poison had entered the child's head. The only way to get it out was to fetch the snake that had bitten the boy. And that was what Malayan Kadungan did. Under the spell of his magic, the snake swam across the Mayyazhi river, plucked out the poison from the Mapilla boy's head and fell dead at Kadungan's feet.

Kadungan was often called Gulikan—the goddess's dancer—because he performed the Gulikan's role at the Thira festival. Kadungan stood expectantly on the veranda.

He had just had a bath, changed and smeared vibhuti over his forehead.

'I was waiting for you, Kelu Achan.' Kadungan knew in advance whom a snake would bite and when.

Kelu Achan hopped on to the veranda leaving a trail of bloodstains on the wet floor. He sat down on the grass mat. Kadungan chanted the naga mantram over him.

'You can go now. But remember, you mustn't sleep for twenty-four hours. If you do, nothing will save you.'

Kelu Achan nodded, took a half-anna coin out of his ear and gave it to Kadungan.

But Kelu Achan did not get back home. He fell down on the way and died.

'Oh my God, my Thiyyan has left me, he's gone away ...' Kurambi wailed for many days and nights. Gradually, her wails quietened to a gentle sobbing. Finally, she resigned herself to her fate.

'IF ONLY HE HAD been a little more fair-skinned,' she began to say as usual as she watched admiringly while Chekku Moopar walked down the street holding his wife's hand.

Clement Sayiv gave his wine free only to policemen. But there was hardly anyone in Mayyazhi who had not been invited to savour Leslie Sayiv's wine. He entertained visitors constantly and loved giving presents. On festive days like Christmas and Quatorze Juillet he served food to the poor people in the dharmasala and showered them with gifts.

Missie bore Leslie two children, Albert and Gaston. Kurambi Amma's son Damu was born the same year as Gaston.

Albert grew up to be a vagrant. He insulted his teachers and ran away from school. Then he took to drinks and women. He joined the French army when war broke out. No one heard of him after that.

Missie's blue eyes used to fill with tears. 'It's my fate, Kurambi,' she would say.

Some said Albert had died in the war, others that he had drowned in a boat disaster on the high seas. There was a rumour that he was living contentedly in France with a wife and children.

'I saw him in Saigon,' said Sergent Kunhikannan.

'Are you sure, Monsieur?'

'I saw him with my own eyes. In the Rue de la Place, holding a bottle in his hand and singing loudly.'

'I don't care where he is as long as he's alive.' Missie wiped her eyes. Maybe Albert was a drunkard and too fond of women. Maybe he did not care for his family. But Missie would always love him, whether he was in Saigon or in some far corner of the earth. It was a relief to know he was alive.

Gaston was not like Albert at all. He was clever at his studies and well-behaved. He completed his higher studies in Pondicherry. Leslie Sayiv had great hopes for him.

'I'll send Gaston to France, Kurambi,' said Leslie, reaching out for a pinch of snuff. 'I'll make him a doctor.'

'Oh God, will you really?'

'Yes, Kurambi. He'll be Gaston Doctor in five years.'

'And will he look after this poor creature if she falls ill?'

'Of course, Kurambi. If you fall ill, my son will take care of you.'

'Oh Sayiv, will I live to see that happen?'

'Certainly, Kurambi. The Mother of Mayyazhi can make anything happen.'

Kurambi turned towards the silvery cross on the steeple, clearly outlined against a pure sky, and closed her eyes. She smiled, lost in a daydream in which Gaston came to treat her, stethoscope in hand.

'Will Gaston take money from me, Sayiv, when he treats me?'

Leslie Sayiv took a pinch of snuff from the ivory snuffbox, closed his eyes and said, 'Gaston is your boy as much as mine, Kurambi.' Kurambi Amma was ecstatic.

When Gaston came to see Damu next day, she made him sit down by her and stroked his golden hair. She saw Leslie Sayiv's lost youth in Gaston.

'I'm not sending Damu to school anymore,' she said to Leslie Sayiv.

'Why not, Kurambi?'

'He's all I have. And I'm growing old. All I want now is to make sure he can look after himself.'

Leslie Sayiv thought for a while and said, 'If Damu is not going to school anymore, tell him to come to the court from tomorrow.'

That was how Damu became a writer of deeds in the Palais de Justice.

When Leslie Sayiv was making arrangements to send Gaston to France, Kurambi Amma went to visit Missie. Seated close together, they talked for a long time about village affairs and their families. They had tea and cake. Kurambi Amma came to the point at last. 'I've been wanting to tell you something, Missie.'

'What is it, Kurambi?'

'I'd like to get Damu married, he's old enough now.'

'He's twenty, isn't he?'

Boys married at eighteen in those days. Mayyazhi men became fathers before their moustaches appeared. Kelu Achan had married

Kurambi when he was seventeen and she twelve. She had come of age only after the wedding. She had shared a bed with her mother-in-law until then.

Kurambi Amma inhaled a pinch of snuff. 'We won't be able to keep an eye on Gaston anymore, now that he's going to France.'

Missie was suddenly lost in her memories. She had only the vaguest recollection of France. She was a white woman only in name now. She spoke Malayalam as fluently as anyone in Mayyazhi. And yet, the mention of France awoke a nostalgia in her. The call of the motherland echoed in her ears.

Kurambi Amma went on, 'Why don't you get Gaston married too before he goes away?'

Missie had had the same thought and welcomed Kurambi Amma's suggestion. Kurambi left, feeling satisfied. But when Leslie Sayiv and Missie spoke to Gaston about his marriage, his face turned as white as paper. 'No, Papa, not now, please.' Leslie Sayiv was astonished at his son's panic.

Gaston refused to consider marriage. His parents were crushed. Their eldest son, Albert, was lost to them and they would never see him get married. They had hoped to make up the loss through Gaston. If Gaston did not marry, how would Clement Sayiv's line continue?

Leslie Sayiv sat in his chair clutching his head in his hands, deep in thought. There's something wrong with Gaston, he thought. He had been bright and energetic as a child but his vitality had dimmed as he grew up. He seemed unhappy and brooded all the time. Something was tormenting him. Some mysterious sorrow that only the Mother of Mayyazhi knew.

'Wait till Damu is married. Gaston will want to get married as well.'

Kurambi Amma started preparations for Damu's wedding. They went and saw the girl and agreed on a date for the ceremony.

Gaston appeared to be avoiding Damu. Damu managed to get hold of him at last, seated alone on the deserted beach with a haunted look in his eyes.

'Gaston, I'm your friend, tell me what the matter is.' Gaston stared silently at the heaving sea.

'Please tell me.' Damu edged closer to him. 'If you won't, I refuse to be friends with you.'

Gaston sat as still as a statue. His blue eyes brimmed with hot tears. At last he told Damu the secret that only the Mother of Mayyazhi knew.

Damu laughed. 'Don't be an idiot. Tell your papa that you want to get married. Or wait, I'll tell him myself.'

Damu went directly to the Palais de Justice and said to Leslie Sayiv, 'Gaston says yes.'

'Are you sure?' Leslie Sayiv's eyes turned gratefully to the cross on the steeple. Wine merchant Clement Sayiv's line could go on now. Gaston's wedding would mark the beginning of a long line of descendants who would in turn claim Count Lally as their ancestor.

Expensive wines arrived from Pondicherry. All the horse carriages in Mayyazhi lined up in front of Leslie Sayiv's bungalow. Everyone in Mayyazhi was invited to the wedding feast. Mayyazhi was steeped in the atmosphere of a carnival until the wedding was over.

'Never in my life have I seen such a fine wedding, Kurambi,' said Kunjakkan as he hobbled along, ladder on shoulder and oilcan in hand.

Kurambi Amma was very happy. Gaston's bride, Teresa, was the daughter of Pondicherry's former mayor, Chevalier Ignas Sayiv. She was young and beautiful with wine-coloured eyes and lips as red as koyyethi flowers.

The day after the wedding, Gaston Sayiv and his wife took the ship to Pondicherry to spend their honeymoon there.

Gaston returned alone. He had changed so much that he was barely recognizable. Long blue shadows lay on his cheeks, his back was bent and his eyes were deep pools of anguish.

'This is sorcery!' exclaimed the people of Mayyazhi.

Damu stayed away from court for a few days. Leslie Sayiv and Missie looked as if their life had been drained away.

The day he came back, Gaston Sayiv went upstairs and closed the door of his room. He never came out again. His world shrank to the space contained within its four walls. No longer exposed to the sunlight, his body became pale and white. His hair grew down to his shoulders. His eyes mirrored an infinite sadness.

Late one night, when Mayyazhi was asleep and the last carriage had left Big Sayiv's house, the sound of a guitar rose from Leslie Sayiv's bungalow.

The music was unbearably sad for Gaston knew that he was impotent.

Time dragged on. Leslie Sayiv had lost Albert much earlier. Now Gaston had become like one dead. Leslie Sayiv never knew happiness again.

He lies eternally at rest now, a cross on his chest, his pain still unmitigated, next to Clement Sayiv who had so proudly claimed to be a descendant of Count Lally.

3

Dasan was born in the deep silence of a pearl grey dawn.

A veil of darkness as fine as hymen lay over Mayyazhi.

Once Kowsu had reached her term, Damu Writer had begun to sleep on the outside veranda.

'Ammè, I can't bear it.'

'Oh God!'

Damu woke up hearing Kowsu moan and went inside. The small kerosene lamp in the room diffused more smoke than light. He saw that Kowsu's eyes were full of tears. Her face looked drained of blood. He noticed blood on his wife's hands and mundu as well.

'What is it, Kowsu?' he asked. Caught in the agony of childbirth, she could not speak.

Kurambi Amma said, 'She's bitten herself.' He winced as if it was he who had been hurt.

'Ayyo!'

'Quiet, my child.' Kurambi Amma sat down by Kowsu and stroked her dishevelled hair. 'You can't escape this if you're born a woman.'

Damu set out to call the midwife. Kurambi Amma was afraid she would not come at this ungodly hour. The night was filled with the silence and emptiness of an eclipse. A grey darkness enveloped the Church of the Virgin. The Mayyazhi river flowed gently beneath the deserted iron bridge.

Damu walked quickly towards midwife Kunhani's house, near the dharmasala. The clatter of horses' hooves and the clink of their little bells broke the silence of the night as he neared the Rue du Gouvernement. The procession of carriages moved slowly under the pale sky along the banks of the river and then over the seashore.

Damu kept to the edge of the street as the carriages went past him. He saw them dozing, their hats on their heads, drunk and sleepy: David Sayiv, Mayor Chekku Moopar, Sergent-en-retraite Kunhikannan and the rest.

'Even David Sayiv's carriage has gone,' murmured Kurambi Amma to herself. He was always the last to leave Big Sayiv's house after supper.

Kowsu had grown quieter after a sharp spasm of pain.

Kurambi Amma could not sleep even after all Big Sayiv's guests had left. She lay awake, listening, her snuffbox at her head. She could make out every carriage in Mayyazhi by the rhythm of its horses' hooves, the sound of its bells and the creak of its wheels. She treasured the sounds of Leslie Sayiv's carriage most of all. Leslie Sayiv was dead now but she still remembered the sound of his carriage.

Damu knocked at the midwife's door.

'Who is that?'

'It's me, Damu.'

'Which Damu?'

'Damu who writes deeds.'

A light flickered inside. Kunhani Amma came to the door with a small kerosene lamp in her hand, her scanty hair knotted over her head. Her long earlobes brushed her shoulders.

'Kowsu's begun her labour. I can't bear to see her suffer, please come.'

'At this hour of the night? No, I'll come as soon as it is daylight.'

He bit down his anger and pleaded. 'I'll give you whatever you want. Please come, in God's name.'

Kunhani Amma's eyes glittered with greed. 'What will you give me?'

'A quarter rupee.'

Kunhani Amma was satisfied. She changed her mundu and went along with Damu.

Kurambi Amma was relieved when Damu arrived with the midwife. The door closed on Damu. He sat outside, smoking beedi after beedi. Kunhani Amma was an experienced midwife and had helped at many births. He was glad she had come, but whenever Kowsu cried out, he was afraid.

'Kowsu, child, don't cry.' Kurambi Amma could not bear to see her suffer either and began to whimper.

The midwife was irritated. 'Go and sleep, Kurambi Amma.'

'My Kowsu! Oh, Mother of Mayyazhi!'

'Get out, will you?' The midwife pushed Kurambi Amma out.

Muttering to herself, the old woman went up to the loft, the same one she had shared with Kelu Achan for over three decades. Where was he now? Perhaps he was hidden among the petals of the chethi flowers in the earthen pot buried in a corner of the room.

She took out her snuffbox from the fold of her mundu, held a pinch to her nose and stretched out on the floor. She could no longer hear Kowsu. Slowly, her eyes closed.

The sound of hoofbeats woke her with a start. A white horse with a bushy mane! Her heart beat faster and her hearing took on the sharpness of a thousand listening ears. The hoofbeats came nearer and the carriage wheels creaked to a halt. There was a sudden silence.

'Kurambi, Kurambi, will you give me a pinch of snuff?'

She recognized the voice of Leslie Sayiv, who had died years ago. She lay helpless, unable to move or make a sound.

Her eyes filled with tears.

'Just a pinch, Kurambi ...'

Minutes passed. The wheels creaked again. The clatter of hooves died away in the distance.

A cock crowed. The church bells rang for morning service. The first rays of sunlight touched the Mayyazhi river.

Damu's happy voice merged with the feeble cry of a newborn child. 'Ammè, it's a boy!'

So Dasan was born. And a little dragonfly flew into Mayyazhi from the Velliyan Kallu, the cluster of rocks in the sea where souls rest between births and which guards in its womb the secrets of the lives and births of the folk of Mayyazhi.

4

Dasan woke up before the crows began to caw, slid down from his bed and went looking for his mother. The hook on his shorts had come undone and they hung down so that the black thread around his waist showed.

'Ammè, isn't it today I'm going to school?'

'You're already awake, son?'

Kowsu, who was lighting the bell metal lamp hanging from the ceiling in the veranda, was surprised. She lighted this lamp with its seven wicks every day at dawn and dusk. Dasan would sit in its glow at dusk and say his prayers and Kurambi Amma would sit beside him with her eyes closed. When Dasan finished reciting all the sacred verses he would pray wordlessly, his palms still joined, 'Make me intelligent. Take care of my Amma, my Achan and my Achamma.'

The past year, Dasan had often started awake from sleep at night and asked, 'Is it morning? Is it time for me to go to school?'

'At this hour?' Damu would exclaim, drawing the child close to him. He would put him back to sleep, tapping his shoulders.

Dasan would get up in the morning before Damu and Kurambi Amma were up. The cross on the steeple of the Church of the Virgin would just have begun to take shape in the pale morning light. The church bells would soon begin to ring for the morning service. They rang three times a day, at dawn, noon and dusk.

'When can I go to school, Ammè?'

'Not yet, son. I'll wake you up when it's time. Go back to sleep now.'

Dasan would feel disappointed. He was in a hurry to go to school and was counting the days. He watched wistfully when Vanaja, the girl next door, set off to school every morning, wearing an ankle length skirt, with kohl in her eyes and flowers in her hair. He felt jealous of her slate and copybooks. In the rainy reason, she carried a small umbrella.

'Why are you crying?'

'I want to go to school, Ammè.' He would burst into tears watching Vanaja until she was lost to sight.

Kowsu would sit him on her lap, wipe his face and try to comfort him. 'You can go next year. You're only a little child now.'

But Dasan's tears flowed unchecked.

He wanted so much to go to school. He wanted to learn everything possible. One day this desire broke all bounds. He opened his box and took out a clean pair of shorts and a shirt. He pulled out a blue copybook from a pile that Damu Writer had brought home and set out surreptitiously.

He had seen the ochre-coloured school building many times. Once when he walked down the Rue de l'Eglise holding his mother's hand, she had said to him, pointing to the building, 'That's the school you'll go to when you grow up.'

Dasan walked on, the image of the ochre-coloured school in his mind. A little farther, he paused doubtfully. Three roads lay before him, one leading east to the Rue du Cimetière, where

Clement Sayiv and Leslie Sayiv lay with crosses on their breasts. To the west, the Rue du Gouvernement led to the banks of the Mayyazhi river. The Rue de l'Eglise was in front of the Church of the Virgin.

Dasan stood at the crossroads, uncertain where to turn.

A group of people gathered around him.

'Who are you, little one?'

'I want to go to school.'

Clutching his book tightly, he looked at them, his eyes full of tears. His sobs grew louder. They were all strange faces, he did not recognize any of them.

'Oh Mother of Mayyazhi, it's Damu Writer's boy!' The sexton had made him out. Someone ran to the court to inform Damu.

'I want to go to school.'

So that was it, thought the sexton. The little boy wanted to run off secretly to school!

Damu Writer came rushing up in five minutes. That was how Dasan's first attempt to go to school ended.

A year had gone by since then and Dasan was finally ready for school. On this day, he would not have to stand uncertainly at the crossroads. The ochre-coloured school in the Rue de l'Eglise had thrown open its doors to him at last.

Kurambi Amma came to the veranda as soon as she woke up and sat down on the mat, her legs stretched out. She took a small pinch of snuff from the tiny ivory box and inhaled. It was the first pinch of the day and reminded her of her first lovemaking.

She put Dasan on her lap. 'You must do well at school, little one.'

'M ... mm.'

'You must become a great man, like Leslie Sayiv.'

She kissed his head. He snuggled into the warmth of her bare, sagging breasts.

'I want to see my little boy in a coat and a hat.'

Intoxicated with the snuff and transported to a distant world of dreams, Kurambi Amma sat still, holding the child close to her. Kunhichirutha came by at that moment. 'What are you dreaming about, Kurambi Amma?' Kunhichirutha laughed, showing her white teeth. She had spent the night at David Sayiv's bungalow and was on her way home. Her gold-bordered mundu was crushed and her oily black hair gathered carelessly in a knot. Her eyes sparkled, even though they were full of sleep.

'You're up early today, Kurambi Amma. What's happening?'

'Dasan is going to school today.'

'Is he old enough then?'

'He's five now. Time flies, Kunhichirutha. Come on in, don't keep standing there.'

Kunhichirutha climbed the steps into the veranda and Kowsu brought her a chair from inside. Kunhichirutha sat down and yawned. She had to make up for so many sleepless nights.

'When did your Sayiv come back?'

'On yesterday's ship.'

'So he can't sleep now if you're not around!'

David Sayiv was unmarried and lived with a butler and servants in his bungalow overlooking the Mayyazhi river. He did not share Gaston Sayiv's fate. Kunhichirutha was proof of his virility.

'He's old enough to be your father!'

'It's old men who really need me.' Kunhichirutha smiled, the sensuous smile that had taken many a man in Mayyazhi captive.

Diminutive in build, Kunhichirutha had a dark, glowing skin and a bold gait. It was small wonder that old men like Chekku Moopar and David Sayiv had succumbed to her charms.

Kunhichirutha walked up to the well in search of Dasan. Kowsu was giving him a bath. Dasan shrank back shyly when he saw her.

'Why are you feeling shy? I'm old enough to be your mother,' laughed Kunhichirutha.

Dasan turned his back on her.

'Why don't you make him a gold chain for his waist, Kowsu?' asked Kunhichirutha, looking at the old black thread that had grown grey with having been on his waist so long. Kowsu had untied and loosened it many times because the child grew so fast.

'You've no idea how hard it is for us,' sighed Kowsu.

Kunhichirutha took out a two-anna coin with King George's head on it. 'To buy yourself sweets in school,' she said. When Dasan hesitated she pushed it into his hand.

Dasan put on a clean pair of shorts and a shirt, had his kanji and took out his slate and books. He had the moist stalks that children used to clean their slates in his pocket.

'Think of God and put your right foot forward when you set out.' He wanted to do as his grandmother said but in his hurry, it was his left foot that he placed on the step.

There were three French schools in Mayyazhi: l'Ecole des Filles, l'Ecole des Garcons and the Cours Complémentaire. Vanaja was in the first one, the girls'. Dasan was in the boys' school, l'Ecole des Garcons. After the Certificat examination, children who wished to do the Brevet went to the Cours Complémentaire.

Dasan held his father's hand as they walked to school. They dropped in at Missie's on the way.

Leslie Sayiv's house was as quiet as a haunted house. An abandoned carriage stood at one end of the courtyard. Leslie Sayiv's white horse with the thick mane had disappeared, but in the silence of the night, Kurambi Amma still heard its hoofbeats.

Missie emerged wearing a long black dress that came down to her ankles. After Leslie Sayiv died, she had worn only black.

'Missie, I'm taking Dasan to school.'

Missie knelt down to give Dasan a hug and a kiss. She gave him a slice of cake. Missie's cakes were famous throughout Mayyazhi. She baked them for Christmas, Quatorze Juillet and other festivals.

Those who were invited to partake of them considered themselves lucky.

Damu could not help glancing at the door at the top of the elaborately carved, carpeted wooden staircase. It was firmly closed. No one had seen it open. Missie went up three times a day with food and set plates and saucers on the low table near the closed door. Cheeru, the maid servant, took away the empty dishes later. No one saw Gaston Sayiv. Damu had not seen him now for years.

At night, the lament that the impotent man plucked out on his guitar, the only reminder of his existence, shrouded Mayyazhi like an anguished dream.

Missie laid her pale hand on Dasan's head in blessing. Her eyes, hollowed out by grief, were full of tears.

As they entered the Rue de l'Eglise, Damu gave Dasan two candles. 'Light them before the Holy Mother.'

They went into the church. Dasan lit the candles, cupped his hands and placed them before the idol of the Virgin. The flames flickered. Rushing in through the arched window, the wind blew out the candles, leaving only the sharp odour of a short-lived flame. Damu sighed.

The big, ochre-coloured school was right in front of the church. Dasan had dreamed about it for such a long time. He stepped in, holding his father's hand, his heartbeats thudding in his ears.

One day when he had no class, Dasan asked Kurambi Amma, 'Who gave birth to me?'

'Your mother, Kowsu, who else?'

'Did I come out of her stomach?'

'Mmm.'

Dasan leaned back on his grandmother's warm breasts. 'Achammè, where was I before I was born?'

Like all grandmothers in Mayyazhi, Kurambi Amma answered, 'On the Velliyan Kallu.'

The cluster of rocks called Velliyan Kallu lay far out to sea like a bright teardrop. All Mayyazhi's children had come from there. The souls waiting to be born in Mayyazhi fluttered over the sunbright rocks as dragonflies.

'Where is Velliyan Kallu, Achammè?'

'Far out in the sea.'

'Can I see it?'

'Only when the sea is calm.'

'Have you seen it, Achammè?'

'Hm ... mm.' She took a pinch of snuff from her ivory box and nodded her head as if she had just woken up from the memories of her previous births.

Next day, on the way to school, Dasan stopped by the sea. It lay calm and silent. Velliyan Kallu could be seen in the distance as if in a dream, the souls fluttering over it like dragonflies. Souls that were waiting to be born or reborn, souls taking a brief rest from the cycle of birth and rebirth.

Dasan stayed on the deserted seashore a long time, gazing out to sea. He was late to school. Two periods of class were over by the time he arrived.

5

Bear Sayiv was dead.

Robert Sayiv, otherwise known as Bear Sayiv, had been one of Mayyazhi's memorable half-French citizens. He was very short, with hair not only on his face and limbs but even on his neck, which was how he had come to be known as Bear Sayiv. He did not live in grand style like Clement Sayiv or Leslie Sayiv. He always wore torn trousers and a shirt of coarse, unbleached cloth with neither collar nor sleeves. He spent the greater part of his life in the toddy shop.

He had not gone beyond the fifth class at school. To him going to school was like being taken to the gallows. Every morning his father, Gabriel Sayiv, used to come up to him with a mug of cold water and say, 'Get up, mon petit, mon cher petit.'

Robert would not move. Gabriel Sayiv would try a few times more to get him out of bed but Robert would not stir. Gabriel would then throw the water on his face and run away. Robert would jump out of bed with a yell, tear at his pillow and roll on the ground. By the time he quietened and came out, Gabriel Sayiv would have taken the keys and left for the salt depot.

Robert never washed his face or cleaned his teeth. By the time he had eaten, Pokkan the tapper would be waiting in the yard with Robert's school bag. Salt merchant Gabriel Sayiv did not have a horse carriage like Clement Sayiv. Since Robert would not walk to school, Pokkan had been appointed to carry him there. Every morning the small-built toddy tapper walked to school carrying on his shoulders the huge, bear-like Robert.

Robert would ask Gabriel Sayiv for money every morning as he set out for the salt depot.

'What do you need money for?'

'To sleep with Kunhichirutha.'

'Damn you!' Gabriel Sayiv would make the sign of the cross.

'Where can I get money from, if you don't give me any? Find me a job, then I won't ask for money.'

In despair, Gabriel Sayiv turned to the priest of the Church of the Virgin. And Bear Sayiv was appointed the bell ringer of the church.

The sun usually rose over the Mayyazhi river to the morning chimes from the church. The day Robert started work, the great church bells resounded through Mayyazhi with the force of a hurricane and were heard many miles away.

But the next day, no morning chimes were heard for the first time in a hundred years. Robert lay fast asleep in the salt depot, dead drunk. He lost the job,

'There goes the Bear,' the children would hoot.

Bear Sayiv spent a great deal of time at the toddy shop, eating and drinking with his friend, elephant-foot Antony, who stayed in the dharmasala. Antony suffered from elephantiasis.

'A bottle of toddy and fish curry for a quarter anna,' said Pokkan, taking off the towel around his head.

Bear Sayiv strode up to him, 'Aren't you Pokkan?'

'Yes.'

Pokkan stood up. Bear Sayiv grabbed Pokkan's toddy and finished it in a few gulps.

'Come out now,' he shouted.

Unni Nair, the shop owner, and the others in the shop watched expectantly.

'Don't thrash him,' pleaded Unni Nair.

'Carry me, rascal,' ordered Bear Sayiv, trying to balance himself on his unsteady legs.

Pokkan stared at Bear Sayiv. Unni Nair and his companions were aghast. This was not the schoolboy Robert, nor was Pokkan young any longer. His back was bent with age. He stood with his palms joined. People crowded around, curious and frightened.

'Pokkan, you had better carry Bear Sayiv,' warned Unni Nair, who knew how hot-tempered Bear Sayiv could be.

Pokkan wound his towel around his waist. Robert sat on his shoulders, his hairy legs on either side of Pokkan's head. Unni Nair and his friends clapped their hands and laughed.

'Walk!' commanded the Bear. Pokkan began to walk, his back bent like a bow. It was broad daylight and the street was full of people. Holding Pokkan's head tight, Bear Sayiv snapped out orders.

'To the church.'

'To the pier now.'

'To the cemetery.'

The old man walked with Bear Sayiv on his shoulders. Gasping for breath, his back nearly broken, Pokkan went around Mayyazhi.

He never recovered from the ordeal to his dying day.

The part-French inhabitants of Mayyazhi kept Robert at a distance. Some ill-treated him, others tried to advise him. He continued to drink, sleep around and pick up quarrels, a disgrace to himself and to his illustrious community.

'PETER!'

Emily shook Peter who lay sleeping, flat on his back. He looked exactly like his father, right down to the thick hair on his body.

'Papa's not back yet.'

The morning chimes rang out from the church. Crows cawed. But Robert Sayiv had not yet returned.

'He's your papa. Go and look for him.'

'He's your man, isn't he? Go and look for him yourself.' Peter turned over and went back to sleep.

Emily set out in search of her husband. The toddy shop in the Rue de la Gare had become more and more of a permanent home to Robert Sayiv as he grew older. Even after midnight he would not leave.

'Sayiv, we're locking up now,' Unni Nair would say, pouring the unsold toddy back into the big cement cask.

But Robert Sayiv would not budge. Someone would heave him up and drag him outside the shop. He would fall asleep at that spot or collapse on the roadside or on a shop veranda. If he had not come home by the time the morning bells rang, Emily would turn to Peter for help.

Emily would look for Robert Sayiv on the wet cement benches on the pier, in the dharmasala, on the veranda of the salt depot or in the Church of the Virgin.

Just as she began to despair of finding him, someone would say to her, 'Your Sayiv's over there, near that gutter.'

Emily would go in the direction he was pointing and find Robert curled up underneath a lamp-post, like a dog. She would shake him awake, help him up and wipe the dried vomit from his chin and moustache. Then she would walk him home, holding his head against her shoulder. Her eyes would fill as they passed the Church of the Virgin.

'Poor thing!' lamented the people of Mayyazhi. This shabby old man, who dragged himself forward with his head on his wife's shoulder, belonged to the clan of Leslie Sayiv, who had owned a mansion and a horse carriage drawn by the finest horse in Mayyazhi, and of Clement Sayiv, in whose veins ran the royal blood of Count Lally.

'DID YOU HEAR THE news, Bear Sayiv, your son is married.'

Robert Sayiv removed the cap lying over his eyes and stared at Paidal, the town's municipal crier. Paidal went down the streets beating his shield-shaped brass plate with a stick on Republic Day when Big Sayiv distributed rice and clothes to the people of Mayyazhi or if a gale threatened. He would open out a scroll with the seal of the Mairie on it and read the announcement loudly.

'I'm telling you, Peter got married.' Robert Sayiv stared at him.

'Truly, Paidal?' Unni Nair and his friends gathered around him.

'A registered marriage at the Mairie. Do you know who the girl is?'

'Who?' asked Unni Nair and his friends in a single voice. 'Janu, Raman Maistry's younger daughter.'

Robert Sayiv's son had married a Hindu girl! Everyone was speechless.

Robert Sayiv, who had been licking the fish curry on his palm, got up and went out.

'Where are you going, Bear Sayiv?'

He did not answer. He hurried down the Rue de la Gare.

Peter had taken his bride home, then gone to the pier with his fishing net. Suddenly, he heard his father shout, 'Son of a bitch, how could you marry a Thiyya girl?'

'I'll marry whomever I like.'

Robert Sayiv flew at Peter's throat. Peter evaded him.

'Take care,' he warned, 'I'll break every tooth in your head.' Robert headed for his house, trembling and cursing.

'Janu is in the house,' Peter called out. 'If you don't behave yourself, Papa, I'll break your bones.'

Robert Sayiv took no notice of Peter's warning. He had decided to have a word with Janu who had cast a spell over his son. He would throw her out of the house.

'Come out, you lowdown creature,' he shouted from the courtyard.

Janu came out. She wore a dotted blouse and a white mundu and had a big pottu on her forehead. Robert Sayiv looked at her windblown hair and her budding breasts. He could hardly breathe.

'Give me some water.' He sat down on the bench, gasping. Janu brought him a glass of salted kanji water.

'Will you have some more, Father?'

He nodded his head, still gazing at her beautiful face. She brought him some more. All that day and the following one, Robert Sayiv kept asking for water. Every five minutes, he would call out, 'Janu, some water for Papa.' A few days went by.

'I can't stay here anymore.' Janu laid her head on Peter's chest and wept. 'Father ...'

'What did he do to you?'

'He's after me all the time.'

She buried her head in his chest and sobbed. That night, Peter did not sleep. He had not failed to notice that Robert Sayiv had not been going out much recently, and that he sat hunched up on the veranda most of the time.

'What happened to your Papa? We don't see him at all these days,' said Unni Nair. 'Who got married, you or your Papa?'

There was loud laughter in the toddy shop. Peter sat with his head bent and gulped down two whole bottles of toddy. And some arrack on top of that. It was past midnight when he left the shop.

The lamp in the house had burned out. The bench on the veranda, on which Robert usually slept at night, was empty. Peter pushed the unlocked door open and slipped in. The old man was moving stealthily outside Janu's bedroom. In the dim light, Peter saw Janu lying on her side, fast asleep.

Robert Sayiv gave a start when he saw Peter. Muttering to himself, he went out and lay down on the bench.

'Get up.'

The old man opened his eyes and saw Peter standing in front of him with a bottle of kerosene and a long rope in his hand. Peter lifted the old man and tied him to the wooden pillar in the veranda. He poured the kerosene over his head, took out a box of matches from his pocket, lit one and set fire to his father.

Robert Sayiv had not possessed a bungalow or a horse carriage, nor had he enjoyed a worthy position in Mayyazhi. In spite of this, he was buried in the cemetery where the great Leslie Sayiv had been laid to rest. They had represented opposing faces of life in Mayyazhi. Born by the same natural laws of creation, they had followed different destinies until they finally disappeared behind time's backdrop.

But the story of Mayyazhi's half-French did not end with them. There were many more, wearing hats and trousers, pampering their mistresses and their pet dogs, distributing rice to the needy for Quatorze Juillet and Christmas, who fostered the glory of the community. Generations of them succeeded one another, each finding new veins for their blood to flow through.

6

'L̲ong, long ago, in France ...'

Kurambi Amma opened her snuffbox, took a pinch and began the story. Dasan lay on her lap, his hands wound around her neck.

'Once there lived, a shepherd girl. Her hair was the colour of gold and her eyes a shining blue. She grazed her goats over the green meadows of Domremy. One day, seated on the bank of the blue river with her goats, she heard a disembodied voice in the sky: "Shepherd girl, your country is in danger."

'She raised her eyes to the sky. St. Michael flew towards her out of the deep azure, his white wings fluttering. The shepherd girl fell on her knees. "Arm yourself. Only you can save France. To battle, shepherd girl!" Brushing his wings against her hair, the saint flew around her.

'The English had invaded her country on all sides. One by one, the kings were being forced to lay down their arms.

'Jeanne remained on her knees, her palms joined and her eyes raised to the sky. The heavenly messenger fluttered his wings and flew upwards. Gradually becoming as small as a pigeon, he disappeared into the blue of the sky.

'Only Jeanne, the shepherd girl of Domremy, could save her country. Her blue eyes full of tears, she abandoned her goats and ran home, the divine voice still ringing in her ears.

'"I'm going to the war."

'"You, child?" Her parents were astonished. But when she told them about the divine command, they fell on their knees as well.

'So the girl went to war. She asked Capitaine Robert de Baudricourt for arms: "Great warrior kings have had to flee, defeated. What can you do against the English, shepherd girl?"

'He laughed at her, ridiculed her, but she was not disheartened.

'She prayed to St. Michael and went weeping to Chinon. When he heard what she said, the heart of Chinon's ruler melted and he gave her weapons and a small army. Holding a sword in her slender hand, she led her army to Orleans. She fought the English, defeated them, liberated city after city and marched victorious to Paris.

'But at Compiègne, the wounded girl collapsed and her delicate, flower-like body lay drenched in blood. The frightened soldiers ran away, abandoning the girl who had fallen on the battlefield. Merchants from Bourgogne passing that way took the helpless girl and sold her to the English for a few pieces of gold. Her enemies were delighted to have the shepherd girl in their power. She had disgraced and humiliated them. They decided to punish her severely.

'They built a fire in the Vieux Marchè and stood her in the middle of the pyre. She was not afraid. She cast her calm eyes upwards and joined her palms. Flames leaped up from all sides. Waves of fire enveloped her but she did not move. With her eyes raised and her palms joined, she burned slowly to death.'

Tears flowed from Kurambi Amma's eyes as the story came to an end. Dasan sobbed. No grandmother in Mayyazhi could tell the tale of Jeanne d'Arc without weeping. Every child in Mayyazhi had grown up with the story and wept over the tragic fate of the shepherd girl who was burned to death. When Leslie Sayiv was a child, Clement Sayiv had taken him on his knee and told him the story. And Leslie Sayiv had related it to Gaston.

Kurambi Amma wiped away her tears with the back of her hand. She inhaled a pinch of snuff and closed her eyes in ecstasy. Dasan leaned back against the pillar and thought of the pyre in the Vieux Marchè and the shepherd girl standing with joined palms in the middle of it. Tears flowed unchecked from his eyes.

Kurambi Amma watched as lame Kunjakkan came along, the ladder over his shoulder and the kerosene tin in his hand. He came every morning to pour kerosene in the lamp in front of Damu's house and clean the smoke-stained glass. Kurambi Amma always asked him to pour a little extra kerosene.

'Oh Kurambi, you know what Soupi Mudalali is like!'

Soupi Mudalali had taken the municipal lamps on contract in an auction. He was a real miser. He would walk down the streets at night, peering at all the lamps. If a single one was burning after midnight, he would be furious. 'You're ruining me, rascal,' he would shout and call Kunjakkan names. Kunjakkan was afraid of him. So he was very careful with the kerosene. The lamp in front of Dasan's house usually burned out long before midnight.

There were, however, a few lamps that burned until dawn—those facing David Sayiv's bungalow, Chekku Moopar's and Sergent-en-retraite Kunhikannan's, in other words, the houses of Mayyazhi's most prominent citizens.

'I want a lamp too,' said Kunhichirutha to David Sayiv. Raman Police lived in the same street as she did, so the lamp was naturally in front of his house.

David Sayiv indulged her wish. The very next day a tarred wooden lamp-post appeared in the dusty lane before her thatched house.

Soupi Mudalali came every day, reeking of attar and wearing his fez cap and squeaky sandals, and called out, 'Is your lamp burning all right, Kunhichirutha?'

'Yes, Mudalali.'

'Tell me if it isn't,' he would say and turn to Kunjakkan to warn him, 'Take care, otherwise I'll break your other leg.'

Kurambi Amma sat Dasan on her lap and told him how Kunjakkan had become lame.

Kunjakkan's grandfather, Kurambachan, lived near the Meethala temple. All the three mandapams of the temple were visible from his house. At sunset, the shadow of the temple flagpole fell over Kurambachan's courtyard.

Kurambachan whitewashed walls for a living. Like most men in Mayyazhi, he too had taken to drinking when he was very young. One evening, in the lean month of Karkatakam, Kurambachan began to crave for a pint of arrack. No one would lend him money. He had nothing left to pawn or sell, having pawned even his coconut scraper two days earlier for a drink. Suddenly an idea flashed through his mind. He wound his towel around his head and stepped into the cold rain.

He stealthily cut down a bunch of bananas from a tree in the temple, wrapped it in his towel and crept surreptitiously towards the arrack shop.

'A quarter bottle and my coconut scraper.' He laid the bananas at Ambu Nair's feet. Ambu Nair was Unni Nair's grandfather and the owner of the shop. He measured out a quarter bottle for Kurambachan and when he finished it, gave him back his coconut scraper.

Kurambachan walked blissfully along the street, the scraper under his arm, singing. It was past midnight. Raindrops still spattered out of a pale sky. A heady fragrance floated out from the champakam tree in the temple.

Kurambachan heard the sound of dancing bells as he reached the temple. A whiteness loomed out of the dark. Kurambachan's heart beat fast. He stood still, his eyes popping out.

'Where are my bananas?'

Gulikan stepped out of the temple, wearing anklets and a skirt of palm fronds. Kurambachan's hair stood on end.

'Where are my bananas?' repeated the apparition.

'Forgive this creature!' Kurambachan fell at his feet.

The deity gave Kurambachan a kick and ran back, hooting, into the darkness of the temple. Kurambachan lay dumbstruck among the fallen champakam flowers. The scraper shot out of his hand. He did not know how long he lay there.

When he got up, he found that his right foot had gone lame.

Kurambachan's son, Kunhikutti, was born lame as well, in his right foot. And Kunhikutti's son Kunjakkan was also born lame in his right foot.

'But Kunhanan isn't lame,' said Dasan.

Kurambi Amma was troubled. Kunhanan was Kunjakkan's son and he was not lame.

'That's because the Gulikan isn't angry anymore,' she said. 'Go and have a bath now.' She helped herself to a pinch of snuff.

Dasan would not go away. On holidays like this, he hung around Kurambi Amma. She would tell him stories and legends. Damu Writer would leave for the court early morning and Kowsu had time only for household chores. Besides, she had to look after Dasan's baby sister, who had just arrived.

Kurambi Amma had no special tasks. She usually sat on the veranda with her legs stretched out and talked to passersby to while away the time. Or she would seat Girija in her lap and play with her.

'One more story, Achamma, please.'

'Go and buy me a quarter anna's worth of snuff.'

'Will you tell me a story if I do?'

'I will.'

She took out a quarter-anna coin with a hole in the middle. Dasan ran to the shop with the coin around his finger and came hurtling back at the same pace.

'Tell me the story now.' He was panting. She transferred the snuff carefully into her snuffbox and tucked it at her waist. Dasan climbed into her lap.

'Which story do you want, child?' Kurambi Amma had exhausted her fund of stories. Many of them had been told over and over again. 'The one about the lion and the rabbit?'

'No, a new one.'

'Where can I go for a new story now?'

She sat for a while, thinking. Then she lowered her voice and whispered, 'I'll tell you a new story. But you mustn't tell anyone about it, all right?'

'I won't.'

Dasan's eyes shone with delight.

Kurambi Amma told him a story she had never told him before.

When Kunhimanikkam was alive, there was no girl as pretty as her in Mayyazhi. Her skin was the colour of beaten gold. The thought of Kunhimanikkam, decked in jewels and wearing a kasavu mundu, haunted the men of Mayyazhi while they slept. Even the white men were disturbed by her. As their ships neared the shore, they would be impatient to be with her.

'Kunhimanikke,' Vaisravanan Chettiar called out from the street with his bundle of silks on his head, 'may I come in?'

Chettiar brought silks from Tamil Nadu and raked in money selling them to the French and part-French women. Jet black and stout, with shining white teeth, Chettiar wore gold rings on eight of his fingers, a gold chain around his neck and a silk shirt.

Kunhimanikkam put her head out. 'Not today, Bernard Sayiv is with me now.'

Disappointed, Chettiar went away reluctantly.

He came again next day, full of renewed hope. 'What about today, Kunhimanikke?'

'Ayyo, Antony Sayiv is here.'

'And tomorrow?' Vaisravanan Chettiar did not give up hope.

Kunhimanikkam banged the door shut. Chettiar walked away with a heavy heart.

Chettiar came right into the veranda next day. He opened his bundle and laid the costliest silks at Kunhimanikkam's feet. Kunhimanikkam looked at the silks greedily and turned them over in her hands.

'Today?'

Kunhimanikkam pretended not to hear. She pulled out a pure white silk saree and held it against herself. 'Can't I come in?'

Chettiar took out his gold watch and chain from his pocket and laid them at Kunhimanikkam's feet.

'Not now. Francis Sayiv is here.'

Kunhimanikkam took the white silk saree and the gold watch and chain and disappeared inside the house. The doors closed behind her.

Vaisravanan Chettiar came day after day and laid gold and silks at her feet. But not once did he succeed in laying hands on her. Chettiar lost interest in his business. He stopped going to Kanchipuram to buy silks. The French women and part-French women complained that there were no silks to buy.

As the days went by, Vaisravanan Chettiar grew thinner and thinner. His eyes sank into their sockets. The gold rings began to slip off his wasted fingers. And he soon drew his last breath without ever having possessed Kunhimanikkam.

Kunhimanikkam used to have her bath in a tank filled with water-lilies. One day, she took off her mundu and stood in the knee-deep water, rubbing herself with warm coconut oil. She untied her long hair which fell down to her navel, covering her breasts.

As she revelled in the water, she heard a whistle from the clump of screwpine on the bank. Cupping her hands over her navel, she looked around her. There was no one to be seen. She went on with her bath among the water-lilies, breathing in the heady fragrance of the screwpine flowers.

Next day, she heard a whistle at the same spot but there was no one to be seen.

The third day, a serpent glided out of the reeds. It stopped by the side of the pond, spread out its hood and savoured Kunhimanikkam's naked beauty.

Kunhimanikkam did not go to the pond for a bath the next day. The serpent came looking for her. It wound itself around a creeper in the courtyard of her house and beckoned to her desperately.

'Mix asafoetida in water and sprinkle it around the house,' advised the sorcerer, Malayan Kunhuraman. 'No serpent can stand its smell.'

Kunhimanikkam did as he told her, but to no effect. The serpent came again and glided into the veranda. Full of distress, Kunhimanikkam rushed to Malayan Kunhuraman.

'He's that bold, is he?'

The sorcerer's eyes burned with fury. He had the power to make a dead fowl flutter its wings or bring back a snake that had struck and make it suck out its own venom from the victim's body.

'Save me!' Kunhimanikkam's kohl-rimmed eyes filled. Her lips, stained red with betel juice, quivered.

Malayan Kunhuraman set off to Kunhimanikkam's house with oil drenched torches and turmeric powder. He sat cross-legged in the centre of the burning torches and drew a magic eight-cornered cone on a copper disc. He chanted a mantram, throwing the turmeric in all directions. When the battle with the serpent was over, he rose to his feet.

'He'll never dare to come here again.'

Kunhimanikkam felt relieved. Kunhuraman went away with the silver coin she gave him. The torches went out and all that was left was the odour of burnt turmeric.

Dawn broke. Crows cawed loudly and beat their wings noisily as they flew over Kunhimanikkam's house. Covered with jewels, she lay lifeless on her silk mattress. The serpent lay dead as well, its hood on her bare breasts.

'Do you know who that serpent was?' Kurambi Amma took a pinch of snuff from her box, inhaled it and went on, 'It was Vaisravanan Chettiar!'

7

THE RAILWAY STATION WAS A MILE AWAY FROM KUNHANANDAN MASTER'S house. Not many trains passed that way. There was a local to Kozhikode in the morning. The Mapillas, who had gone home to spend the night with their wives, usually came back from Vadagara and Nadapuram by the morning train.

Kelan dropped a Mapilla at the station and went to Kunhanandan Master's house. He brought his jutka to a halt and called out, 'Are you ready, Master?'

Kelan's horse did not have the speed or poise of Leslie Sayiv's. Its ribs were clearly visible underneath its skin. Its mane was infested with fleas. It looked like an overgrown dog. Kelan got down from the carriage and smoked a beedi, leaning against his horse.

Kunhanandan Master gazed at himself in the mirror. The hair above his temples had grown quite grey. At thirty, he looked like an old man. Two weeks in the hospital had fattened him up a little, but his face still looked swollen and jaundiced.

Continuing to stare into the mirror, he murmured to himself, 'Kelan's jutka is here again. I have to get ready to go to school now. I'm starting all over again. I'm not dead!'

'What are you muttering to yourself?'
'That I'm not dead, Leelechi.'
Leela grew pale.
'I never thought I'd come out of the hospital alive.'
Leela tried to change the subject. 'Kelan is waiting for you.'
   Kunhanandan glanced at the mirror once more. His eyes shone with the happiness of being alive. Picking up the books that lay on the bed, he ran down the stairs, forgetting that he suffered from a heart ailment. The sound of his heartbeats excited him.
   'Master's looking fine.' Kelan threw his beedi down.
   'Tell me Kelan, did you really think I'd come back alive from the Kozhikode hospital?'
   'What do you mean, Master? You're so young.'
   Kelan was perturbed. He knew that Master, young as he was, had contracted an incurable disease. He opened the jutka door. Master climbed on to the leather seat, still redolent of the attar that a Mapilla passenger had used. The carriage jolted to a start.
   The school was only two furlongs away, but Master was not strong enough to walk the distance, so he had to go by jutka. His bloated body, drained of blood, could grow inert at any moment. While he lay on the hospital bed covered up to the head with a blanket, he had thought of his heartbeats as the heartbeats of approaching death. The burden of death oppressed him all the time.
   'Anyhow I'm not dead now,' he said to himself as the jutka clattered on its way. He felt comforted. The joy of being alive ran through his veins. I'm alive! Happiness flooded him from head to foot. He felt carried away by sheer delight.
   This awareness of being alive that he often experienced had become his greatest source of happiness. As the jutka rolled forward rhythmically, he thought of an incident from the past.
   Late one night, he had gone out to urinate. The cross on the church steeple gleamed in the pale starlight. Lamps glowed on the

tarred wooden lamp-posts. He could hear the breathing of the sea. Squatting on the ground, he had suddenly become aware of his existence. Intoxicated with the thought of being alive, he had got up without urinating and walked away.

Although he knew he was not allowed to walk too long or be exposed to the dew, he had wandered over the deserted roads in his thin mundu—through the Rue de l'Eglise, the Rue du Gouvernement, the Rue de la Prison. Even his hair had throbbed with the joy of existence. He had forgotten himself totally. He had gotten back home only at dawn. He had found it difficult to climb the steps and had reeled over and fallen down, frothing at the mouth. The neighbours had come running up when Leela screamed. Kelan had rushed with the jutka to the doctor.

Master had not regained consciousness for twelve hours and had had to stay in bed for a week.

He had been sickly from the time he was a child and had swallowed innumerable medicines to no effect. Ramutty Vaidyar from Azhiyoor had said it was tuberculosis and prescribed a kashayam. Goat's milk was considered a potent remedy for tuberculosis in those days.

'Keep the goat tied to his cot. Give him the milk warm and fresh, straight from its teats.'

Kunhanandan's father bought a goat that very day from the Vadagara market. Master had been a little boy in shorts at the time. The goat was tied to the bedpost and milked twice a day. The room stank of goat all the time.

The goat finally ran dry. Kunhanandan Master's father died. And Master continued to be ill. He stumbled through school and reached the tenth class. He was too ill to go on. The tenth grade examination was important. As soon as he passed it, he was appointed a teacher in the Ecole des Garcons.

'So you want to teach?' Kunhikutty Ammaman expressed displeasure when he learnt that Kunhanandan, who could barely hold himself straight, was going to teach. 'Your father made enough for you to live on.'

'I can't waste time doing nothing.'

'Sick people should stay at home.'

'I'm not so ill that I have to stay in bed all the time.' He hated being thought an invalid.

Teachers were scarce at the time. Kunhanandan could not work for more than fifteen days in the month but he would not give up. When he found it difficult to walk to school, he arranged for Kelan to take him by jutka.

The jutka went through the Rue du Cimetière and arrived at Sekharan's teashop.

'Stop for a minute,' Master said. Dasan was walking down the road holding Girija's hand.

'Get in.' Dasan hesitated. Girija's large eyes widened in wonder. She had never been in a jutka. 'Come on, get in.' They got in.

'Your younger sister?'

'Oui, Monsieur.'

'Which class?'

'First.'

Girija loved the way the jutka jolted. Master talked to Dasan. He was Dasan's class teacher.

The jutka stopped in front of the Ecole des Garcons. Dasan and Master got down.

'Kelan, drop Dasan's sister at her school.' Kelan drove fast through the Rue du Gouvernement. Girija's school was in the Rue de la Prison.

Soon this became a routine.

Dasan stood first in the examination that year. Kunhanandan Master had grown very fond of the intelligent boy who had about him a seriousness beyond his years.

'Tres bien!' He congratulated Dasan.

Kunhanandan Master could not talk loudly because of his ailment. He would talk at length about Napoleon and Rousseau in a very soft voice. He was always clear and concise and never scolded his students.

'How can he teach when he has something wrong with his heart?' Kurambi Amma would ask with amazement when Dasan sang his teacher's praises.

Like Kunhanandan Master, Gaston Sayiv had also been crippled by life. But the two men had chosen completely different ways. Master knew he might drop dead at any moment but he found happiness in being alive, while Gaston lived in a prison he had built for himself. Gaston wanted to return to the seed which had borne him, while Kunhanandan Master longed to pour himself into the world and be a part of it. They were entirely opposite poles.

After Kunhanandan came back from his treatment in Kozhikode, he began to sow the seeds of communism in Mayyazhi. He hung up three framed pictures in his front veranda. The middle one was of Karl Marx, with Lenin and Stalin on either side.

'Who are all these people with moustaches and beards?' Kunhichirutha climbed into the veranda and gazed at the pictures. 'Is the one in the centre a sanyasi?'

A smile fluttered across Master's face.

'And this one with the moustache—is he the Commissar?' She pointed at Stalin.

Commissar Lorrin Sayiv was Mayyazhi's Chief of Police. He had a moustache like Stalin's.

'That's a great man.'

'Greater than Big Sayiv?'

'Much, much greater.'

Kunhichirutha was dumbstruck. No one could be greater than Big Sayiv in her eyes. And not only in her eyes and Kurambi Amma's but in the eyes of everyone in Mayyazhi. There were those who even believed that Big Sayiv was a divine incarnation. How could this moustachioed person on Kunhanandan's veranda be greater than him?

'Here, Kunhichirutha, have some coffee.' Leela held out a glass of black coffee with coconut grated into it. 'The Chettichi hasn't yet brought the milk and there's none left.'

'I just had some at David Sayiv's bungalow.'

'Now that you have your Sayiv, you're not interested in our coffee anymore.'

'Do you think he'll marry you one of these days, Kunhichirutha?'

She blushed at Master's question. She drank the coffee and put down the empty glass on the bench. As she was leaving, she pointed to Stalin's picture and asked. 'That picture there, will you give it to me, Master?'

'Not that. What about another one?'

'All right then, one with a moustache like that.'

Master nodded. He watched her walk away, the wide kasavu border of her mundu gleaming in the mellow sunshine.

Other people besides Kunhichirutha were intrigued by the picture on Master's veranda.

One day, Secrètaire Karunan, who was Sergent-en-reatraite Kunhikannan's son and Big Sayiv's right hand, came riding that way. He stood in front of the pictures and exclaimed angrily, 'Il est communiste!'

8

THE MUNICIPAL LAMPS HAD BURNED OUT. UNNI NAIR'S TODDY shop was closed. Even Bandman Kanari, always the last to leave the shop, had gone home, singing. Silence had fallen over Mayyazhi.

In her bed over the granary, Kurambi lay with her eyes wide open, unable to sleep. She could not sleep in the daytime either. She would call out to anyone who passed by and talk to them in order to while away the time.

In the old days, she had spent a lot of time telling Dasan stories. She had told him the legends of Jeanne d'Arc and Vaisravanan Chettiar many times. He had never tired of listening to them.

But Dasan was no longer a child. He had moved away from the world of legends and fantasies, and Girija had taken his place.

'Long, long ago in France there lived ...' Kurambi Amma sat Girija on her lap, opened the ivory snuffbox, took a pinch of snuff and began the story. When it was over, her eyes were full of tears and so were Girija's.

She knew that Girija would also grow up and lose interest in the stories after a while. Only the stories themselves would go on. And there would always be grandmothers to recount them. Dragonflies fluttering over the Velliyan Rock would come to Mayyazhi to listen to them.

Dasan was engrossed in a book. Damu Writer was busy arranging the documents that he had sat up all night to draft.

Kowsu came up to Damu. 'There's no rice.'

'We'll buy some in the evening.'

'What will the children eat when they come home from school?'

Ready to go to the court with his umbrella and documents, Damu hesitated for a moment. 'Ask for a measure of rice next door.'

'I can't. If you're not ashamed, I am.'

Sukumaran, who was a greffier, a senior officer in Big Sayiv's government, lived next door. Kowsu had not yet returned the rice she had already borrowed from his wife. How could she ask for more now?

Damu looked perplexed. 'I'll see if I can find a way.'

He sighed, tucked his documents under his arm and went down the steps.

'Bring me some snuff on your way back,' Kurambi Amma pleaded. The ivory snuffbox was empty most of the time these days. There had been a time when she had needed only a quarter anna's worth. Now, lying awake all night, even a half anna's worth was not enough.

Dasan had already set off for school. As he walked along holding Girija's hand, he thought, there won't be lunch for us today.

But he came home to find his plate filled with steaming hot rice.

'Where did you get the rice, Ammè?'

'Don't worry about that, child.'

'Is it from next door?'

Kowsu did not answer. She leaned against the door, wiping her eyes. Dasan could not bear to eat. He got up and went away.

'Things will be alright, Kowsu. Just wait until Dasan grows up.' Kurambi Amma tried to comfort her.

At sunset Dasan said his prayers and sat down with his books. Kurambi Amma said to him, 'You must study hard and become a big officer.' Her eyes turned to the cross on the steeple. 'Oh Mother of Mayyazhi, bless Dasan.'

She watched him study by the light of the little kerosene lamp. The books he read were about strange things and were written in a language she did not know. She understood only a few words of French. In the old days, when Leslie Sayiv asked her if she was all right, 'Ça va?', she would shake the thakkas swinging in her earlobes and say, 'Oui, Monsieur.'

She often sat up until midnight, listening to him read. She would say to herself, 'One day my Dasan is going to be a notary like Leslie Sayiv.' Intoxicated by the snuff, her eyes half-closed, she dreamed of Dasan riding in a horse carriage, wearing a coat and a hat.

The municipal lamps in the street had burned out. Bandman Kanari's song had faded into the distance. Dasan was still at his books. His head was full of thoughts of the examination.

Big Sayiv's guests had dispersed for the night. The carriages clinked their way home, carrying Mayor Chekku Moopar, David Sayiv and Sergent-en-retraite Kunhikannan. The thudding of the sea below Big Sayiv's hill only deepened the silence.

As she lay awake in the reddish glow of the kerosene lamp, Dasan's image faded slowly from Kurambi Amma's eyes. She lay still, her ears attuned to sounds in the distance.

Was that a carriage coming nearer? Those hoofbeats! Her heart throbbed wildly. Her hearing sharpened a thousandfold.

The hoofbeats sounded closer now. The wheels of the carriage creaked over the uneven road and the bells on the horse's neck jangled. Suddenly, it was quiet. The carriage must have stopped in front of the house.

The bells tinkled as the carriage doors were opened. 'Kurambi, Kurambi ...'

She recognized Leslie Sayiv's voice. Death had not stilled it.

His boots crunched as he got down from the carriage. 'Will you give me a pinch of snuff, Kurambi?'

'Of course, Sayiv,' she wanted to say, but her tongue would not move. Nor her hand, to take out the snuffbox at her waist.

The old bench creaked. Leslie Sayiv must have sat down on it and put his hat on his lap.

'A pinch of snuff. Just a pinch. Won't you?' he pleaded, in despair.

There was silence after that. Then the bench creaked again and she heard the sound of boots going down the steps. Bells jingled and the carriage wheels groaned.

The hoofbeats faded into the distance.

Kurambi Amma burst into tears.

'Achammè!' Dasan looked up from his books. Kurambi Amma was seated on her bed, sobbing wildly. Dasan looked at her for a moment, then went back to his books. It was not the first time this had happened. It had become a habit with Kurambi Amma to wake up at midnight and weep.

'Ammè!' Damu was angry. 'Don't you realize Dasan has an examination to prepare for? What a time to wake up and cry!'

'I don't know what is wrong with Amma,' said Kowsu, who had woken up as well. 'She cries every night like this.'

'Maybe she had a bad dream. Go to sleep, Kowsu.'

Kurambi Amma wiped her eyes with the back of her wrinkled hand and lay down. A little later, cocks began to crow. Kurambi Amma dropped off to sleep at last. Who could understand her anguish?

DASAN KEPT READING, HIS eyes reddened with fumes from the kerosene lamp.

The Certificat Examination was drawing near. He had never failed. He was considered the brightest in his class. His teacher had often said, 'I'm lucky to have students like you. I'm sure you'll do marvellous things.'

There were one or two children in his class who were better than him at mathematics. But their general knowledge was poor. Kunhanandan took a special interest in Dasan and chose books for him from the school library because he was a voracious reader. That was how Dasan had read Hugo's *Hernani* and Beaumarchais' *Le Mariage de Figaro*.

Kelan's carriage stopped in front of Dasan's house. Kunhanandan Master put his head out. 'Come on, Dasan and Girija.'

Master had made a detour to pick them up.

'Will Dasan get through the examination, Master?'

Master smiled. 'How little you know your child, Writer.'

'He's rather weak in mathematics.'

'Not enough to fail in the exam.'

As the carriage began to move away, Master called out, 'Send him to me in the evenings until the exam is over. I'll take care of the mathematics.'

Damu Writer was happy. 'He's all I have, my only son. I can't relax until he's settled in a career.'

'Dasan won't disappoint you. I'm sure of that.'

Dasan's habitually serious expression deepened when he heard this. I must try not to let my father down, he thought. I'll work hard, score high marks and get a first. Then I'll find a secure job and help the family. I don't want Amma to beg for rice, I don't want Achamma's snuffbox to be empty.

The carriage wheels made long, curved trails on the dusty road.

Dasan did not go out to play as usual in the evening. As soon as he came from school, he gulped down a tumbler of jaggery-sweetened coffee and ran to Kunhanandan Master's house, mathematics book in hand.

It was the first time he had been there. He had only seen the house from outside. It was big and two-storeyed. Two lions were sculpted in cement on either side of the gate. A small girl stood at the entrance.

'Is Master home?'

The little girl stared at him. She wore a long skirt. Her anklets tinkled as she ran inside.

'Come in child.' Leela came out to the veranda.

Master lay on his cot reading Rousseau's *Le Contrat Social*. His bare body was as yellow as turmeric. The hair which used to grow thick on his chest had begun to fall and underneath was a waste of skin.

He taught Dasan until eight o'clock. Leela brought tea twice. Dasan realized that he had forgotten how tea tasted with milk and sugar, which were luxuries in his house.

Sometimes he heard the soft tinkle of anklets and looked up to see Chandrika at the door.

Dasan went to Master's house regularly every day until the day before the examination. When the results came, he stood first in the Certificat.

DASAN'S EYES WIDENED IN astonishment when he saw himself in the full length mirror. How long his limbs had grown! How had this happened? No more playing with marbles. No more squabbling with Girija. No more tantrums. He was a young man now.

He did not regret his lost childhood. He wanted to grow up fast, become an adult.

He suddenly caught sight of his parents in the mirror. It was the first time they were seeing him in a mundu. His mother's eyes filled with tears. 'I can hardly make you out, son.' She smiled through her tears. His father sighed and sat down on the easy chair in the veranda.

Dasan gazed at himself again. Once upon a time, my soul was a dragonfly, fluttering over the Velliyan Rock. He was lost in thought for a moment, full of wonder at the mystery of life and death.

Kurambi Amma, who had been seated on the veranda with her legs stretched out, stumbled to her feet and hugged Dasan. She threw a towel over her sagging, bare breasts, took Dasan's hand in hers and said, 'Come with me.'

Dasan guessed they were going to Missie's house. Kurambi Amma always took him there whenever any important event took place. The hot sun of the month of Makaram had the warmth of the womb. They walked along the blazing road to Missie's.

'Missie, look who's here.'

Missie stared at Dasan, astonished.

'How big you've grown, child, bigger than your Papa.' Missie's wrinkled hands fondled Dasan's neck, ran down his back. Her fingers felt cold.

Missie brought him a piece of cake, the same kind she had given him when he first went to school and then again when he passed the Certificat.

Kurambi Amma thought of Gaston. 'Gaston,' she called, looking towards the stairs, although she knew he would not answer. It was years since she had seen him. He must have heard her call out to him. She could see his room, its doors were firmly shut. No one had seen them open. They would not open even if the earth shook or it rained fire, she thought.

Kurambi Amma sighed and sat down next to Missie. Reading her thoughts, Missie's smile dimmed. A disquieting silence fell.

'It's my fate, Kurambi.' The tears welled up in Missie's blue eyes.

'I'll pray to the Holy Mother, Missie. He'll come to his senses one day.'

Dasan stopped eating the cake. He too was thinking of Gaston, who had been a riddle to him for many years, whose secret had haunted him until he had learnt the meaning of the word *impotent*.

Dasan went to Master's in the evening in his full-length mundu. Leela smiled, 'This suits you.' Chandrika stood shyly behind her mother.

Dasan wore a mundu regularly from that day, a coarse, black-bordered one that brushed his ankles. He was a young man now, aware of his responsibilities. He held up his head, a look of seriousness on his face.

9

It was the month of Mesha. Dark rain clouds blew over Mayyazhi, piled up over the cross on the church steeple and cast black shadows over the river. Below Big Sayiv's hill, the sea grew heavy with the threat of a gale.

Kelan's jutka clattered over the deserted street and came to a stop in front of Dasan's house.

'Where's Master?' asked Dasan.

'Ammaman is not well,' answered Chandrika from inside the carriage with a quiver in her voice.

Dasan's heart thumped with fear. He knew what Master was suffering from. It frightened him to think of Master's precarious journey over the frail bridge of life.

Girija climbed in beside Chandrika. Dasan did not get in. 'I'll walk,' he said.

The jutka rolled off leaving behind a yellow cloud of dust. Dasan tucked up his mundu and hurried to Master's house. Master had been working very hard of late and neglecting his health.

Smallpox was raging in Mayyazhi. Bhargavan and Sisupalan of the health centre had visited all the houses and tried to vaccinate everyone, but had met with little success. The Mayyazhi folk were more frightened of vaccination than of death.

Till well past midnight, corpses rolled up in mats were carried along the Rue du Cimitière accompanied by flaring torches. When oracles and sorcerers failed to control the disease, devotees brought Veluthachan out from the church.

The cortege bearing his idol wound slowly through the streets. The church bells chimed sadly.

One morning, Bandman Kanari appeared in the street, trumpet on shoulder, holding up his baggy trousers.

'I saw it with my own eyes,' he said, gasping for breath. 'What did you see, Kanari?' asked Kurambi Amma.

'The battle between Veluthachan and Vasoori Amma.'

In a voice filled with awe, Kanari described the battle which had taken place in the vicinity of the Church of the Virgin the night before. Veluthachan had been on a white horse and was armed with a lance, while Vasoori Amma had worn a white saree and had had her hair streaming over her back.

Kurambi Amma mixed some cowdung with water and placed it in an earthen pot on her doorstep. She believed that cowdung kept away Vasoori Amma, the goddess of smallpox.

'Ammè, I'm hungry.' Girija called out to her mother from the street.

'Don't call out so loudly, child,' warned Kurambi Amma.

'Why can't I?'

'If you do, Vasoori Amma may come running instead of your own Amma.'

Girija looked terrified.

'We've all been vaccinated,' said Dasan, 'how can we catch the disease?'

'Who are you to decide that? I warn you, don't talk so lightly about Vasoori Amma.'

'It's a virus that brings the smallpox, not Vasoori Amma,' Dasan laughed.

Kurambi Amma covered her ears with her hands.

Master stood at his window at night, watching the flickering torches move in the distance. His heart ached.

He paced up and down all night long. Until now, the fear of his own death had been his only anxiety. The very word 'death' was like a whiplash to him. He was prepared to make any kind of sacrifice in order to live an extra day. Now, he shuddered at the thought of the poor fishermen on the seashore, dying of smallpox.

When he arrived at school in the morning, his eyes were inflamed with the lack of sleep. Front bencher Cyril's Papa, the sexton of the Church of the Virgin, had died the day before. One of the burning torches he saw had been for Cyril's Papa. He could not bring himself to teach that day.

'The sexton was still alive when Kelappan buried him,' said the jutka driver, Kelan, on their way home from school. Master's face grew pale.

Master and his friends usually spent the evenings in the Vignanaposhini Library. Master had worked hard to establish the library, which was situated above Chettiar's grocery shop. There were about five hundred books, including the French classics, in glass fronted cupboards, and a few benches and chairs.

'Why are you so quiet today, Master?' asked Vasutty, observing Master's silence.

'Do you know how the sexton died? Kelappan buried him alive.'

Master wrung his hands. His eyes were wet. Vasutty was busy arranging books. There was a young boy named Pappan with them, a pupil of the Cours Complémentaire.

'It's time we did something, Vasutty.'

'What can we do, Master? They hide from Bhargavan when he goes to vaccinate them. Let them suffer.'

'Don't say that, Vasutty. They don't realize the risks. We must go to them and do whatever we can.'

Vasutty's heart leapt in fear. The seashore, where the fishermen lived, was filled with victims of the smallpox. He could not face the thought of going there.

'Kelappan will bury all of them alive unless we do something about it.'

Kelappan cared for the sick who had been abandoned by their relatives. He laid them out on banana leaves and gave them medicinal potions. He had been dead drunk when he buried Cyril's Papa alive.

'Don't come unless you want to, Vasutty. I'm going anyway. I'm a communist, I can't sit back and do nothing.'

Pappan looked up from the paper he was reading, his eyes burning. 'I'm coming too, Master.'

Master's face lit up.

They went to the fishermen's huts the same day and poured water into the parched throats of the afflicted. They rescued old Marikar just as Kelappan rolled him up in a mat to bury him.

Kunhanandan Master's uncle, Kunhukutty Ammaman, rushed up from Azhiyoor to warn him. 'You're playing with fire. You're not even strong enough to stand on your own feet. First take care of yourself, your love for others can come later.'

'How are other people's lives different from mine, Ammaman?'

The next day he stayed away from classes and visited the sick again. Pappan accompanied him.

A few days went by. Clouds gathered over Mayyazhi, dissolved in rain and poured over the town. Soon, Mayyazhi was freshly washed and clean. Bright drops of water dripped from the leaves. The sun shone over the waterlogged rice fields. The cross on the church steeple sparkled.

'That Kunhanandan is a marvel!' said Kurambi Amma. He had earned everyone's admiration.

But when the first showers came, Master took to bed. His fingertips turned as blue as if they had been poisoned. The doctor came from Thalassery every day to see him. He stopped going to school.

When Dasan entered, Master was lying in bed with his eyes closed. Books and magazines were scattered over the bed.

'Why aren't you in school?'

'I'm on my way.'

'Why didn't you go in the jutka?'

'I wanted to see you, Master.'

Dasan came up to the bed. Master's chest, which had grown smooth and hairless, heaved painfully.

'You're late, Dasan. You'd better go,' said Master without opening his swollen eyes.

Dasan lingered for a moment, looking thoughtful, then picked up his books and went to school.

Dasan began to visit Master every evening after school. Pappan and Vasutty would be with him and sometimes Kanaran as well. Kanaran was the first to wear khadar in Mayyazhi. He was a dark-skinned young man with glistening teeth.

Leela and Chandrika joined them only if the others were not there.

Leela would ask, 'Have you had tea, Dasan?'

'Yes, before I started.'

'Have some more.' She would take him to the kitchen. Seated on a low stool while she made the tea, Dasan would listen to her talk about her visits to Singapore. Chandrika's father worked there, in a shipping company.

'Don't you want to go to Singapore again, Leela Edathi?'

'I'm too old now, child.' Leela smiled shyly. She was older than Kunhanandan Master but did not look her age. 'Who will look after my Kunhanandan if I go away?'

'Amma is frightened of the sea.' Chandrika would stand leaning against the wall, her anklets tinkling every time she moved.

Chandrika's father, Bharathan, travelled a lot. He had come home recently after having been at sea for three years. He had landed in Madras and taken a train to Mayyazhi. He was short and plump and had a watch with a gold strap. It needed three men to lift his luggage and carry it home. Bharathan's arrival was an event in Mayyazhi.

'And who is this?' he had asked seeing Dasan. He had not recognized him.

'Don't you know him? He's Damu Writer's son.'

'You were so small when I last saw you.'

Bharathan took off his shirt and trousers and put on a lungi. He was fun-loving, he talked and laughed and joked all the time.

'You had the first rank for the Certificat, didn't you?'

'Yes.'

'You must be first for the Brevet now.' Bharathan laid his hand on Dasan's shoulder.

Dasan walked with Bharathan and Master to the wine shop in the Rue de l'Eglise. A posse of policemen were enjoying their drinks and joking with each other in a mixture of French, Tamil and Malayalam.

'You're young enough to be my son, Dasan, and Kunhanandan is your teacher. All the same, don't hesitate if you want to join me for a drink.'

The boys of Mayyazhi took to drink before their moustaches sprouted. But Dasan had not yet touched alcohol. He spent most evenings on the seashore, looking at Velliyan Kallu and meditating on that enigma of life and death gleaming in the distance. He often lost count of time. Sometimes, as he walked home in the dark, he wished he could have a drink, he wished he could drink himself senseless. But he had promised himself that he would not. How could he, while his father struggled to keep the impoverished family alive?

'Come on Dasan.'

Bharathan took hold of Dasan's hand and took a step forward. Master was watching them closely.

'Thank you Bharathetta. I can't.'

Bharathan went into the wine shop by himself. Dasan prayed silently, may I always have the strength to refuse.

10

The waves of the national movement beat against the shores of Mayyazhi. A group called the Mahajana Sabha was formed with Kanaran as its chief. Its aim was to win freedom for Mayyazhi from the French.

Early one morning, while Kunhanandan Master was standing in the courtyard cleaning his teeth with burnt rice husk, Kunhichirutha appeared in the street. She was on her way back from David Sayiv's bungalow. The sleep of several nights had gathered heavily in her eyes.

'Master, Master!'

'Yes, Kunhichirutha?'

'Did you say the white men should leave Mayyazhi?'

'Yes, I did.'

Kunhichirutha's face grew pale. 'Where can they go, Master?'

'Back to their own country.'

'All of them?'

'Yes, all.'

'Even David Sayiv?'

'Yes, even David Sayiv.'

Kunhichirutha looked dazed. If anyone else had said it, she wouldn't have believed it. But Master could not be wrong. She began to walk back home slowly, looking perplexed, a lost look in her eyes.

'Poor thing, you really frightened her,' said Leela who had been watching the scene from the veranda.

'But David Sayiv will have to leave one day. And all the other white men as well.'

'Oh God, speak softly. If someone hears ...' Leela was afraid. But Kunhanandan was unmoved. He seemed sunk in thought.

Not many in Mayyazhi could accept the fact that the white men had to leave. Only a few seemed aware of the need for freedom and you could count them on the fingers of your hand.

Kunhanandan Master went to Damu Writer's house to speak to him.

'Freedom? What does that mean, Master?'

The deed writer could not even understand the meaning of the word. He knew that the world outside Mayyazhi was in flames but he had always felt that Mayyazhi did not belong to the world. He was always preoccupied with his bronchial cough and his domestic woes. He was used to reading deeds, not newspapers. All he heard every day was the racking cough rising from his sputum-filled lungs or his wife's perpetual refrain: there's no rice, no oil, no sugar. Most people in Mayyazhi were like the deed writer. Master was in despair, he could not figure out how to inspire them with the ideal of freedom.

'They're as thick-headed as buffaloes. How can we sow the seeds of freedom in them?'

Vasutty continued to stack the books on the shelves in the library. Pappan's head was buried as usual in a newspaper. Both of them turned to Master.

'There's no use just talking to them,' said Pappan, 'They will have to be shaken awake.' Pappan worshipped Subhash Chandra Bose and often used to say he wanted to form an army like the INA.

Pappan and Kanaran argued all the time. Kanaran admired Gandhiji deeply. He had once gone away with a khadar bag on his shoulder, joined the Dandi salt march and been sent to jail.

Kanaran belonged to a very wealthy family. He had left school after the tenth class. He could have become a teacher like Kunhanandan but was not interested in a job or in his family's affairs. His only link with the family was his father, who had noticed that the boy sat upstairs all the time, brooding.

'What is it, Kanaran? Tell me, I'm your father. Is it money you want?'

'No Father.'

'Is it a girl?'

'No.'

He did not want money or a wife. His father could not understand what else he could possibly want at his age.

Once his father died, Kanaran was free. He gifted his house, his land and the shops in town that his father had left him in his will to his sister. All he took when he left home was the faded khadar bag he had taken to Dandi. He slept in the office of the Mahajana Sabha, on a towel spread over a wooden bench.

Vasutty's story was different. Pokkanachan, his father, used to climb coconut trees to make his living. One day, when it rained, he had slipped and fallen. He could not climb trees after that. He was bedridden now. An old cracked earthenware pot kept under his bed served him as a chamberpot. His tongue, however, never stayed still. 'Go on,' he would say to Vasutty, 'wander all over the place. You never think of your crippled father, do you?'

Vasutty worked in the Treasury as a clerk.

'I'm going to resign,' Vasutty said. 'I don't want to work for the white man anymore.'

Pokkanachan and Kallu Amma stared at him in disbelief. Neither could speak for a while. Then Kallu Amma said, 'You have a crippled father and young sisters. Just think of them, son.'

Vasutty contemplated, the rain pouring outside silently.

'Go to work, son. Clean your teeth, have some kanji and go.'

Kallu Amma pleaded with him but he would not go.

The fire in the hearth died out. Vasutty's little sisters cried with hunger. Pokkanachan lay on his cot and cursed. Kallu Amma bore her lot in silence. Squatting on the floor of the mud hut, she lamented, 'Oh God, why don't you put an end to me ...' But Vasutty did not relent. He had foreseen all this. He carried on his secret meetings and discussions.

Kunhanandan Master organized study classes, paying scant attention to his health. The slogan of 'Freedom!' began to be heard in many parts of Mayyazhi.

Dasan's Brevet examination was drawing near. There were six students including him taking it this year. It was the highest examination that could be taken in Mayyazhi and was a constant topic of conversation.

'Who'll be first this year?'

'The Brigadier's son, who else?'

'What about Secrètaire Karunan's son?'

'Sekharan? He's dumb!'

'Secrètaire Karunan's son doesn't have to be brainy to pass an exam.' Unni Nair, the toddy shop owner, laughed, screwing up his eyes. Everyone knew that Secrètaire Karunan was Big Sayiv's right hand and that his word was law.

The candidates for the examination sat up studying all night. The teachers were kept constantly busy. They stayed away from school and coached the students at home.

Dasan did not succumb to the examination fever however. Every morning, he sat outside the Bibliothèque Publique, the state-owned library, waiting for it to open. As soon as it opened, he would devour the newspapers greedily. The war was spreading to the Middle East. The Indian Army had confronted Italy under the leadership of Lord Wavell. America was about to join the war.

'Will Burma fall, Master? If the Japanese take Burma, who will give us rice?'

Dasan talked to Kunhanandan Master about the war for hours together and read every newspaper and magazine he could lay hands on. It saddened Dasan to think of the war. His tender mind was troubled. Why did men fight among themselves?

'Only in a communist society can we hope for a world without war. Global communism is the only remedy,' said Master.

Dasan walked around looking like a young Christ, a Siddhartha, his mind filled with agonising thoughts of the war and its sufferings. Master tried to dissuade him from thinking too much about the war. 'It's for us older ones to worry about,' he urged. 'Go back to your books now.'

'If you don't study hard, Dasetta, you won't have the first rank.' Chandrika came into the room, her anklets tinkling.

'Did you see my new necklace, Dasetta?' She pulled it out from under her blouse. Its links were shaped like grains of wheat. It had a pendant in the shape of a banyan leaf with a tiny image of the child Krishna carved on it. Krishna had a peacock feather on his head and a flute in his hand.

'Does it look good on me?'

'Mm ... m.'

'Do you know how many sovereigns it is made of ?'

'Five.'

'Such a small necklace? It's just three sovereigns!' She giggled. 'I wanted a manimala with little gold beads but Amma said this looked pretty.'

Leela had promised to make her the pattern she wanted for her wedding. 'Anyway, why make jewels for you? You never wear them,' she had said.

Chandrika had a lot of jewels. Bharathan made her new ones every time he came home. But she seldom wore anything except her silver anklets, which she wore all the time.

The sun sank in the sea beyond the Velliyan Kallu, making Mayyazhi dark. The light came on in Secrètaire Karunan's mansion, in Sekharan's room on the first floor. His voice could be heard in the street, reading aloud.

'Go home and study, Dasan.' Master forced him to leave. Dasan did not want to study. Seated before the smoking kerosene lamp with his books open, he began to think again about the war raging in distant countries. A worried Damu Writer watched him silently, a muffler wrapped around his throat. He had come home early because his cough was worse. He lay down on the easy chair in the veranda and got up only when it was time to eat. He no longer sat up late at night drafting deeds.

'Everyone else is working very hard. Do you want to fail?'

'I won't fail.'

'You will if you don't study hard. I've been watching you for some days now. What's on your mind? What are you brooding about all the time?'

Dasan did not answer. Huddled over his books, he looked silently at his father.

'If you fail, I'll kill myself. I'm warning you.'

What could the matter be? Dasan seemed worried all the time. Damu went back to his easy chair and gazed into the darkness.

Damu spoke to Kunhanandan Master, who consoled him. 'Don't worry so much. There's nothing wrong.'

'Will he get through, Master?'

'Who will if he doesn't?'

'I want to send him to Pondicherry to do the Baccalauréat. I don't have the money, but I want to do it somehow. Even if I have to beg or starve, Master, I want to do that for him.'

'Good. Go ahead then and make your arrangements.'

The deed writer was relieved.

On his way back home, Secrètaire Karunan stopped him in the street. He put his head out of the jutka. He always covered his overgrown, curly hair with a net and wore a hat over it.

'How is your son's preparation going?' Karunan was always afraid that Dasan would do better than his son. 'He was first in the Certificat, wasn't he?'

'Yes, Monsieur.'

The Secrètaire grunted and drew back his veiled head, feeling desperate. The jutka jolted to a start and was soon lost to sight over the slope in the road.

Kurambi Amma's turn came next. She inhaled a pinch of snuff and came up to Dasan. 'You must work very hard, my boy.' She looked at his eyes, reddened by the thick fumes of the kerosene lamp. While she watched him study, she dreamed that he had grown up, that he was wearing a hat and boots and driving around in a horse carriage like Leslie Sayiv.

It struck eleven, then twelve. One by one, the street lamps that Kunjakkan had lit flickered and went out. Mayyazhi lay dark and silent.

Supper was over at Big Sayiv's mansion A long line of carriages moved forward under the pale sky, carrying the drowsy guests back home. Sergent-en-retraite Kunhikannan's carriage was missing. He would never partake of Big Sayiv's hospitality again.

The silence of the night was not disturbed even by the sound of the sea. Not a leaf stirred. Dasan read quietly.

As usual, Kurambi Amma heard the crunch of Leslie Sayiv's boots.

'Won't you give me a pinch of snuff, Kurambi?'

How could she give Leslie Sayiv, long dead, a pinch of snuff?

She burst into tears.

The kerosene lamp in Dasan's room continued to flicker until dawn. As day broke, Dasan began to doze, but only for a few moments. He shook himself awake and went on reading.

ONLY DASAN AND SEKHARAN got through that year. Dasan stood first. His success was the talk of Mayyazhi. Damu heard the news in court while drafting a document. He put down his pen and rushed home, gasping for breath.

On the way he saw Edouard Sayiv, Principal of the Cours Complémentaire and one of Dasan's teachers.

'Félicitations!' he congratulated Damu, 'Vives félicitations!'

All the way home, the people he met congratulated him. He held his head up proudly and his bent back straightened. He almost choked with excitement. He was only a poor clerk, living precariously on the pittance he earned by drafting and copying deeds. But today, everyone was gazing at him with respect and wonder. His son had passed, while Mayor Chekku Moopar's had failed. His son had beaten Secrètaire Karunan's. Tears welled up in his sunken eyes.

Dasan was summoned to Big Sayiv's great white house the next morning. He could not figure out why. Did Big Sayiv want to congratulate him in person? No student of the Cours Complémentaire had ever been summoned to the bungalow.

'There goes the deed writer's boy,' remarked someone seated in the teashop. All eyes were on Dasan. He walked with confidence. The policemen guarding the bungalow made way for him. He went up the path in the middle of a garden filled with exotic plants and flowers.

Another armed policeman stood on the veranda. The floor was covered with a red carpet and the cushioned chairs were polished to the sheen of glass. There was an old painting resembling Van Gogh's *Le Champ de Blè* on the wall and a huge statue of the President of the Fourth Republic stood majestically in the corner.

The pleated silk curtains at the door parted and Dasan heard the crunch of shoes over the carpet. Secrètaire Karunan moved aside hurriedly. Pipe smoke and the odour of burning tobacco wafted through the room.

There was a moment's silence. The crash of waves could be heard below the bungalow.

Big Sayiv's voice rose over the rumble of the sea:

'L'Etat se rèjoit de ton succès.' The State takes pleasure in your success.

'Poursuis tes ètudes.' Go on with your studies.

'Va á Pondichèry.' Go to Pondicherry.

'L'Etat t'accorde une bourse.' The State grants you a scholarship.

'L'Etat s'occupe dèsormais de toi.' The State will look after you from now on.

The silk curtains parted and footsteps crunched over the carpet again as Big Sayiv left.

Dasan came out through the guarded gateway, intoxicated with joy and pride.

11

DASAN WAS BUSY PREPARING TO GO TO PONDICHERRY FOR HIS HIGHER studies.

'Who will buy me snuff, child, when you go?' Dasan had been buying Kurambi Amma snuff from Chettiar's shop for years. For a quarter anna in the old days and now for half an anna.

'I can go and buy it, Achamma,' said Girija. She had stopped going to school. She had come of age recently. Girls from good families did not go to school once they came of age. They were seldom allowed to go out at all.

'You? You're a big girl now. How can you go to the shops by yourself?'

'Why, will someone catch hold of me if I go out?'

'Young girls can't go out as they like.'

Girija was quiet by nature and never really wanted to go out much, except to Chandrika's house. Chandrika and she were close friends.

'Never mind the snuff,' said Kurambi Amma. 'I want you to do well at your studies.' She hugged Dasan, stroked him with her ageing hands. Her eyes filled with tears. She could not bear to think that she would not see him for a year or two. He had never been away from her from the day he was born. Holding him on her lap for hours together, she had fondled him, told him so many stories. She had watched him grow, inch by inch, into a young man. She had wept with joy when he passed the Brevet.

'Will you remember your Achamma when you're a big man in a hat and coat?'

How can I forget you, Achamma, thought Dasan, it is for all of you that I live.

'There's nothing I want from you, child, except the half anna to buy my snuff until I die. Will you give me that?'

'I'll buy snuff for you as long as I live.'

Kurambi Amma wiped her eyes. Girija and Chandrika packed his clothes in a steel trunk. He had managed with one shirt all these days, wearing it only when he went out. Big Sayiv had sent him some money for the journey and he had bought new clothes with it. More than half the trunk was filled with books. Kunhanandan Master had given him a long envelope to be handed over to Subbaraman, a professor in Pondicherry who was working for the freedom movement. Dasan knew it contained information on the political situation in Mayyazhi and the problems that the freedom fighters faced.

Chandrika had been at Dasan's house all the time over the last few days. She came very early the morning he was leaving. When he woke up, he saw her leaning against the table and talking to his mother. Fresh from her morning bath, her wet hair was in a loose braid and her kohl-rimmed eyes were sparkling.

She hurried into his room when she realized he was alone.

'Dasetta—'

'What is it, Chandri?'

'Will you write, Dasetta?'

'To whom?'
She did not answer. 'When will you be back?'
'I don't know.'
'For the summer vacation?'
'Perhaps.'

She heard a voice outside and left the room hastily, her anklets tinkling in unison. Dasan felt a twinge of sadness as he watched her go, even though he did not believe in romance.

Kunhichirutha came to say goodbye just as he finished his bath.

'What will you bring me from Pondicherry?'

Did she want silks and jewels like those that Vaisravanan Chettiar had brought for Kunhimanikkam?

'I don't want anything, child. Don't forget me when you're a big man, that's all.'

Kunhichirutha took a betel leaf from the box that Kowsu held out to her. 'I want to come to Pondicherry too. God willing, I'll come and see you there, Dasan.'

'Why stop with Pondicherry, Kunhichirutha? You can go to France with David Sayiv after all.'

'God willing, I'll go to France as well, Kurambi Amma.'

Kunhichirutha chewed on her betel leaf and her red lips grew redder. She got up, gave Dasan her blessings and left. He remembered how she had blessed him on the day he first went to school. And given him two annas to buy sweets. He watched her walk away with her swan-like gait. Time had gone by, but Kunhichirutha still looked the same.

Kelan's carriage pulled up in front of the house. Dasan lifted up his trunk and took leave of all of them. Kowsu looked anxious. Who would care for her son in Pondicherry? Who would feed or nurse him if he fell ill?

'Stop crying, Kowsu. Don't see him off with tears.' Damu Writer chided his wife. 'Dasan, you haven't forgotten anything, have you?'

'No, Father.'

'Let's go then.'

Unthinkingly, Dasan put his left foot forward. An ill omen. He had done the same thing on his first day at school.

Father and son climbed into the carriage which would take them to the small railway station. Everyone had gathered on the veranda. Amma and Achamma dabbed at their eyes. Girija hid her tears behind a smile. Chandrika stood behind her, her face pale, her eyes fixed on the jutka.

The jutka creaked forward.

'Goodbye, all of you.'

12

Policeman Andru got up at dawn and hurriedly put on his hat and leggings. He had to be on duty at Big Sayiv's mansion at five-thirty. It was still dark. The church steeple and the cross on top were shrouded in blue mist. The sea bordering the Rue de la Rèsidence looked grey and the casuarina trees standing guard over it had a pale gleam. Fishermen carrying heavy loads slung on poles across their shoulders could be glimpsed like shadows on the iron bridge in the distance.

Andru stopped outside Big Sayiv's house, startled.

Libertè!

A huge poster was stuck on the wall with the word written elegantly on it in red ink. Andru was furious when he discovered what it meant: freedom! He knew people were running around the town shouting slogans but he had never imagined that they could be so impudent. His jaw trembled with, anger.

Policeman Palani, gun in hand, stood dozing inside the small guardroom at the entrance. He started awake when he heard Andru's footsteps.

'It's a lie, a lie!' Palani did not believe Andru at first. When he saw the poster, however, he began to sweat in spite of the cool sea breeze. He had been on guard all night. Some insolent fellow had done this right under his nose. If word reached the Commissar's ears, it would be the end of him.

'Andru, sauvez-moi,' he begged, his grey moustache trembling in fear. 'Save me, think of my wife and children.'

If the poster could be removed before anyone saw it, Palani would escape punishment. But Andru would not allow that. The more Andru thought about it, the angrier he grew. The rascal who did this had to be caught, no matter who he was, he thought to himself. He set off for Brigadier Venkayya's house, paying no attention to Palani's pleas.

The Brigadier lived above the police station. He came out of his room yawning. When he heard what had happened, his puffy face turned red.

'Let's go.' He tucked a pistol in his belt and sprang into the jeep. Andru got in as well. Raising whirls of dust that dissolved the mist hanging over the Rue de la Prison, they rushed to Commissar Laporte's house.

'Where could those death-mongers be off to at this time of morning?' asked Kallu, seated in front of the dharmasala, lazily picking lice out of her tangled hair.

Elephant-legged Antony, another inmate of the dharmasala, raised his head and looked at Brigadier Venkayya in awe. Unlike most of the policemen in Mayyazhi who were a dull lot, drinking incessantly and running after women, Brigadier Venkayya was as ferocious as a tiger.

Commissar Laporte was exactly like the Brigadier. An unfortunate incident had occurred the day he disembarked in Mayyazhi from the ship that had brought him from France. Elephant-legged Antony had an atrocious habit of never using the latrine attached to the dharmasala. Brigadier Venkayya took Commissar Laporte around the town the day he arrived. The Commissar visited the Church of the Virgin, then the Maine and the Palais de Justice and entered the Rue de la Rèsidence. A row of bungalows lined the left and the Mayyazhi river flowed down to the sea on the right. Big Sayiv's mansion was set in a garden with casuarina trees surrounding it. The gulmohar trees lining the pier were ablaze with red flowers.

The Commissar thrilled to the beauty of Mayyazhi. Red gulmohar flowers rained over him as he walked down the pier. Revelling in the lovely view of the sea, the river and the trees in bloom, he suddenly caught sight of elephant-legged Antony squatting on the bank of the river, smoking a beedi. Coming as he did from the land of Lamartine's verses and Manet's paintings, he could not bear such an ugly sight. Before Brigadier Venkayya quite realized what had happened, the Commissar's foot shot out. Antony scrambled up with a cry and ran away, dragging his afflicted foot. The same day he was deported from Mayyazhi on the orders of the Commissar.

But where could Antony go? He had been born in Mayyazhi and had grown up there. It was his home. He returned to Mayyazhi the same day. Ever since, he had been trying not to appear within sight of the policemen.

The Commissar's jeep came to a stop in front of Big Sayiv's mansion. He saw the poster, the harbinger of the impending storm, pulled it off the wall, tore it into a thousand shreds and flung them into the Arabian Sea.

Brigadier Venkayya and his minions set out in search of the traitor who had put up the poster. The poster became the talk of the town.

The people of Mayyazhi feared the goondas more than the policemen. All of them were heartless, particularly Achu.

'Shall I tell you who put it up?' Unni Nair poured frothing toddy into Achu's tumbler.

'Who?'

'Kunhanandan Master, who else?'

'That half-dead creature?'

Achu had suspected Master himself. But Master was very ill and confined to bed. He could not go out at all.

'If it's not him, it's his friends,' said Andru.

Achu grunted. He knew, of course, that Master and his friends were trying to make trouble.

Andru and Achu emptied their toddy glasses, got up and went out. With a face that was always flushed and grim and blazing red eyes, Achu was a man of few words. As he stepped out with his mundu tucked well above his knees and his head held high, the earth seemed to tremble beneath his feet. 'Achu, whoever it is, see that you break his bones,' Unni Nair called out behind him.

Achu and Andru walked to Kunhanandan Master's house. The news had spread by now. The Commissar and the Secrètaire were trying to figure out the political fallout of the poster. But Achu and Andru were not interested in politics. They saw the incident as an arrogant act that challenged the authority of the police and the goondas. Achu's blood boiled with the indignity of it.

Master knew that the police and the goondas had been watching him closely. Leela had warned him constantly: 'Be careful, Anandan, that Achu is wicked.'

'What harm can he do to someone like me who is half dead?'

Master had realized that his activities were considered provocative. The framed photographs of Lenin and Marx looking down from the wall had incensed the police and the goondas. The poster would have been the last straw.

'Master, we're afraid for you.'

'Mayyazhi doesn't need sick people like me, Pappan. It needs strong young men like you and Uthaman. What use am I now to anyone? I'm just counting my days ...'

'Please Master, don't say that. You'll live a long time yet.'

Uthaman looked distressed. He was the son of Malayan Kurumban, the sorcerer, the healer of snake bites. Malayan Kunhiraman, who had tried to save Kunhimanikkam from Vaisravanan Chettiar when he came disguised as a snake, had been Uthaman's paternal great-grandfather. Uthaman was a student of the Cours Complémentaire. He practised black magic and healed snake bites. Pappan often argued with him.

'You call yourself a communist?'

'Why not?'

'You have to be a Marxist in order to be a communist and a materialist in order to be a Marxist. Are you a materialist?'

'I am.'

'Don't you know that materialism and sorcery don't go hand in hand?'

'Look Pappan,' Master intervened, 'Uthaman practises sorcery for a living. There's no faith involved.'

Uthaman had no belief in his family profession. For generations, there had been sorcerers and healers of snake bites in his family. They had incarnated divine Theyyams for the festival at the Meethala temple. For Uthaman, it was a means of earning a livelihood and nothing more.

Someone shouted from the street, 'Anyone there?'

They recognized Achu's threatening voice. Uthaman's heart missed a beat.

Achu entered, followed by Policeman Andru.

Master came out, gathering up the folds of his mundu. Pappan and Uthaman stayed inside the house. Pappan rolled up the sleeves of his shirt. If Achu had come to make trouble, he was ready for him. Leela stood behind the door, her heart thumping. None of the women in Mayyazhi had ever dared face Achu. She prayed silently.

'What's the matter, Achu?'

'I came to find out what the matter is.'

Achu looked at Master from head to foot. At the greying stubble of hair on his face, his sunken eyes, his pale lips. He looked as if he had got up from his deathbed. But Achu was not moved.

'I'm going to ask you something, you have to tell me the truth.'
'Go ahead.'
'Who stuck the poster on Big Sayiv's wall?'
'I don't know.'
'You had better tell me the truth. You don't know me. I don't care if you're ill. I'll thrash you until you don't have a tooth left in your mouth.'
'Who are you to ask about the poster on Big Sayiv's wall? What right do you have to question me? I don't know who did it. And if I did, I wouldn't tell you. I'll tell those who have the right to ask. Now get out.'

Clutching his mundu, Master tore into the house, choking with anger.

'The scum. Imagine him coming to question me!' He lay down.

Feeling deeply insulted, Achu waited uncertainly for a moment, unsheathed penknife in hand. Then he muttered something and hurried away with Andru.

'Oh my God!' Leela heaved a sigh of relief. 'Now, will you tell me who put up the poster?'

'That one there.'

Master pointed to Pappan. Pappan smiled, a lighted beedi held tightly between his teeth.

Leela was astonished. 'I didn't know you had the guts.'

Pappan continued to smile. 'I'll stick one on Big Sayiv's back if need be.'

13

Activists of banned political parties, murderers and thieves from Malabar and Travancore often came to Mayyazhi seeking asylum. The police from those states did not have access to Mayyazhi which was a French possession. Achu, a criminal of this kind, had come to seek refuge in Mayyazhi. No one knew where he had come from, not even Kurambi Amma, an eyewitness to every drama that unfolded in Mayyazhi.

Seated on the veranda with her legs stretched out, Kurambi Amma helped herself to a pinch of snuff as usual. Kowsu was busy cooking lunch. Damu was expected back from the court any moment.

A young man passing that way stopped at the gate. He was short, stout and fair-skinned. His mundu was tucked up above his knees.

'Who's that?' asked Kurambi Amma, who knew everyone in Mayyazhi.

'I don't know, Amma. He seems a stranger to this place,' said Kowsu, peering through the smoke-stained kitchen window.

Kurambi Amma gazed at the stranger, her hand shading her eyes. He came into the courtyard. Kurambi Amma got up. Kowsu came out and stared at him curiously. Suddenly, to their shock, they saw the unsheathed penknife in his hand.

'Who are you?'

'I'm Achu.'

'Achu?'

'Don't worry, old woman.' Achu pulled the bench towards him and sat down. Kurambi Amma was irritated by his arrogance.

'Give me some rice.'

'You didn't tell me who you are.'

'Never mind who I am. I asked you to give me some rice.'

'What a thing! Do you think this is a dharmasala serving food to passersby?'

'Mind your words, old woman.'

Kurambi Amma's nostrils twitched with anger. Who did he think he was, this stranger from nowhere? How insolent he was!

'Be quiet, Amma,' said Kowsu.

Kowsu brought him water. Achu washed his face and went in. Kowsu set a brass plate for him and a low wooden stool to sit on. Achu ate enough rice for three, belched, washed his hands and spread the mundu he was wearing on the bench. He lay down in his red cotton underwear.

By the time Damu arrived, Achu was fast asleep and snoring loudly, his mouth open. The deed writer had heard of Achu. He went in without a word.

'Why don't you drive that rascal away?' Kurambi Amma lost her patience.

'No one can drive him away.'

'Who is he?'

'He's not from here. But he hangs around with the police and no one can lay hands on him. It's better you keep quiet, Amma.'

Achu had been in Mayyazhi only a few days, but he had already become a friend of the police and the goondas. The day before, he had worked himself into a fury and beaten up everyone in Unni Nair's toddy shop. He always carried an open penknife. The deed writer knew all this.

Achu woke up and retied his mundu around his waist, over his red underwear.

'Who lives here?'

'I, Damu the deed writer,' said Damu politely.

'Do you know who I am?'

'I do.'

'Listen then. If you behave, I'll be good to you. But if you cross me ...' He flung his knife into the air, caught it as it fell and left.

He walked to the toddy tapper Kumaran's mud hut, knowing Kumaran would be away at this time of day. His daughter Kamala was alone at home ...

Kumaran came to seek revenge, tapping knife in hand. Achu knocked him down. Turning his back towards the sea, Achu declared, 'I'll rape every woman in Mayyazhi!'

The policemen drowsing in the arrack shop nearby clapped their hands.

'Now there's a man for you,' said Kallu admiringly, seated on the veranda of the dharmasala, picking the lice from her hair.

Achu had neither home nor family. All he had was an open penknife. If he was hungry, he entered the house nearest him and demanded food. No one dared refuse him. If he was sleepy, he went into the first house he saw. If there was an easy chair or a bench on the veranda, he lay down on it. Otherwise, he would call out, 'Bring me a mat and a pillow.'

He never bothered to find out whose house he had entered. He ate in the deed writer's house many times, often knocking on the door late at night. No one ever objected. Kowsu always fetched him a mat and a pillow.

And so Achu settled down permanently in Mayyazhi and put down roots. Very soon, he became a part of its destiny as well, since he was one of the principal actors in the tragic drama that was to unfold in Mayyazhi.

14

Malayan Kurumban died at the age of seventy.

He had been performing the ritual Thira dance at the temple festival and practising sorcery since he was twelve.

The temple deities now needed someone whom they could possess, a new pair of feet to dance. Would the Vellattu ever be able to drink the rooster's blood again?

The deities came out of their divine mysteries at the silent hour of midnight or in the blazing noonday and wandered around, invisible to the eyes of the Mayyazhi folk. The gods became visible only when Kurumban incarnated them in the temple courtyard.

'Who will suck out the poison when a snake bites us?' asked Kunjakkan. Snakes crawled all over Mayyazhi in the rainy season. Kunjakkan had been bitten twice, once in the rice fields and then on a lamp-post. Both times, Kurumban had saved his life with his sorcery.

'Who'll exorcise the ghosts now?' asked Kunjakkan's son, Kunhanan. He was frightened of ghosts.

'Uthaman, Kurumban's son. Who else?'

'But he's a communist.' Unni Nair added up the sums of money his clients owed him on the table with a piece of chalk.

Kunhanan looked doubtful.

'Uthaman's a smart lad all right.'

Uthaman was a sturdy young man with dark, oily skin, strong hands and legs and curly hair.

As Kunjakkan and Kunhanan sipped their toddy, Kuramban's body was taken that way. A couple of Malayans, tribals from the east, carried the dilapidated wooden bier infested with woodworms. Kunhanandan Master, Vasutty and Pappan were all in the crowd that followed. Uthaman walked in the shadow of the bier. In the sunshine, his ear-studs glinted as brightly as the tears in his eyes.

Kurambi Amma came out of her house as the bier came in view. Kurumban's body was covered from head to foot with a white cloth. Only his pale bald scalp was visible. She recalled the many deities she had seen Kurumban incarnate at the Thira festival—as Gulikan, clad in palm leaves and wearing a headgear measuring over thirty feet; as Kuttichathan, dancing in a trance with a basket and baton in his hand; and as Vellattu, hooting as he lacerated his head with a curved sword ... Kurumban had danced these roles for as long as Kurambi Amma could remember.

'So he's gone as well,' she sighed.

Uthaman lighted the pyre for his father's cold, rigid body. When the flames began to blaze high, Kurumban stood upright in the fire, writhed and fell back.

'Come on,' said Master, placing his hand around the sobbing Uthaman's shoulder. 'In our life, we act all kinds of roles—blackmarketeers, thieves ... But your father died playing the roles of gods. We must be happy for him.'

Everyone had left, except Master, Vasutty and Pappan.

When the fire died out, they accompanied Uthaman home and went on to Master's place.

'If only the gods had died too, with Malayan Kurumban,' murmured Pappan. The gods were as much his enemies as policemen and goondas were. He hated them. There were no gods in his dream world. He often said, 'If I had my way, I'd change every temple into a library.'

'Do you think Uthaman will take Kurumban's place in the Thira festival? I doubt it.'

'If he doesn't, his family will starve.'

'How can a communist like him become a temple dancer?'

'Listen, Vasutty, all of us have many roles to act in life. Surely, playing God can't be worse than any of them.'

'But Master, one must at least be a believer to play that role.'

'You can be a pujari without believing in God. Bhakti has an aspect that we do not always understand, Vasutty, it can simply be a profession. And that is how Uthaman will have to see it.'

They continued to argue about Uthaman's future.

Meanwhile, with Kurumban's death, the burden of the family fell on Uthaman's shoulders. When the mourning was over, his mother said, 'Don't go back to school.'

Seeing his mother's tears, Uthaman held his anger in check.

'If you go back to school, we'll starve.'

Uthaman did not need to be told this. But he did not know what to do. He wanted to educate himself and find a respectable job. This sudden calamity had upset his plans.

'Why don't you say something, son?'

Avoiding his mother's eyes, Uthaman gazed at the parched rice fields. After a long time, he said, 'I can't perform at the Thira festival or cure snake bites.'

He had no desire to follow in the footsteps of his forefathers and become a sorcerer.

His mother was shocked. 'The Gods will be angry, son.'

'How can they be angry? They don't exist.'

This was another shock to her. She would rather have believed that there were no human beings on earth than that there were no gods.

The deities of Meethalambalam were fierce. They loved you if you loved them. But if they were crossed, they would destroy your tharavad. There were families in Mayyazhi that had been ruined this way. And families that had been blessed by them as well. Lame Kunjakkan was living proof.

The fire in their hearth ceased to burn. The family starved. Dechu, Uthaman's elder sister, threatened, 'I'm hungry. Wait and see, I'll run away with some man.' Uthaman was adamant. He would never practise sorcery, even if he had to starve. In the end, Uthaman's mother turned to Kunhanandan Master for help. 'Unless you tell him, he won't change his mind, Master.' She sat down at his feet. 'We haven't cooked for three days. I have nothing left to sell. Save us, Master.' Master sent Pappan to fetch Uthaman.

'If you don't want to be a sorcerer, you'll have to find other work. You can't let your mother starve, it's not right.'

'What sort of work can I find, Master?'

'You can roll beedis or plough the rice fields.'

'I'm not used to that kind of work.'

'Then do what your family has always done. Your father spent his life in the service of the gods. His family can't be left to starve now.'

Uthaman went away without a word.

Next day, he got up at dawn and had a bath in the stagnant green water of the family tank. He changed, placed a sandalwood mark on his forehead and sat down on the cloth-covered chair in the veranda, the chair his father had used. As the sun grew hotter, he saw Kunhanan coming across the rice fields.

'What is it?'

'Last night ...' Kunhanan's face grew pale, as if he had a fever. 'I was going home from Unni Nair's toddy shop ... It was pitch dark, the church dock struck twelve. Someone called out from behind, 'Here you, Kunhanan ...' He looked terrified.

'I walked on as though I hadn't heard. The call came again. When I turned ...'

'When you turned?'

'It was Bear Sayiv.'

Kunhanan sank to the ground, too weak to stand or speak.

Uthaman was amused. Bear Sayiv had been dead for years, burned alive by his son, Peter. But he was careful not to laugh, for if he did, his family would starve. He took a length of black string, muttered a mantram over it and tied it on Kunhanan's hand.

'Go home. Bear Sayiv won't bother you anymore.'

Kunhanan wiped the sweat from his forehead. He took an anna from the pocket of his unbleached shirt and offered it as a fee.

Uthaman watched Kunhanan walk away over the rice fields and thought to himself—there goes the first man I've deceived.

He threw the anna coin at his sister, who was seated on the front steps, picking lice from her hair. 'There, you don't have to run away with some fellow now, Dechu Edathi.'

Uthaman stopped going to school. The fire in Malayan Kurumban's hearth burned every day now, wafting the smell of cooked dry fish. And the day of the temple festival drew nearer.

There were two important festivals in Mayyazhi—the Feast of the Virgin and the Thira festival. Although the Thira temple belonged to the Thiyyas, every caste except the Mapillas came to watch the celebrations. The Mapillas were forbidden to enter the temple premises.

'Not that we mind if you enter,' Choyi Moopan would say. 'It's just that Kuttichathan won't like it.' Kuttichathan was one of the main temple deities.

'In the days when Choyi Moopan's father, Raman Moopan, ruled over the tharavad ...' Kurambi Amma began her story, and Girija listened, while her grandmother's fingers ran through her hair. Girija was not a child anymore now, but she still listened to the stories and legends that Kurambi Amma told her. As the old woman talked, Girija's mind would wander through her own dreamscapes. She would imagine her ideal man—firm-chested, with hairy arms and legs, reeking of beedis and sweat.

'Are you listening, child?' Kurambi Amma would ask her from time to time and Girija would murmur, 'Yes, Achamma.'

'Raman Moopan had a Muslim friend named Keyi Mapilla who owned many rice fields and coconut groves. He was a rich and generous man.

'"Hey Moopan," he said, "I must come and watch your Thira festival this year."

'Moopan and Keyi were seated in Moopan's courtyard, drinking tender coconut water.

'"Oh Keyi, that would be a sin against the gods."

'"Look, if Nairs and Christians can enter your temple and Pariahs can watch the Thira, surely I can watch it too."

'What Keyi was saying made sense, thought Moopan. Even Mayyazhi's scavengers came to watch the Thira, after all.

'"As you like, Keyi."

'"Will you go back on your word?"

'"Of course not."

'That night, Moopan curled up under his blanket wearing only a mundu. The moonlight was pale. The oil lamps in the temple had burned out. Moopan woke with a start. Kuttichathan stood outside the window in the moonlight, basket and baton in hand.

'The deity who had watched over his tharavad for generations! A chill ran through Moopan's spine.

'"Rama," Kuttichathan's eyes blazed at the window like live coals. "Take care. Or I'll wipe out your tharavad."

'Kuttichathan turned his back on Moopan. His yellow silk fluttered. Hooting, he rushed away, the sound of his dancing bells gradually growing softer. Moopan saw the deity disappear into the shrine.

'Moopan did not keep his word to Keyi. And Keyi Mapilla never spoke to Moopan again in his lifetime,' said Kurambi Amma.

Girija was lost in her daydreams. When she idled in bed during her periods or drowsed under her blanket through the long afternoons in the month of Karkatakam, she would feel overpowered by the odour of sweat and beedis.

She woke up suddenly to the sound of firecrackers going off one by one seven times in the temple. The ceremonial flag had been hoisted, the festivities had begun. The first festival after Malayan Kurumban's death.

'Who'll perform the Thira this year?'

'Who but Uthaman?'

Kunjakkan, Kunhanan and their companions were seated in the toddy shop, discussing the Thira festival. Kurumban was dead, his son Uthaman had to perform the ritual dance. That was the tradition.

'But will he?'

'If he doesn't, he'll pay for it. You can't play the fool with Kuttichathan and Gulikan.'

True, Uthaman practised sorcery now and cured snake bites. But would he dance the Thira? No one in Mayyazhi was sure. If no one performed the ritual, Kuttichathan and Gulikan would destroy Mayyazhi.

'I'll perform the Thira,' Uthaman announced. 'But I won't observe the fasts.'

Thira dancers were not permitted to eat meat or fish during the festival time. They had to observe celibacy. Uthaman made it clear that he would defy these rules. That very evening, he bought a basketful of sardines. His mother and sister were petrified with fear.

'Why are you frightened of Kuttichathan and Gulikan, mother? If we Malayans didn't incarnate them, they would not exist.'

His mother sobbed, covering her ears with her hands.

Uthaman left the fish in the kitchen and went to the veranda to smoke. Twilight grew into night, and still there was no smell of fish curry. He went to the kitchen. Dechu was seated by the fire, blowing her streaming nose.

Uthaman cooked the fish himself and ate it. But he was not satisfied with this. Next day, he went to the dharmasala at dusk. The temple bells were ringing and the oil lamps glowed bright.

'Ah, look who's here ... Uthaman!'

Kallu was delighted. Though he was a tribal, Uthaman was a hot-blooded youngster. Her usual clients were drunken policemen. At this auspicious time of year, tribals who performed the Thira ritual dance would carry within them the presence of God. It was God himself who would sleep with Kallu tonight.

Kallu picked up her mundu from the mat and wrapped it around her. Gathering her unbound hair, she said to herself, 'There's a real man, now.'

The news spread like wild fire that Malayan Uthaman had eaten fish and slept with Kallu.

'It will rain fire now—it will be the end of us.'

The Mayyazhi folk went hysterical. Chanduvachan, one of the village elders, went to meet Moopan, the head of the Meethalath family who owned the Thira shrine. He had already heard the news.

Chanduvachan said, 'We can't allow Uthaman to perform the Thira. It would be inviting disaster.' Moopan listened quietly.

'If Uthaman does wrong, the gods will punish him,' was all he said.

There were no Thira performances on the first two days of the festival. Only poojas and prayers were offered. The Thira performances began on the night of the third day. The shrine and its surroundings were crowded even before dusk. Chandrika and Girija were in the crowd.

'Is your skirt new?' asked Girija, running her fingers over the blue silk.

'Yes, Achan sent it to me.'

Bharathan had sent a packet of clothes from Singapore through a Mapilla who had come to Mayyazhi on a visit. The girls wandered around the bangle stalls. There were bangles of every conceivable colour. Girija looked at them longingly.

She had asked her father for a four-anna coin to buy bangles. 'We don't even have three quarter annas to buy rice,' he had shouted, 'and you want bangles!'

Chandrika bought half a dozen black glass bangles. The Chetty who sold them to her slipped them on her hand himself. All of them had to go on her right hand as she wore a watch on the left one.

When they came out of the bangle shop, Chandrika asked, 'Does Dasettan write?'

She used to think of him often, especially when she had new clothes or bangles.

'We haven't heard from him for a month now.'

Chandrika walked quietly beside Girija, her head bent. Dasan wrote to Kunhanandan Master regularly. She looked secretly at the letters. They were all written in French. Chandrika went to an English school, so she could not read French. But she still examined every word with care. Once she had seen her own name in a letter. Her heart had beaten fast. She had tried hard but had not been able to make out what Dasan had written. Nor had she the courage to ask Master. She had spent three sleepless nights wondering what he had said about her.

There were lights everywhere. The rhythmic beat of the Keli had started, announcing a Thira performance. The drummers stood in rows, with caparisoned elephants behind them. The glowing oil lamps illuminated the figure of the Vellattu in his yellow silk, his long hair flying, sword in hand.

Uthaman would perform as Gulikan at midnight. The women settled down in the viewing hall, Kurambi Amma and Kunhichirutha amongst them. Mayor Chekku Moopar was seated in the special pandal put up for him and with him were David Sayiv, Commissar Laporte Sayiv, Secrètaire Karunan and Brigadier Venkayya. David Sayiv's eyes often wandered to where Kunhichirutha was seated, wearing a mundu with a golden border. Kunhanandan, Vasutty and Pappan were all in the crowd.

Uthaman lay on a mat in the thatched shed while an old tribal painted his face with rice powder and vegetable colours.

Then he sat up and a little tribal boy tied the heavy dancing bells on his feet. Uthaman took out a bottle of arrack, gulped down a mouthful and hooted. The sound that came from him did not belong to him alone, it was the sound of Malayan Kurumban, his father Malayan Kunhukutty and the generations of Thira performers before him.

The little tribal boy came out of the shed, lamp in hand. Uthaman followed and then a drummer. Darkness and silence lay over expectant Mayyazhi.

The drummers and pipers stood in rows before the temple. Uthaman paid tributes to the divinities enshrined in all the three mandapams and climbed the seven steps to the stone platform in the middle of the courtyard. Two men held up a sheet of white cloth to screen him. No one was permitted to watch while he put on his headgear. It needed four people to hold up the frame of the bamboo and palm leaf headgear, high as five men. The heavy structure was fastened in such a way that it stood up behind his neck.

Dynamite crackers resounded. The drums thudded. The sheet of white cloth was whirled away. Carpenter Raman fainted when he saw the Gulikan.

Gulikan descended the stone steps slowly, balancing himself on sticks. His towering headgear swayed, threatening to sweep him off the ground. The devout moved out of his way. Escorted by drummers and lamp-bearers, Gulikan reached the temple facade and began the first stage of the performance. The long shadow of his headgear swayed over the courtyard, dimly lit by oil lamps.

As the dance grew faster, the balancing sticks were discarded. Gulikan began to dip and sway in the yellow light, his enormous headgear caught in the whirlwind movement of the ritual dance. The headgear dipped and rose against the skyline. At the climax of the ritual dance, Uthaman faltered and fell on his face.

The drums thudded to a sudden stop. The spectators were transfixed.

In the flickering lamplight, Uthaman could be seen writhing, his neck broken under the weight of the towering headgear.

'Lord, bear with me.' Moopan fell at the feet of the deity in the sanctuary and wept bitterly.

Uthaman's mother and sister left Mayyazhi after his death. And so the family in which generations of Thira performers had been born and reared disappeared from Mayyazhi.

There were many rumours about Uthaman's untimely death. The Mayyazhi folk were sure that the gods had punished him.

Only Kunhanandan Master offered an explanation: 'After all, he was a novice. He should have been more careful.'

15

Having passed the baccalauréat, the highest examination, Dasan completed his studies in Pondicherry. There was great rejoicing on the day he came home. No one slept at all the night before.

'My little one must have grown into a big man,' Kurambi Amma repeated a hundred times. 'He'll come home wearing a hat and coat.'

All Mayyazhi discussed Dasan. Vasutty and Pappan talked about him too in Kunhanandan Master's house.

'He must be a big man now,' said Pappan, echoing Kurambi Amma.

Vasutty frowned: 'Does studying in the white man's college make one a big man?'

'Vasutty, we're only against the white man's rule. Why should we be against his culture?'

'How can you accept their culture and oppose their authority at the same time?'

'I can do it. I don't know about you.'

'You're a fool then and a fence-sitter.'

Vasutty sounded irritated. Everyone was singing Dasan's praises. But it was the white man who had awarded him his high qualification and Vasutty resented this. Pappan found it hard to understand Vasutty's resentment. Why was he against Dasan? Vasutty was not jealous by nature. Master was silent and thoughtful. After all, he knew Dasan better than the others did.

'Vasutty, don't be annoyed. Wait till Dasan gets here. I'm sure you'll understand him. Be patient.'

'What are you hinting at, Master?'

'Be patient, Vasutty. You'll understand, I promise you will.'

Master lay down, his head resting on his hands, and looked at the ceiling.

Vasutty and Pappan were at the railway station the day Dasan arrived. The deed writer was there before them. A man named Purushu, who worked in the Secrètariat, was also there. He was Secrètaire Karunan's right hand. Pappan and Vasutty wondered why he had come.

Policeman Andru and Achu were talking to each other on the station platform. Porter Kunhanan rang the bell to announce that the Mangalore Mail would soon come in.

Kunjakkan and elephant-legged Antony had also arrived by that time.

The train drew up on the platform.

Dasan stepped out of a third class compartment with a gunny-cloth bag in his hand. He was dressed in a white mundu and a short-sleeved shirt. He looked emaciated, but his face was calmer, more serious than it used to be.

The first person he saw was his father. The scant hair on his bald scalp was completely grey and his back was bent like a bow. Dasan walked up to him.

'How are you, Achan?'

'I'm coughing and wheezing all the time. Not a wink of sleep at night.'

'What does the doctor say?'

'No medicine can cure me, child.'

'You mustn't say that.'

Dasan placed his hand on his father's hot shoulder. The deed writer held out his sweating hand for Dasan's bag.

'I'll carry it myself, Achan.'

'Where's your box?'

'I didn't bring it. The handle broke.' Dasan smiled feebly. He noticed his father's face darken. The deed writer looked closely at his son. They walked on.

'Do you remember us?' asked Pappan.

Remember them? He had asked about them whenever he wrote to Master.

'How's Master?'

'Just the same. He manages to move around the house a bit. I wonder how long he can go on like this.' They were outside the station now.

'Here I am,' said Kunjakkan. Elephant-legged Antony stood behind Kunjakkan scratching his head. Dasan took out an eight-anna coin from his pocket, gave it to Kunjakkan. 'For both of you.'

They bowed and moved away, one dragging his lame leg and the other his elephantine one.

Purushu, who had been waiting in the government car, got out and gave Dasan a sealed envelope.

Dasan opened Big Sayiv's message. All eyes were riveted on him. The deed writer's heart missed a beat. A message delivered by Big Sayiv's representative was bound to be important.

Big Sayiv had signed it himself. He was delighted at Dasan's success. He congratulated him. Dasan could choose a scholarship to

France for further studies or a job in the Secrètariat, whichever he preferred. He was requested to report at the residence next morning.

Dasan's face dimmed and his face grew even more serious. He folded the letter and put it in his pocket.

'What's in the letter, son?'

The deed writer could not contain his impatience.

'Big Sayiv wants me to study in France or work in the Secrètariat.'

The deed writer felt very happy. He took a few seconds to collect himself. He raised his eyes to the cross on the steeple.

The sun grew hotter as they walked down the road. Bare rice fields lay on both sides of them. Malayan Uthaman's ruined hut could be seen on the farther side of the rice fields, on the left.

'Did you know? Uthaman is dead.'

'Master wrote to me. Such a sad thing ...'

The image of a short, dark boy with ear-studs glinting against the black skin of his face flashed through Dasan's mind.

The passersby looked at Dasan with respect. Hundreds of eyes watched him from behind the doors and windows. Dasan paid them no attention. He could not stop thinking about Big Sayiv's letter. It was more than he had expected. If only the circumstances had been different, he would have been so happy.

Would he ever be happy again? He had chosen his path. It was not the path of happiness.

His heart felt heavy. Pappan and Vasutty went to their own houses. The deed writer gripped Dasan's hand tight and his eyes grew moist. Was not his family's destiny being reshaped? He would not have to break his back any longer, drawing up documents. Nor would he be poor. He would soon reap the fruit of his good deeds. It was for this that Dasan had been born as his son.

Dasan loosened his father's grip gently as they came into the lane where Master lived.

'Let me see Master for a moment.'

'You can go later, can't you? Your mother's waiting, counting the minutes.'

'I'll be home in a moment.'

Covering his head with his shoulder cloth to protect it from the scorching heat, the deed writer hurried home to give Kowsu the news. Our son is going to France. My son and yours. How can we bear so much happiness, Kowsu?

Master was half asleep when Dasan went in. He looked very pale and thin. The stubble on his cheeks was grey. Leela was seated at the foot of the bed.

'Chandrika's father says we have to take him to Vellore for an operation.'

'When will Bharatettan come home?'

'In five or six months.'

'Would Master survive until then?'

Leela moved a chair towards him, but Dasan did not take it. He did not want to wake up Master. He could come back in the evening.

Amma would be waiting, he thought. Professor Subbaraman had given him some papers to be handed over to Master. He would bring them in the evening.

As he stepped out of the house, a voice he had almost forgotten called from behind: 'Dasetta ...'

He stopped. The tinkle of anklets came nearer. He saw her at the door, standing with her head bent.

How beautiful she was. Her hips had blossomed gracefully. Her braided hair, half done, fell on her shapely waist.

'When did you come?'

'Just arrived.'

She stood there for a moment, in silence, pressing her forehead against the door.

'Which class are you in?'

'The tenth.'

Her fingers moved unsteadily over the door.

'Dasetta ...' Her fingers were suddenly still and her head bent lower. She whispered, 'I've come of age.'

'When?'

'It's eight months and fourteen days now.' Her eyes darted away shyly.

He smiled at her. So you've been calculating the months and the days to spring this surprise on me?

'What did you bring me from Pondicherry?'

He felt guilty. He had not brought anything, for Chandrika or anyone else. All he had in his bag were his clothes, his books and the letter for Master.

Confused thoughts tumbled through his mind. Chandrika was one of them. He was so distracted by his thoughts that he hardly realized he had reached home. Amma, Achamma and Girija were in the veranda, waiting for him eagerly.

Amma ran up and hugged him.

'Why didn't you write? I was so worried.'

He had not written to them for a long time. Not because he did not want to, but because studies and political activities had kept him very busy. Most days, he had slept only four or five hours.

Kurambi Amma was deeply disappointed when she saw Dasan in his white mundu and short-sleeved shirt. Was it for this that he had gone to the white man's college in Pondicherry?

'Where's your hat and coat, Dasan?' She had hoped to see him dressed like Leslie Sayiv.

Dasan tried to comfort her: 'I'll become a Sayiv one day and wear a hat and coat.'

'Dasan will soon have to wear a coat, Amma. Big Sayiv is sending him to France.' Kowsu said proudly.

Kurambi Amma took out her snuffbox and helped herself to a pinch of snuff.

Dasan had a bath and sat down to eat. Girija served him.

Like Chandrika, she too had grown up.

'I could hardly make you out, you've grown so much.' Girija lowered her eyes shyly.

'It's time we looked around for a young man,' said Kurambi Amma.

'I've already found someone,' the deed writer said.

'Who?'

'David Sayiv!'

'Oh God, will Kunhichirutha allow that?'

Achan, Amma and Achamma laughed. Girija slipped behind the door, blushing.

In the evening, when Dasan started out, the deed writer reminded him: 'Don't forget to go and see Missie.'

She knew he was back. Would she have baked his favourite cake?

It was a long time since he had walked through the Rue de l'Eglise.

People looked at him admiringly. He doesn't look stylish or haughty, they said to each other. You would never know he had been to a white man's college.

'There's a young man for you,' said one of the customers in Sekharan's teashop. 'He's proof that passing exams doesn't turn you into a Sayiv.'

Dasan went straight to Missie's bungalow. He could hardly recognize her. She looked like a ghost of her old self. She wore a black dress that came down to her ankles. Her red hair, thin as a rat's tail, was gathered over her head with a piece of string. Her body was bent like a bow. Was this the beautiful, blue-eyed, golden-haired woman who used to walk hand-inhand with Leslie Sayiv on the beach?

'I can't see very well, child.' She ran her fingers over Dasan's head and cheeks.

Still, she had baked his favourite cake, the same pretty one she always used to make. She sat by him as he ate.

He wanted to enquire about Gaston, but he could not find the words. He did not want to hurt her. Gaston was still shut up in his room upstairs. Time had gone by, but the impotent Sayiv still stayed by himself, cut off from the outside world. Perhaps he would never come out, he would die in solitude.

As he came out of Missie's house, Dasan saw Vasutty and Pappan on the pier, under the Republic Memorial, smoking beedis.

'What are your plans?' Vasutty held out a beedi. Dasan lit it and sat down by them.

'You'll be off to France, now, won't you?'

'Don't ask me anything now, Vasutty.'

Dasan had felt as if his head were on fire ever since he had read Big Sayiv's letter this morning. On the one hand, he had to consider his father who had grown prematurely old with sickness and worry. On the other, there were the ideals that had moulded his life.

'You're not going to France, then?' Vasutty was amazed. 'Then it's the job in the Secrètariat you want. Good. You can become another Secrètaire Karunan.'

'How little you know me, Vasutty.' He did not want to say more.

They sat on the pier until dusk. The sea shone in the darkness.

At home, they were talking about him.

Amma asked Achan, 'What will he study in France?'

'Let him learn to be a doctor. We don't have anyone in the village to take care of the poor when they fall sick.'

So they gilded their dreams with gold ... Dasan saw the joy with which they looked at him and realized that he had never seen his parents so happy.

The happiness would be short-lived. He was about to destroy it, wrench it from them and give them tears instead.

Many people would be ruined. That was Mayyazhi's destiny. He felt it was better to be the cause of his parents' tears than other people's. At least his parents' tears were his own.

'You have to be at Big Sayiv's at ten tomorrow morning, don't you?'

'I've ironed your mundu and shirt, Etta,' said Girija.

He ate silently, not looking at them. Kurambi Amma came up and patted his head.

'You'll go to France in a ship, over the seven seas, won't you?'

He sighed. All night, he could not sleep. He smoked innumerable beedis. In the morning, he went to his father, his eyes still heavy, and said gently: 'I'm not going to France, Acha.' The writer was dumbfounded.

'I don't want the job in the Secrètariat either.'

His tone was calm. His father heard him in stony silence.

The silence grew unbearably heavy. He heard his mother sobbing in the kitchen.

This is only the beginning of an endless stream of tears, he thought.

Give me strength.

16

The people of Mayyazhi could not believe that Dasan had refused to meet Big Sayiv. It seemed to them that Dasan was being very arrogant. For the most part, all of them were eager to catch a glimpse of Big Sayiv, to hear him speak a few words.

Leela was very distressed. 'The deed writer had pinned his hopes on him. How will he endure this?' She knew how desperate things were for Damu Writer.

But Kunhanandan Master's eyes, dark with the shadow of death, lighted up with a strange gleam. 'Dasan's decision may ruin his family, but it will bring our country good fortune.'

'It's you they will blame in the end, Kunhanandan. They'll say you forced Dasan into this,' said Leela.

'That is an accusation that will make me happy.'

'Tell me the truth, did you persuade Dasan to do this?'

'No, he is better educated and better informed than I am.'

Leela fell silent.

'Dasan will do many more astonishing things. He will rewrite our destiny, Leela Edathi. Wait and see ...'

Master grieved for the deed writer, but Dasan's decision had gladdened him. He could die in peace now. Dasan would follow in his footsteps and carry on what he had started.

There was one more person who was delighted—Vasutty. All his doubts about Dasan were set at rest.

Vasutty and Pappan found Dasan's house still and quiet, like a house of mourning. The deed writer's easy chair was empty.

'Anyone at home?' Vasutty called out. There was no answer. After a while, Girija came to the door. 'Ettan is not here.'

'Where has he gone?'

'I don't know.'

Girija's face was tear-stained. Dasan had gone out in the morning and not come back for lunch. And anyway, what would he have eaten if he had come back? No food had been cooked that day.

Vasutty and Pappan looked for Dasan everywhere. Beneath the Republic Memorial, on the beach, in the library, in all the haunts where he could usually be found. But he was not anywhere.

'Maybe he is trying to calm his thoughts,' said Pappan. 'Let's leave him alone.'

Chandrika went out in search of him, too. For the first time, she had worn a half-saree, a pink one, over her white skirt. She had thought of Dasan as she stood before the mirror, placed a black pottu on her forehead and tied a ribbon in her hair. She set off for school with her umbrella and books and stopped in front of the temple. She said a silent prayer, 'Please God, let me meet Dasettan on the way.' She turned from the Rue de la Gare into Mayyazhi's main street, the Rue de l'Eglise, which linked Thalassery with Vadagara. The Church of the Virgin and the Vignanaposhini Library were both situated on it.

She peered into the library. But he was not there.

She walked on, observing both sides of the road although, she kept her head bent. Achu passed by her with his mundu tucked up, flashing his unsheathed knife. Then came Kunjakkan hobbling along with the ladder on his shoulder and the kerosene oil tin in his hand. Policemen zigzagged along the road after an early morning visit to the wineshop. The only person she did not see was Dasan.

Chandrika's school was in the Rue de la Prison. She slowed down as she came up to it. Would Dasettan be on the pier?

Her heart was heavy as she went into class.

When she came home in the afternoon, she asked her mother whether he had come there, but he had not.

She washed her face at the well and made a pretence of eating. She was not hungry at all. She had to be back at school at two. The sun was burning hot. The cross on top of the steeple shone like the tip of a sword.

She looked for Dasan again in the library, but it was empty. Who would come there to read in this searing heat?

After school, she took a different route home, sure that she would find Dasan at the pier. Her heart beat fast as she turned into the Rue de la Rèsidence. Pappan and Vasutty were seated under the dome of the Republic Memorial. But not the person she wanted to see.

She decided to go to Dasan's house, pretending that she wanted to meet Girija. Surely Dasan would be there. Where else could he be?

Girija came out looking forlorn. She made an effort to smile and asked, 'When did you start to wear a half-saree?'

'Today.' Chandrika glanced into Dasan's room through the corner of her eye. A big book lay open on the bed, but there was no sign of the reader.

'Sit down,' said Girija. Kowsu and Kurambi Amma were not to be seen, nor Damu Writer. He had obviously not gone to the court, his faded umbrella hung on the door. The house seemed sunk in sorrow.

But Chandrika saw nothing of all this. All she knew was Dasan was not there. She left quickly. She knew Girija would be puzzled by her behaviour, but she could not bear to stay.

Chandrika stayed by the window, gazing at the road until her mother reminded her to change. 'You don't need a half-saree at home. Just a skirt will do. You're not such a big girl as all that.'

Kanaran and Kunhanandan Master were discussing something seriously. Vasutty and Pappan joined them later in the evening.

Pappan asked Chandrika, 'When did you start wearing a half-saree?' Paying no attention to him, she continued to stare at the road.

Amma reminded her again at dinner time, 'You still haven't taken off your half-saree? Who are you waiting for?'

Chandrika did not answer, she ate mechanically, her eyes fixed on the dark space that lay beyond the pools of light spilling from the smoky municipal lamps.

Master's house was two-storeyed and Chandrika's room was upstairs. She went to her room after dinner, but could not concentrate on her books. Every time she heard a voice downstairs, she would peer down to find out who it was.

The municipal lights burned out. A cock crowed from somewhere in the distance.

Chandrika took off her half-saree at last and, holding the pillow against her cheek, she began to cry.

They were the first tears she shed for Dasan.

17

When Brigadier Venkayya was transferred from Mayyazhi, he was replaced by Brigadier Chettiappa. Chettiappa arrived on a rice cargo ship from Pondicherry. A group of policemen and goondas came to welcome him, under the leadership of policeman Andru. Achu was one of the group.

Brigadier Chettiappa was sleek and fat with a stomach that protruded from his khaki uniform. His skin was as black as rosewood and his teeth were white and shining.

Every evening, he went for a walk, escorted by Achu and Andru, wearing a pale yellow silk shirt and a mundu with a golden border draped around his bulky stomach. He wore a gold chain on his neck and rings on all his fingers. He reminded everyone of the legendary Vaisravanan Chettiar, who had transformed himself into a serpent and made love to Kunhimanikkam.

One day, Chettiappa and his companions went to Bandman Kanari's hut in the Rue du Cimetière. Leaning against the coconut tree in the courtyard, Kanari's wife Nani gazed at Chettiappa with awe. Her daughter Devi was by her side. Both of them looked very youthful.

The Brigadier turned to Andru, 'Who's the young woman?'

'Madame Kanari,' answered Andru. Achu explained to Chettiappa who Kanari was. Chettiappa had a long look at Madame Kanari. As he walked on, he turned back to look at her a couple of times.

Kanari played the trumpet in the only band in Mayyazhi. Though he was neither white nor half-French nor an officer, he always wore a coat, trousers and a hat. No one had ever seen him in a mundu. Thin and bony, he looked like a scarecrow in his Western clothes. He had work only if there was a death or a wedding in Mayyazhi. Every day, he would sling his trumpet over his shoulder and go straight to Unni Nair's toddy shop. He would come home only at midnight. He would then practise on his trumpet. His ear-splitting trumpeting could be heard until cockcrow.

Brigadier Chettiappa rented a two-storeyed house in the Rue du Cimetière. He could not sleep at all at night because of Kanari's dreadful trumpeting.

'Take the wretched trumpet away from him,' the Brigadier ordered policeman Andru angrily. And for first time in many years, Mayyazhi did not hear Kanari's trumpet that night.

The festival of Vishu came and went. The rains broke by the end of May accompanied by winds. No one got married. No one died. Kanari could find no way to buy himself even a drop of toddy. His only hope was that someone might die. Staring out into the unceasing rain, he went over the list of people who were very sick. Only Thomas Sayiv was likely to succumb suddenly. He was a diabetic and had been bedridden for a long time.

Kanari prayed hard, his eyes fixed on the rain-soaked cross on the steeple.

'Ten candles for you, if he dies today.'

As the rain continued unabated, Kanari curled up on the veranda, his trumpet in his arms. He could not sleep. He knew he would not be able to sleep until he had a half bottle of toddy inside him. Suddenly he heard an inner voice say that Thomas Sayiv would die before dawn.

He started up, put on his coat with the brass buttons and slung his trumpet over his shoulder.

'Where are you going at this time of morning? The toddy shop isn't yet open.'

'Thomas Sayiv is dead,' he said to Nani.

Kanari would have work if Thomas Sayiv died. But he would spend all his earnings at the toddy shop. And Unni Nair would thrive. Nani turned over and went back to sleep.

'Is someone dead?', asked Kunjakkan, seeing Kanari rushing out in his bandman's uniform.

'Yes, Thomas Sayiv.'

'Our Lady is merciful, at last she's called him.'

Kanari hurried off to Bandmaster Pathrose's house. His huge drum stood against the wall. Above it was a framed picture of the Virgin and a lamp that always stayed alight. Pathrose's eyes gleamed hopefully. The fire had died out in his hearth as well.

'Thomas Sayiv is dead.'

Pathrose looked at the lamp and made the sign of the cross. Then he quickly put on his coat and trousers and slung his drum over his back.

They gathered the other members of the band on their way to Thomas Sayiv's house. It was still drizzling. The pier was waterlogged. Wilted gulmohar flowers floated over it.

Thomas Sayiv's dog barked when it saw the bandmen. His son, Joseph, came out. He was surprised to see all the bandmen standing in a row in his courtyard.

'What's the matter?'

'Isn't Thomas Sayiv ... dead?' Kanari stammered.

Joseph raised his hand and sprang into the courtyard. The dog broke loose and barked furiously. Kanari couldn't remember exactly what happened next.

Unni Nair roared with laughter. Later, when he saw Kanari seated in a corner, clutching his head, he felt sorry for him and gave him a free tumbler of toddy.

The rain stopped by evening. Warm sunshine lay across the wet roads. Brigadier Chettiappa suddenly appeared in front of Kanari's house, wearing silk clothes, rings on eight of his fingers and slippers that creaked.

'Madame Kanari! Oh Madame Kanari,' he called out.

Nani was picking lice out of her daughter's hair. Tiny baby lice wriggled between the teeth of the fine toothed wooden comb.

'Is Monsieur Kanari at home?'

'Devi's father has gone out,' she said. Devi hid behind her.

Kanari was Nani's man, but they had little to do with each other. They seldom spoke. Kanari generally slept on the veranda. Nani made a living for herself and her daughter by washing the neighbours' clothes and braiding palm leaf mats.

Chettiappa climbed into the veranda to talk to Nani. He had fallen for her the day he saw her. While leaving, he called Devi and gave her a rupee from his leather wallet.

'You go to school?'

'No.'

'Don't you want to?'

'I don't know.'

Devi went back to her mother. A bright green note. She couldn't believe her eyes.

Next day, Chettiappa sent for Kanari. Kanari was very frightened. He had been afraid of Chettiappa ever since he had forbidden him to play his trumpet at night. His knees knocked together when he saw the Brigadier.

'Remember, I asked you not to play your trumpet? I'm ashamed of myself for doing that.'

Chettiappa came smiling down the steps. 'You can play your trumpet now.'

Kanari's fear melted. Chettiappa opened his leather wallet. Kanari went away happily to Unni Nair's toddy shop.

That night, the Mayyazhi folk heard Kanari's trumpet once more.

A few days later, Kurambi Amma witnessed a strange sight: Brigadier Chettiappa, wearing a silk shirt and creaking slippers, and Nani, in a yellow saree and new slippers and jasmine in her hair, walked past her house.

'Where are you going Nani?'

'To the cinema,' said Nani proudly. The touring cinema had just come to Narangapuram.

Kurambi Amma had never been to the cinema. Not many in Mayyazhi had experienced that good fortune.

'You are lucky, Nani.'

Kurambi Amma took out her ivory snuffbox and helped herself to a pinch of snuff.

18

Dasan gazed out of the window. Mayyazhi was bathed in warm sunshine. Bells echoed from the church for evening service and birds flew across the river to their nests.

Dasan's eyes were heavy and swollen with sleep. It was six months since he had returned from Pondicherry and he had done nothing but sleep, or smoke endlessly standing at the window. His chest had begun to hurt with the innumerable beedis he smoked.

'What is the point in brooding like this? You can't undo what you have done,' his mother said to him. She had realized that he was suffering, but had not understood why he had refused to go to France. She was certain that he had a good reason. Her son would never make a mistake, she was sure.

'Etta, why don't you shave and have a bath? I'll draw water from the well for you,' Girija said. She had been the first in the house to shake herself free of the shock Dasan had given them. It was true that she had dreamed of her brother going to France and becoming a great man. She had built her own castles in the air and had wept bitterly when, like her parents, she had succumbed to the death-like silence that had enveloped the household. But she had suddenly opened her eyes to reality.

'Have a bath and eat,' urged Amma, 'You'll fall ill if you don't eat properly, son.'

Dasan had taken to going out at odd hours and returning whenever he liked. What would happen if he went on this way?

One day, at last, he thought he would shave. Girija filled a pot with water from the well. The water had the scent of the earth and the cool feel of a tender banana sapling.

When he came in after his bath, Girija smiled, 'You look handsome, Etta.'

She was at the age when girls admired men reeking of sweat and beedis. She worshipped her brother, loved his thick moustache, the grave look in his eyes, the gentleness of his speech. How lucky the girl who married her brother would be ...

Suddenly, she thought of Chandrika. She could read Chandrika's mind clearly now. One day, she would ask her, 'Are you in love with my brother?'

Girija ironed her brother's shirts and mundus, brought him a lighted wick from the kitchen when he wanted to light a beedi, made him a cup of tea every now and then when he spent the day at home. Kowsu Amma was attentive to his needs as well. Slowly the house was eased of its weight of sorrow. But the pain Dasan had caused cut deep into their hearts. Would they ever be healed again? Damu Writer's family somehow struggled on, hiding their sorrow.

Life came back to the house gradually.

Only Damu Writer could not surface from the depths into which Dasan had plunged him. He never smiled now. He lay in bed for many days, nursing a persistent cold and fever. His chest ached all night and he found it difficult to breathe. For nights together, he could not sleep.

He went back to work before he was fully recovered.

Kowsu scolded him, 'What do you think you are doing?'

The deed writer tucked his documents under his arm, hooked his umbrella over his fist and said, 'Destiny has ordained that I should never rest.'

'Stay in bed at least one more day and go to work from tomorrow.'

Dasan heard what his father said. His heart felt sore like a festering wound. It hurt him to watch his father walk out of the house with his files, but he could do nothing.

Sometimes, he felt confused. But it never occurred to him that what he was doing was wrong. He had thought deeply before he took his decision. He felt as if his father's sorrow was his own and shared in it. Who was there to share his own pain?

Dasan knew that his pain would be healed only when Mayyazhi's sorrow was alleviated. His well-being was linked with that of his country. But where was Mayyazhi's freedom? As far away as Velliyan Rock, where unborn souls hovered like dragonflies ...

'We do not have even a grain of rice for tomorrow.'

Dasan watched and heard. Times were changing around him, but the poverty in his house remained unchanged.

Was there no way to help his father without accepting Big Sayiv's bounty?

He began to give tuition to Nathan's children, Chandran and Latha. Soon, three more children arrived. All five came to him after school and he taught them until half past six. Then he hurried to Pappan's house, where they had a study class every evening.

The children brought him a sum of twenty rupees. When they paid him for the first month, he took the money to his father, a stack of faded five, two and one rupee notes.

'What's this?'

'The fees the children paid me.'

'Give it to your mother.'

Damu Writer stared into the distance and would not touch the money.

His mother refused to take more than fifteen rupees. Dasan heard her say to Girija, 'He's a young man, he's sure to need money for himself. For a glass of tea or a bundle of beedis ...'

Kurambi Amma said softly, 'He's only got himself to blame.'

Dasan used the five rupees to buy a month's ration of beedis and some snuff for Achamma.

When Chandran paid him for the next month, he said, 'Tomorrow, we won't come.'

'But the exams are coming, you can't afford to waste a day.'

'We'll never come here again.'

'Why?'

'My father said you're a communist.'

He was amused. Chandran was a child, he would not understand if he explained to him—I'm not a communist, I'm a human being.

He avoided Nathan when he saw him in the street next day.

A few days later, the other children stopped coming.

'The stars say it's a bad time for him,' lamented Kurambi Amma, who regretted the children not coming, more than any of them.

All Dasan did now was sleep. Or stand at the window, smoking.

19

Madhavan drove Dasan and Chandrika in the horse carriage to the railway station. Madhavan was the son of Kelan, the old carriage driver who had died.

'I'm so happy, Dasetta.'

'Why?'

'Because I'm alone with you.'

Dasan was perturbed. Where would this take them?

'What are you thinking about, Dasetta?'

'Nothing.'

'That's a lie. Tell me.'

Chandrika brushed the strands of hair blowing across her cheeks and smiled, looking at him.

Her mother had not liked the idea of her going to the station with Dasan.

'You're no longer a child to go around with a young man.'

'But it's Dasettan ...'

Dasan was no stranger, they had grown up together and gone to school together in the same horse carriage.

'I don't mind, Chandri. But people will wag their tongues ...'
She combed her hair, lined her eyes with kohl and placed a black pottu on her forehead.

'You're becoming insolent,' Leela said, as Chandri left with Dasan.

The horse carriage jerked forward.

Seated on the wooden bench placed outside Unni Nair's toddy shop, Kunjakkan, Kanari and Antony were enjoying their morning drink. The carriage turned into the Rue de la Gare. Rice fields filled with rainwater lay on either side. The shadow of the moving horse carriage fell across the glowing water.

In the station, the train had been announced. The two rail tracks that emerged from the green shadows in the distance broke up into myriad paths.

Only Bharathan got down from the train at their station. He had not brought much luggage this time. Last year, he had come home on holiday. This year, he had come for the sole purpose of taking Kunhanandan to the hospital in Vellore for surgery. He was the only person who could do this. His uncle Kunhukutty, who lived at Azhiyoor, was too old. Besides, he had not travelled much and would not be able to take Kunhanandan on such a long trip. As for Kanaran and Vasutty, they were too busy with their political activities to take care of Kunhanandan Master.

In spite of this, Kanaran had offered once to take him to Vellore.

'Let's go to Vellore. Dasan will come too.'

'To Vellore? What for?'

Master hated the very mention of surgery.

Doctor Seethi, who had been looking after Master, had suggested an operation. 'There's not much I can do for him now,' he had said to Dasan.

Madhavan opened the carriage door. Chandrika sat next to Dasan, opposite her father, Bharathan.

'How are you, Dasan?'

Bharathan had heard about Dasan's brilliant performance in the Baccalauréat and of how he had rejected Big Sayiv's generous offer.

'Busy with study classes and underground activities.' Dasan smiled. 'We have many plans. It's such a pity that Master is so ill. The next time you come home, great events would have taken place.'

'You're playing with fire. Take care, Dasan, that's all I have to say.'

Dasan knew that he had to undergo an ordeal by fire. He would lose much and suffer much.

'I'm ready for anything.'

'May all go well with you, Dasan.'

The horse carriage stopped in front of the house.

Master heard the carriage come to a halt and then Bharathan's voice. It was as if he was nailed to the bed. He had given up teaching quite some time ago. It was months since he had shaved or taken a bath or gone out. His beard lay thick on his yellowed face. He knew why Bharathan had come all the way from Singapore. To take him for an operation ...

'How do you feel now?' Bharathan came up to the bed. He wished he had not asked that question, it was so meaningless. His heart ached. He had always had a deep affection and sympathy for Master. He wished he could see him cured.

'Will the doctor come today?'

'He hasn't been here for a week.'

Master tried to hide his despair with a feeble smile. When Dasan had gone for Doctor Seethi the last time, he had refused to come, saying he could do nothing.

'Even the doctor has forsaken me, Bharathetta.' Master's voice choked. He wanted so much to live. He had taken such pleasure in his existence. And yet, fate had brought him to this state.

Bharathan brought the doctor that evening. The doctor felt that surgery offered the only chance of survival. If he did not have the operation, he could die any moment.

'Let's take him to Vellore tomorrow. I'll come with you,' said the doctor. 'If you decide not to take him, don't come and bother me again.'

'Master will never consent to an operation.'

Dasan understood Master better than any of them. Master felt that he would not survive an operation.

When the doctor left, Bharathan and Dasan went to Master's room. 'Kunhanandan, you must have heard what the doctor said.' They knew from his face that he had. He was pale and the fear of death was in his eyes. 'We'll go to Vellore in the morning.'

Master lay with his eyes closed.

'Why don't you answer, Kunhanandan?'

'I don't want an operation.'

'How long will you live like this?'

'Until I die.'

Bharathan paced up and down the room. After a while, he stopped by Kunhanandan's bed.

'I won't force you. If you really don't want the operation, I'll board the ship next week.'

Bharathan went out. Dasan stayed behind in Master's room.

'Do you want me to go to Vellore, Dasan?'

'No, I know how you feel about it.'

'If I go to Vellore, I know I'll never come back alive. I might live a little longer if I don't have the operation. Let me live as long as possible. Even if I can live one extra day, I'll be so happy.'

Master gasped for breath. His eyes protruded from their sockets.

No one spoke to Master again about having an operation. Bharathan sailed for Singapore a week later.

ONE RAINY DAY, WHEN Dasan lay in bed reading, he heard Chandrika's voice outside.

'Is Dasettan in?'

Dasan got up and went out to the veranda. Chandrika was drenched and her black pottu had spread all over her wet forehead. Raindrops dripped from the ends of her oily hair.

'Uncle wants to see you.'

'What's the matter?'

'He's very ill.'

Were Chandrika's eyes wet with the rain or tears? Dasan grew anxious.

Carrying his umbrella he rushed out with her. They ran all the way.

Master lay as he always did, with his eyes closed. Leela stood near him, crying.

'Master ...' He knelt down by the cot and called softly. Master looked so weak, Dasan thought he was barely alive.

Master moved his head slightly. He opened his eyes with difficulty. He seemed to want to say something. Dasan bent down to listen.

The sun had set. Darkness was gathering outside. It was still raining heavily. The church bells were inaudible in the swish of the rain.

'There was so much that I wanted to do for our freedom movement. Now, I can't do anything. I'm not worried though, I have confidence in you.' Master paused between each word. 'I wanted to ask you to join the movement the day you finished your Certificat exam. It was for your father's sake that I checked myself. It made me so happy when you came in yourself. Now you will have to carry on what I started. That makes me really happy.'

Master's chest heaved like a rough sea. He struggled for breath.

'I've never been a healthy man a single day of my life. I spent the greater part of my existence in this bed. Though I'm over forty, I've never touched a woman. Still, I'm a satisfied man. Can you hear me Dasan?'

'Yes, Master.'

'I am not sure why I sent for you. I wanted to tell you that I am happy, even though I'm in this condition. Only death can destroy my happiness.'

'Do happiness or sorrow really exist in our world, Master? Only life exists ...'

'Yes, only life ...'

THE DAYS WENT BY. Lying in bed, Master watched summer succeed spring outside his window. When the first raindrops fell on the hot earth, he trembled as if the rain was coursing down his own body. He found new rhythms and melodies in the incessant rain. When the sky brightened after the rain, he shared the warmth of the sunlight with the wet earth and the plants.

One day, as the sun rose over the Mayyazhi river, his awareness of existence suddenly intensified. As the joy of being alive entered into him like the waves of the sea, he had convulsions and his mouth foamed.

Even when he died, his eyes remained open in a ceaseless protest against death.

20

The rains had been over and the month of Karkatakam had started.

Damu Writer was very ill, he could not perform the annual bali rituals for dead ancestors on full moon day. He was ill all the time now. Apart from his chronic asthma, he had developed other ailments like a backache and swelling of the limbs.

Two more days to full moon. 'I can't do the bali rituals. May the dead forgive me,' said Damu.

'Let Dasan do them if you can't,' said Kurambi Amma. Dasan, the only other man in the house, had never performed these rituals before.

When everyone insisted, he consented to perform them.

The bustle in the kitchen started the day before full moon. Many kinds of payasams had to be prepared for the dead ancestors.

Girija got up at dawn and had a bath. Her hair still wet, she served the payasam on banana leaves, filled a vessel with water and went to the southern room, which was kept apart for the ancestors.

Kelu Achan's bones were preserved there in an earthen pot, under the cowdung-smeared floor.

'Think of your grandfather, little one, keep his image in your mind,' said Kurambi Amma coming up to the door. Girija invoked her grandfather, who had died of a snake bite long before she could remember, and placed the payasam and water on the floor.

She came out and closed the door. Then she served out some payasam on another leaf, lighted an oil-drenched leaf torch and went to the southern courtyard. The offerings meant for the spirits called Biran, Pena and Bhandaram were always placed outside the house, with a lighted cloth torch, because they were the spirits of people who had died evil deaths. 'Those who drowned are called Biran,' Kurambi Amma had explained to Dasan when he was a child, 'those who hanged themselves are Pena and those who died of smallpox are Bhandaram.'

Kurambi Amma and Dasan bathed, put on wet clothes and cooked turmeric rice over a fire in the courtyard. They then served the rice on banana leaves and sprinkled karuka grass and sesame seeds over it. Kneeling by the side of the leaves, they clapped to the crows, inviting them to come and accept the offerings.

'Not a single crow, Achamma,' exclaimed Girija who was watching from the veranda. What had happened to the crows that came every morning and perched in the yard and on the well parapets, cawing with hunger?

Kurambi Amma knelt and clapped over and over again.

'They'll come,' said Dasan. 'It's a busy day for them today.' The same rituals were being performed in almost all the Hindu houses in Mayyazhi that day.

At last a crow flew towards them, but it suddenly changed direction because it heard someone else clap louder.

'Eight o'clock, oh God!' Kurambi Amma felt desperate. Where had all the ancestors gone? Why were they staying away? She clapped her thin hands repeatedly.

Dasan stopped his efforts to attract the crows and sat down on the steps. He felt chilly, in his wet mundu.

'Come, come,' Kurambi Amma called out again, looking up at the sky and clapping her tired hands. 'Come, come ...'

Kurambi Amma's heart was heavy and she felt like crying. Her voice grew shriller.

The sun climbed higher. A crow flew up at last and landed near the banana leaf. It ate the turmeric rice and sesame seeds and gazed at Kurambi Amma with a drunken look. It was a miserable crow with bald patches on its scraggy neck.

'Come here,' Kurambi Amma called it nearer, affectionately. The crow cocked its head to one side and looked at her. It lifted a wing and scratched underneath with its beak. Then it flew down and perched on Kurambi Amma's banana leaf.

'So you've come at last, thank God!'

Kurambi Amma stared at the crow. It pecked at the side of the leaf and scattered rice and sesame seeds in all directions with its feet. Then it pecked at a few morsels again.

Kurambi Amma's eyes filled with tears as she watched it.

'What is it, Achamma?'

'That's your grandfather.' Kurambi Amma burst into tears.

Was it really Kelu Achan, the scraggy crow with the bald neck?

THE FESTIVAL IN THE Church of the Virgin was as important in Mayyazhi as the Thira festival in the Meethalambalam temple. As soon as the month of Kanni began, Kunhukutty Achan could be seen balanced on a wooden box suspended from the high steeple, whitewashing the walls of the church. This marked the start of the preparations for the festival.

The Padiri, the priest, came out and seated himself on a chair under the mango tree with his stole around his shoulders and his cap on his knees. The Kappiyar, the sexton, stood next to him with a sheet of paper in his hand. They would now auction the land for the stalls and booths for the festival.

'A booth near the lamp-post, ten by eight feet.' The Kappiyar read from his paper and looked around. Bangle sellers from Mangalore, halva makers from Kozhikode, hypnotists and gamblers from unknown places, they had all come to bid for a shop or a booth.

'Ten rupees.'

'Ten and a quarter.' That was the bangle seller.

'Ten and a half.' The hypnotist.

'A quarter rupee more.' The gambler.

And so it went on until the bangle seller bid for fourteen rupees.

'Fourteen rupees. Once. Twice. No one?' The bangle seller looked around anxiously. Everyone was silent. The Padiri moved in his chair.

The land near the lamp-post went to the bangle seller.

The festival started at noon on 5 October, with a single blast of dynamite. There were two blasts on the second day and three on the third. On the tenth and final day, there would be ten deafening blasts.

Stalls selling glass bangles, marigolds, crosses, candles, images of saints and angels had come up all around the church.

Pilgrims flocked to Mayyazhi. An endless stream of visitors flowed from the railway station and the bridge.

'Do you think all these people have really come out of devotion?' Pappan watched the crowd from the Vignanaposhini Library, which was right in front of the Church. You could watch the festival from start to finish from there. 'They've all come to drink liquor.'

'You mean this whole crowd is here to drink?' Dasan laughed. Bhakti can make people more intoxicated than liquor.

The library was full of people. Once the festival started, all sorts of people, who normally never came to the library, would flock in to watch the festival.

The Mother of Mayyazhi, as the Virgin was known, loved her devotees, just as the Thiya gods, Gulikan and Kuttichathan did. And exactly like them, she made short work of her enemies too.

One of the many legends Kurambi Amma had recounted to Dasan as a child was that of the origin of the Mother of Mayyazhi.

'Once upon a time,' she said, 'a ship that was going over the vast expanse of the Arabian Sea sailed into the shadow of the Velliyan Rock. Suddenly, it was grounded, as if the anchor had been dropped. The captain and the sailors were stunned for there was no obstacle in sight. Three days and three nights passed. The ship refused to move.

'The sailors fell on their knees and prayed, their eyes raised to heaven.

'"Install me in Mayyazhi." The captain heard a voice. It came from the idol of the Virgin in the ship.

'The captain obeyed the divine command. He went ashore with the idol and placed it at an isolated spot.

'The ship moved.

'Our church is built at the spot where the captain placed the idol.' Kurambi Amma opened her ivory snuffbox, took a pinch of snuff and inhaled with her eyes half-closed.

Dusk. The sun dipped into the great calm sea. The cross on the steeple was etched clearly against the limpid sky.

The church bells pealed, gathering into themselves the grandeur of the sea and the sky. They resounded through Mayyazhi. The bells would ring continuously until the urukan, the procession bearing the holy image of the Virgin, came back to the church after circling the town.

'Look, there goes the urukan,' said Kurambi Amma as she sat in the veranda with her snuffbox open and her eyes closed, carried away by memories of bygone festivals.

The awesome bells swayed above the sexton, who lay suspended from the bell ropes. As he rang the huge bells, he swung between the earth and the sky, following the violent movement of the bells.

The procession wound its way through the Rue de l'Eglise with chariots, flags and coloured lamps. The scent of burning incense spread through Mayyazhi. Thousands of pilgrims moved with the procession, singing the praises of the Mother of Mayyazhi in many languages.

Even after dusk, the sun refused to set over Mayyazhi.

The procession came back to the church after four hours. The bells stopped ringing at last. As he let go of the ropes he had been pulling for hours, the exhausted Kappiyar fell down, losing consciousness. Blood dripped from his hands. For two whole days, the people of Mayyazhi had not slept. Men wandered around the church, drunk.

Housewives were tired of cooking for guests. Only one house stayed dark and silent—Leslie Sayiv's. Missie who had always made cakes for the festival for as long as people could remember had not done so this year. Anyway, even if she had baked a cake, who would have eaten it? In the old days, people had come in carriages to her house and feasted and drunk the whole night long. Why would they come now? There was no one at home.

The man of the house, whose task it would have been to welcome guests, had shut himself away behind closed doors, doing penance, his hair and beard growing thicker with the years.

It was on the first day of the festivities that Missie lost the vise of her right hand and leg. She fell down while mixing the batter for a cake and her head hit the floor.

Mambi, the maid, shouted for help. Gaston heard Mambi's cry as he drowsed with his guitar against his chest. He got up, opened the door a little and peered out.

He saw Mamma lying prone on the floor. His heart turned over. He opened the door a little wider and began to go down the steps.

Just then the neighbours arrived, having heard Mambi's cry for help. Gaston withdrew at once.

It was twenty-five years since he had gone downstairs. Although he had been born and bred in Mayyazhi, its people had become strangers to him. Sometimes, he peered out through the thick curtains at the window. He looked at the people walking along the Rue de la Rèsidènce or seated on the pier, but did not recognize any of them.

Gaston felt only one emotion now—pain. Pain for his lost manhood. The pain of losing Teresa who had not stayed with him even a week. It was this pain that his guitar strings tried to express night after night, spreading its music over Mayyazhi. It haunted those who were asleep, disturbing them with bad dreams.

Pathrose and Policeman Chathu laid Missie on the cot. She was unconscious and her head was bleeding.

Someone ran to fetch a doctor.

Gaston longed to know what had happened but did not come down. He could hear voices downstairs. He was afraid of people. A conflict raged in his mind. His mother lay dying, the mother who had wept unceasingly for him over the last twenty-five years. But he could not move to go to her. The voices frightened him. How could he go amongst them?

No, I can't go. Gaston locked the door from inside. He paced up and down the room.

Missie regained consciousness next morning. She opened her eyes and looked around her. She saw Kurambi, Damu, Dasan, Pathrose and Policeman Chathu.

'Gaston ...' Her lips moved. All eyes turned towards the staircase. The door upstairs remained closed.

The tears ran down Missie's cheeks. She lay in a faint, her eyes closed. Two small, pale feet could be seen outside her long black robe.

Damu could not bear it any longer. He looked at the stairs and cried out, 'Gaston, come down. Your mother is dying ...'

Behind the closed doors, Gaston's footsteps quickened.

Missie's eyes stopped moving. Her body trembled from head to foot. 'Gaston ...' Kurambi Amma wailed in despair.

Damu stood on the bottom step of the carpeted stairs and called as loudly as he could, 'Please come down, Gaston.' Gaston did not answer.

Damu began to go up the stairs slowly, holding on to the banisters. Everyone's eyes were fixed on him. He came to the closed door and called out again. There was no answer. He knocked repeatedly. Gaston did not reply. There was only the sound of frenzied footsteps moving inside the closed room.

Damu came back, still leaning on the banisters for support.

That evening, Leslie Sayiv's Missie drew her last breath.

Everyone except Gaston was at her bedside.

The beautiful Missie, who used to walk in her flowing white silk dress on the seashore, hand in hand with the charismatic Leslie Sayiv, lay still on the rosewood cot on a faded sheet.

With Missie's death, the curtain fell on the golden age of Mayyazhi's half-French citizens. An era ended with her passing away. She was the last link in the line of rich and generous half-French who had lived dignified and noble lives. The half-French would continue to play a role in the life of Mayyazhi, but they were never to achieve the same measure of greatness and nobility. Poverty and its attendant evils were to force them to lead mean lives. Beggars and prostitutes were to be born amongst them. Missie's death marked the start of a tragic journey that was to destroy their very roots.

People crowded to Leslie Sayiv's house when they heard of Missie's death. Her closest friend, Kurambi, wept her heart out, seated next to the bier. Dasan and Girija, who had loved her delicious cakes, bit their lips to keep from crying.

Gaston still paced up and down his closed room.

Finally, the mourners went home, and the bungalow was empty.

It was past midnight. The sea was quiet under a clear sky spattered with stars.

After years, the door that had remained closed upstairs opened. Gaston's pale face appeared above the stairs. Golden hair streamed over his shoulders and a long, golden beard flowed under his chin. His blue eyes were as calm as the sky. Holding on to the banisters, he came down slowly.

Missie lay on a silken bier in Leslie Sayiv's empty living room, under the glittering crystal lamp, her hands crossed on her breast.

Gaston went up to the bier and looked at his mother's face. He knelt down beside her and said, 'I've no one now, Mamma, no one.'

He lay his head on his mother's breast and sobbed until the sun rose over the Mayyazhi river.

21

On days when there were no study classes, Dasan spent the evenings by himself on the beach, looking at the sea. He could see Velliyan Rock clearly when the sea was calm, like a silver streak in the distance. On such days, he would think of the souls hovering over it in the interval between death and rebirth and his thoughts then somehow seemed more profound.

Vasutty and Pappan were with him sometimes. They discussed the freedom movement. Kanaran never joined them. Older than any of them, he was often involved in some serious activity connected with the movement.

'I'll kill all of them,' said Pappan. 'I see no path before us except that of bloodshed.' Blood-red dreams blossomed in Pappan's eyes.

'It frightens me when you talk about bloodshed,' said Dasan. 'A drop of human blood is worth more than a crown.'

'Are you going to become a Gandhi then?'

'No, I don't want to be a Gandhi or a Marx. I just want to be a human being.'

Dasan gazed at the sea. It was high tide and Velliyan Rock was obscured behind the rising waves.

'Master didn't have the good fortune to see the white men leave. Will we see it happen, Dasan?' Vasutty sighed.

'The white men must go. History will see to it. As for us, we must act. We'll have to suffer, watch our parents shed tears. We might even die. No matter what the consequence is, we must act ...'

Pappan was impatient. 'The movement started nearly twenty years ago. What have we achieved? How long must we wait?'

Pappan often confided in Dasan and was closer to him than to Vasutty. His ardour increased with every day that passed. He talked incessantly of bloodshed. It distressed Dasan to listen to him.

'Communism is humanism,' Dasan reminded him one day. He was afraid that Pappan would do something radical.

Next day, Dasan was summoned to Pondicherry to take part in a meeting that could decide the fate of Mayyazhi. Kanaran had insisted that Dasan attend it. He spoke the white man's language like a white man, and could argue well.

Kanaran took him to the library in the morning and they had a long discussion. Dasan came home at noon, bathed in perspiration.

'Can't you spare even a minute to have the gruel I've cooked for you?' Kowsu was upset to see her son look so hot and tired. He spent all his time at discussions and meetings, neglecting to eat and sleep. Would all this ever end?

'Have a bath, Etta,' said Girija. She had drawn water from the well. Her arms, covered with bangles, were wet to the elbow.

'I've no time, I'm leaving ...'

'Where are you going?' Kowsu asked.

'To Pondicherry.'

'Can't you have a bath and eat something before you go, son?'

How could he stay? The Mail train was due any moment and he had to drop in at Leela's on the way. He was not sure when he would get back from Pondicherry. He, Kanaran and all the others lived now in constant fear of being arrested.

Damu Writer had come back from the court for lunch and lay on his easy chair in the veranda.

Dasan went up to his father. Damu looked up from his newspaper.

'I'm leaving for Pondicherry ... to attend the meeting of the Indo-French Congress.'

'Hmm.'

'Will you bring me a blanket from Pondicherry, Dasan?' Kurambi Amma asked. Kunhichirutha had told her that there were good blankets in Pondicherry. David Sayiv had bought her one when he went there on business.

Dasan hurried to Leela's house. The maid servant said she had gone to her parents' place.

'Has Chandrika gone as well?'

'No, she's having a bath.'

He hesitated. He couldn't wait until she came out but she would be very upset if he did not tell her he was going.

He put down his bag and walked up to the closed door of the bathroom.

'Chandrika ...'

'What is it, Dasetta?' She was surprised.

'I'm leaving for Pondicherry by the Mail. Open the door if you can.'

'Just a minute, please.'

'I can't wait. The train is due any minute now.'

He stood uncertainly before the closed door.

'Please Dasetta, don't go,' she begged from behind the closed door.

As he was leaving, the door creaked open. The fragrance of seasoned oil and soap wafted out with her. She had hurriedly gathered a voile sari with black polka dots on it around her. He could make out that she was not wearing a skirt underneath. Water dripped from her hair on her neck and shoulders.

'When will you be back, Dasetta?'
'Soon.'
'Will you write to me?'
'Write?' He laughed. 'I'll be back in four days.'
'Please come back soon.'

The radiance in the liquid pools of her eyes dimmed. She held on to the door with wet hands, the black bangles on them clinking softly. When she leaned forward, he caught the scent of her wet hair.

He picked up his bag and walked away hurriedly.

No one was at the railway station to see him off this time. There was no horse carriage. He was not going to Pondicherry for higher studies in a French college. He was going to attend a meeting which would shape Mayyazhi's destiny.

PAPPAN SCRAMBLED UP FROM the roadside, his shirt torn across the middle. The palm of his right hand was stained with the enemy's warm blood. He found it difficult to balance himself on his shaking feet.

In front of him lay the Commissar, inert, clutching a handful of hair that he had plucked from Pappan's head by the roots.

Pappan saw people run towards him and noticed a policeman's red cap amongst them. The boundary of the town lay just behind. He must hurry to safety, he had to get away. Perhaps never to return ...

He looked at Mayyazhi one last time, as it lay spread out before him. At the church steeple etched against the sky and the cross above it.

'Mayyazhi, goodbye,' he whispered through lips coated with blood. He walked away on unsteady legs. He crossed the boundary safely before the screaming crowd could get to him.

'Forgive me, Mayyazhi. I do this for you, so that your days of subservience may end soon ...'

Pappan stumbled over the long stretch of road and disappeared.

When the people of Mayyazhi heard the news, they were stunned. Vasutty quickly made his escape. Kanaran went underground.

Seated on the veranda, Kurambi Amma inhaled a pinch of snuff. A jeep came crashing up to the house and stopped. A handful of red-capped men got out.

'Where's Dasan?'

'In Pondicherry. He went by the Mail today.'

Kowsu came to the door.

'Isn't your son here?'

'No.'

The policemen pushed Kowsu aside and rushed in. They flashed their torches under the cots, behind the doors, then went out, disappointed.

Damu Writer came home from court just then.

'Where's your son?' The policemen didn't allow him to answer. The bundle of deeds and umbrella he was carrying fell down from his hands. A feeble cry rose from his throat.

The jeep roared away, carrying Damu Writer. Its noise drowned Kowsu's cries.

Kanaran and Vasutty escaped, but many others associated with the freedom movement were caught by the police. Some were innocent. Most of them were sent to the Mayyazhi jail, while some were taken to the jail in Pondicherry, Damu Writer amongst them.

DASAN ESCAPED FROM PONDICHERRY before the meeting was over. The warrant for his arrest had been sent to Pondicherry since he could not be traced in Mayyazhi. Changing from a bus to a train then back again to a bus, he made his way to Mayyazhi.

The railway station was just outside the boundary dividing French Mayyazhi from British Azhiyoor. He knew he could not go beyond that point.

He looked at the cross on the steeple and the lighthouse on Big Sayiv's hill. He felt he had lost his home and his country. Pappan's radical act and his father's arrest had shattered him.

Passersby looked at him suspiciously and talked to each other in hushed voices.

Kanaran and Vasutty soon joined him.

'You heard, Dasan?'

'Yes.'

'I was worried for you.'

'Why worry for me? My father ...' He could not go on. His head spun in the heat of the noonday sun.

'What has happened has happened. There's no use lamenting.'

Kanaran put his arm around Dasan's shoulder. Vasutty followed them. They tried to comfort him as they found their way to Porter Kunhaman's house. The house, which lay just east of the railway station, belonged to Kanaran. He had moved in there with Kunhaman since he didn't have anywhere else to go now. He could not bring himself to ask Porter Kunhaman to vacate.

Dasan felt better after a bath and a meal. Reason began to prevail over emotion. At the moment when he gave up the scholarship to France and the post that Big Sayiv had offered him, he had felt as if he was looking into a magic mirror showing him his future. He had known then that many ordeals lay ahead of him. He must learn to endure the worst. He must have the strength of a rock.

It took him two days to find Pappan. Neither Kanaran nor Vasutty had seen him. In the evening, when Dasan was going down to the river bank, he suddenly came face to face with Pappan. He had changed. His eyes were sunk in their sockets. An untidy stubble covered his face.

'I never thought you would do this, Pappan.'

'Are you blaming me too?' Pappan's eyes flashed fire. He snarled like a tiger.

'I can bear it if that Gandhian Kanaran finds fault with me. But I can't take it from you.'

'No Pappan, I don't blame you.'

Dasan went on, 'If only you could have pierced the Commissar's body without hurting him, wounded him without shedding blood ...'

Dasan hated pain and bloodshed. But he had realized that there were occasions when it was necessary to inflict pain and shed blood. And he could understand Pappan's feelings.

'Someone else would have done it if you had not. But you wanted to do it yourself. So you saved someone else from the sin of murder. I think that shows courage.'

'No more philosophising,' growled Pappan.

Pappan had gone without food the last two days. Having nowhere to sleep, he had curled up on a shop veranda at night.

He had a huge house in Mayyazhi. His father lived in Colombo. He didn't remember his mother at all. She had been laid to rest under the earth before he could recognize the world around him. He had neither sisters nor brothers.

Pappan is lucky, thought Dasan. He is a free man. If only I could be free like him, he thought. His father in jail, his helpless mother, his sister and grandmother, their images were like festering wounds in him. He thought, if only I had been alone in the world ...

'Come, Pappan.'

'Where?'

'Where we are staying, Kanarettan, Vasutty and I. You're one of us after all.'

'But the others may not like it.'

Pappan knew that he had dealt a blow to Kanaran, the Gandhi of Mayyazhi, from which he would never recover. 'I'm telling you, come with me.'

Pappan moved in with them reluctantly in Porter Kunhaman's house. Kunhaman's woman cooked rice gruel for them. They spent the greater part of the day in discussion and argument. In the evening, they sat on the banks of the Mayyazhi river, smoking all the beedis they could lay their hands on.

Days of pain and solitude. Would he ever know peace of mind in his life, Dasan asked himself.

Maybe when he returned to Velliyan Rock, in the form of a dragonfly ...

22

FIELDS FILLED WITH NEWLY PLANTED PADDY LAY IN FRONT OF HIM. Beyond them was the Mayyazhi river that flowed beneath two iron bridges and then merged into the sea, in the shadow of Big Sayiv's white bungalow.

How many times, Dasan thought, I have watched the river and the sea flow into each other, from the pier carpeted with red gulmohur flowers ...

Memories of childhood warmed his heart, like rays of sunshine on rainy days. He did not notice Chandrika approaching. When he saw her, he was taken aback. How did she know he was here?

'So you're staying in Porter Kunhaman's house?'

'How did you know?'

'Amma told me, she wants you to come and stay with us.'

He had known Leela would say that. They had moved to the family house in Azhiyoor, outside Mayyazhi, now that Chandrika was in college. It was easier for her to catch the morning train to college from there.

'Tell her I'll come in the evening.'

'Why not now?'

'I've some work.'

'You'll surely come in the evening?'

'I'll try.'

Chandrika wore a saree now. Her hair was in a loose braid, half-done as usual. She still wore the anklets that made her footsteps tinkle.

'Dasetta, will you walk with me as far as the railway line?' she asked. Happy to be with her, he put on a shirt and followed her through the fields.

'Where does the railway line end, Dasetta?'

'Where it begins.'

'And where does it begin?'

'Where it ends.'

She burst out laughing. He laughed too and realized that it was days since he had done so.

He had no news of his father. He had no idea how his mother and sister were. Were they able to keep the fire burning in the hearth? Was Achamma able to get a pinch of snuff now and then?

'You'll come this evening?' repeated Chandrika as she left. He watched her go down the road that ran parallel to the railway line.

That evening, he went to Leela's place. The house was near the railway station. It was low roofed and two-storeyed with a great deal of wood work. There were banyan trees in the compound. Haystacks were heaped in high cones everywhere. Even by day, the rooms were dark. Dasan had been there often with Kunhanandan Master.

'Stay here with us,' said Leela's uncle. 'Think of this as your home.'

'I'll come as often as I can, isn't that enough?'

'No, come and stay with us,' he insisted. 'Why must you stay at Porter Kunhaman's when you can stay here?'

'Even if Kunhanandan is gone, there's all of us,' said Leela.

Dasan had been part of their family when Master was alive. He had come and gone as he pleased and there had been occasions when he had slept in Master's house at night.

'Bring us two glasses, Chandrika,' called out Chandrika's uncle, taking out a bottle of arrack.

'Dasan doesn't drink, Ammaman.'

'Is that true, young fellow?'

'I've never had a drink.'

'Well, you needn't refuse out of respect for me. Kunhambu and I started to drink together when he was twelve. Respect is something you feel in your heart.'

Kunhambu, Ammaman's eldest son, had died of a snake bite, like Kelu Achan, Dasan's grandfather.

Ammaman poured a little arrack into both the glasses.

'Please, not for me.'

'Drink it up, young man.'

He had often longed to get drunk in Unni Nair's shop, not in order to enjoy himself, but to forget everything that had happened. But how could he enjoy a drink, while his father languished in prison and his mother and sister starved?

'Don't force him. He's got trouble enough to handle.' Leela came to his rescue.

Ammaman didn't try to persuade him anymore. He poured the arrack from Dasan's glass into his and gulped it down. In a little while, he started to talk about the brahmarakshassu, his favourite topic while he drank.

'Tell me, Dasan, what is a brahmarakshassu?'

'I don't know.'

'What the hell did the white man teach you in Pondicherry then? When Parasuraman threw his axe into the sea, a piece of land emerged. That's Kerala. Did the white man ever teach you that? Well, Parasuraman brought some people from the north and installed them in the land. They were scholars who had learnt the sacred texts and tantric practices. Their ghosts are known as brahmarakshassus.'

The brahmarakshassus, the spirits of the learned brahmins, were immortal. Moving with ease from body to body, they existed through generations, over aeons of time.

Dasan sat listening to the stories for a long time. He got up when it grew dark.

'Where are you going?' Leela was surprised. 'I'm going home.'

'This is your home.'

'I know, Leela Edathi. But if I stay here, all of you may share my father's fate.'

'It's I, your Leela Edathi, who tells you not to go.'

'Forgive me,' Dasan said gently. 'I'm a fire that consumes itself and others. Those who love me have to be careful.'

He walked away quickly through the darkness to Porter Kunhaman's house. A plate of gruel would be waiting for him there. And a coarse screwpine mat to sleep on.

That was all he needed.

THE VERANDA WAS LIT by a hurricane lamp hanging on the door. Kanaran and Vasutty were waiting for him.

'Dasan, we have news.' Kanaran's white teeth gleamed bright in the glow of the oil lamp. 'The governor has agreed to a referendum.'

Kanaran took out a telegram from the pocket of his khadar shirt. It had come from Pondicherry.

'Our sufferings are over, man, over,' Vasutty exclaimed, overjoyed.

Dasan, however, did not think it was such great news.

He had guessed that the government might agree to a referendum. But what would the outcome be? He was not sure the outcome would be good.

Dasan put the telegram back on the table.

'You don't seem very enthusiastic.'

'Let's see what happens at the referendum.'

The governing council soon followed with an announcement. The municipal election, which was to be held in October, would be a prelude to the referendum.

'It's a trap. They know we won't win the municipal election.'

'But the people of Mayyazhi are with us. Surely you know that ...'

'Maybe some of them are. But will they have the guts to say so?'

There were people who believed in the movement in their heart of hearts, like the teachers and students of the Cours Complémentaire. But the arrest of Damu Writer and the others had frightened Mayyazhi badly. No one dared talk about the freedom movement in public.

Lawyer Raman had been the Mayor of Mayyazhi for more than twelve years. He had been elected unanimously every term. No one had dared to oppose this government sympathizer until now.

But the wind began to blow in another direction. Sukumaran came forward to stand against Lawyer Raman. He was a young man in government service who had been working quietly in the background for the freedom movement.

As the election drew near, Kanaran, Dasan and the others could hardly sleep. They did their best from outside Mayyazhi. They wrote personally to people in Mayyazhi, requesting their support. Two young men named Paputty and Bhaskaran led the activities in Mayyazhi.

A government order was issued almost immediately. Paputty and Bhaskaran were forbidden to leave Mayyazhi until the election was over. In spite of this, Paputty swam across the river at night under cover of darkness.

'They might arrest you and Bhaskaran. If both of you are caught, there'll be no one to work for us.'

'God is with us, Kanaretta.' Paputty wrung out the water from his clothes.

He was very young and had joined the movement when he was still a student at the Cours Complémentaire. Thanks to Achu, he had lost a front tooth.

'Stay with us here, son.'

'Then who will do our work in Mayyazhi?'

'Better to be here than in jail.'

'I'll go to jail if I must. Let me do whatever I can until then.'

Paputty blew on the hot black tea Vasutty had brought him and drank it. The cold night wind blowing across the river made him shiver.

'It looks as if they won't give any of us election cards,' said Paputty.

No one could vote without a card.

'What will we do if they give cards only to their own people?'

No one had an answer to Paputty's question.

'I had a feeling this would happen. That's why I was not enthusiastic about the election.'

'Then why have an election at all, Dasan?'

'It's a mockery.'

Dasan paced up and down the yard. The wind still blew across the river. Pale moonlight lay over the rice fields. A cock crowed somewhere.

'Law and justice do not mean anything to them. We should take knives to them, cut out their entrails.' Pappan's eyes blazed. He had been quiet until then.

'We'll force them to give us election cards.'

Kanaran held his head in his hands. None of them slept that night. They talked until the sun rose. As the river began to glimmer in the pale light of dawn, Paputty swam back to Mayyazhi.

Mayyazhi became tense as the election drew nearer. Something was bound to happen. Everyone was filled with fear.

23

The twenty-first of October 1948.

Paputty and Bhaskaran walked to the Mairie to claim their voting cards. About fifteen sympathizers went along with them. Paputty was happy that there were so many of them.

They walked in procession. People watched with bated breath from the roadside. It seemed as if something was going to happen.

The group passed the Palais de Justice and arrived at the Mairie.

'Our cards!'

'Give us our cards!' they shouted. Mayor Raman, an old man, came out of the office.

The Mayor's face grew red. What impudence! He looked at Policeman Kumaran, his eyes blazing with anger. The policeman turned his face the other way.

'All those who have a right to vote must be given cards. Give us our cards!'

The crowd climbed into the veranda. The Mayor shouted for help but no one responded.

They pushed the Mayor aside and entered the office. They pulled open the almirah doors, took out the voting cards stacked inside and threw them on the floor. The ground was soon scattered with old, faded papers. Chairs and tables lay overturned. The rebels heaped the papers on the road and set fire to them.

Bhaskaran climbed up the building and tore down the flag that had flown there for over a century. A saffron, white and green flag suddenly appeared in his hand and began to flutter from the top of the Mairie, an old yellow building.

The rebels who had taken over the Mairie gathered on the road. There were about a hundred of them.

'Come on ...'

Dasan, who had been waiting impatiently outside Mayyazhi, called exit to his companions. Vasutty, Pappan and a few other young men followed him.

Two armed policemen with red caps, gleaming rifles in hand, guarded the entrance to the town.

'Wait, Dasan,' shouted Vasutty, but Dasan had started to walk towards the border. Vasutty was frantic. Dasan could not bear to wait any longer. The people of Mayyazhi had woken and entered the battlefield. He walked on.

'Dasan, they'll kill us ...'

But Dasan would not stop. He found it impossible to shut out the call to battle that rang in his ears. Vasutty tried to prevent Pappan from following Dasan, but Pappan brushed him aside. The other young men were just behind.

They rushed to the boundary dividing French Mayyazhi from Azhiyoor, a village in Malabar.

Mayyazhi resounded with cries of victory. People ran about wildly holding the Indian national flag in their hands. Dust rose from under their sweating feet.

The policemen, who attempted to confront them, stood petrified for a moment. Dasan took no notice of them and walked into Mayyazhi.

No one stopped him. Those in power seemed paralysed with shock.

Dasan led the rebels into an awakened Mayyazhi. They hurried through the Rue de l'Eglise, past the imposing church. The cross on the steeple, high up above them, bore witness to their victory.

The teachers and students of the Labourdonnais College came out and joined them. Clerks working in the offices put down their pens as well and came out to join them.

They marched through the Rue du Gouvernement, spreading bloodstains over Mayyazhi's breast.

They took over the Government establishments one by one. Finally, they arrived at Big Sayiv's bungalow, shouting slogans. Their clothes were soaked with blood. Songs of freedom rose from their throats.

Dasan forced open the rusted iron gate of the bungalow. His right eye was bleeding. His mundu and shirt were in tatters.

Big Sayiv stood at the arched glass window, binoculars in hand, watching the unfolding drama silently. His eyes, bluer than the sea crashing against his ancient bungalow, blurred with tears.

'Don't shoot,' he ordered. The policemen watched in despair, their hands itching to pull the triggers of their rifles, as the rioters entered forbidden territory.

In a short while, innumerable flags with the saffron, white and green started fluttering over Mayyazhi. The shimmering sky was reflected in the undulating sea. A breeze blew in from the distant Velliyan Kallu, the abode of Mayyazhi's souls.

Mayyazhi was free.

DASAN WALKED HOME IN triumph.

Girija saw Dasan turn the corner near their house. Excited, she ran out into the courtyard. It had been so many months since she had seen her brother.

They had all barred their doors when the uprising began and stayed inside. None of them had realized what was taking place in town. They had heard slogans, cries and curses from the street. People were running helter-skelter.

'Is it my Dasan?' Kurambi Amma came down from the loft. She hobbled into the veranda, her back bent double.

Dasan's right eye was swollen. There were bloodstains on his cheek. He could hardly hold himself upright and walk.

Everything seemed like a dream now. He felt as if Mayyazhi had won freedom years ago. The national flags that he had seen fluttering everywhere as he walked home seemed part of the dream.

'What has happened to your eye, Ettan?'

Girija could hardly bear to look at Dasan. His shirt and mundu were torn and he was splattered with blood.

'Give me a glass of tea, Girija.'

He sat down on a bench in the veranda. Girija's eyes filled with tears.

'Water will do.' He corrected himself hastily. They must be starving. He wondered whether they had even kanji water in the house. And he had thoughtlessly asked for tea.

'Is my son there?'

Dasan heard his mother's trembling voice from inside.

'Is Amma ill?'

'She's been in bed ever since Achan was taken away.'

Girija bit her lip to keep from crying. Dasan gulped down the water she had brought him and got up.

'Don't go in like this. Amma won't be able to bear it. Please wash and change, Etta.'

Dasan longed to see his mother—the most unfortunate woman in Mayyazhi, with her husband in jail and her son in exile—but he did not go in. He sat down again on the wooden bench infested with bugs.

'Achamma, why don't you say something?'

She stared at him. Dasan's behaviour had intrigued her. Why had he refused Big Sayiv's offer? Why had he gone underground? He had been educated in Pondicherry, he was intelligent and knowledgeable. No, Dasan could do no wrong.

But when Damu was arrested, she had realized what was taking place. Dasan wanted the white men to leave Mayyazhi. Kurambi Amma's heart broke. Had it been anyone but Dasan, she would have cursed him.

'Are you angry with me, Achamma?'

She didn't answer. She continued to stand before him, motionless.

Dasan understood his grandmother's emotions. Her heart would be weighed down by sorrow when the white men left Mayyazhi the next day. He knew that she would grieve deeply and weep while Mayyazhi blazed with joy.

'Achamma, I have no grudge against Big Sayiv or France. Please believe me ...'

Kurambi Amma came up slowly to Dasan and sat beside him. She caught his hands in her skinny ones.

Dasan heard footsteps at the door.

He was shocked to see the change in his mother. She seemed to have shrunk, become as small as a child. Her hair had thinned. Dark circles had appeared under her eyes.

'You're back, my son. But your father ...'

The words stuck in her parched throat.

There had been no news of Damu Writer since he was taken away to the jail in Pondicherry. Was he alive?

'Were you born only to bring misery to all of us?'

'Amma, our troubles are over. Mayyazhi is liberated.'

The saffron, white and green flags were flying over Mayyazhi in the gentle sea breeze.

'Etta, will Achan come back now?'

'Yes. I'll go and get him.'

Hope glimmered in Girija's eyes. She had already heated some water. She made Dasan lie down and held a warm towel to all the aching parts of his body. His eyes closed when the warmth penetrated his skin. As steam rose from his lacerated body, he began to doze. He breathed the pure air of freedom as he slept contentedly.

Girija watched him sleep, lying in bed with his face pressed against the pillow. She had cherished her own dreams about him. Unlike Kurambi Amma, she had never imagined him in trousers, and a coat and hat. She had dreamed that he would get a fine job and buy her a saree with his first salary.

Her hopes died as she watched him now. All she wanted was for him to be all right, for all to go well with him.

Dasan could not sleep very long. Every minute was precious. Mayyazhi cried out to him. True, Mayyazhi was now in the hands of her people. But that was not enough. Big Sayiv and his entourage were still in the bungalow. They had to leave. Only then would the storm in Dasan's life be stilled.

'Etta, where are you going?' asked Girija, when he pulled on his shirt. She had had a bath and was in a freshly washed saree and blouse, as he always remembered her.

'I have to go.'

'Not today,' she said. 'You need rest.'

'I cannot rest now. I have to go. Tell Amma.'

Happy because Dasan was back, his mother was still asleep.

He hurried out. Crowds thronged the streets. Many looked bewildered, even afraid. They had not quite understood what had happened. All they knew was that something had changed.

Unni Nair opened the toddy shop at noon. He had closed it the day before when the rioting started. All the regulars were inside, drinking greedily to make up for the day they had missed.

'I don't understand,' Unni Nair looked confused. 'Kunhanan, do you know what is happening?'

'No,' Kunhanan shook his head, glass in hand. He had not opened his provision store today. All the shops in Mayyazhi were closed. 'Something terrible is going to happen.'

'Nothing terrible will happen. We are free now and can rule ourselves,' said Balan, an employee of the Mairie. Everyone looked at him.

'The white men are leaving.'

'Where can they go, Balan?' Unni Nair was puzzled. 'This is their country, isn't it?'

'No, their country is across the sea.'

Balan smiled. Unni Nair could not quite believe him. There had been white men in Mayyazhi ever since he could remember. They could not, would not go away.

'All I wish is that the white men won't leave before I die.'

'Your wish will not be granted, Unni Nair. They are packing up. They may leave even today.'

Unni Nair heaved a sigh. Kunhanan found that the toddy would not go down his throat.

They saw Vasutty walk past, his mundu hitched up above the knee.

'Vasutty, God will not forgive you,' Unni Nair cursed him with an aching heart.

'Do you think Vasutty, Dasan and all the rest will go to hell then, Unni Nair?' Balan smiled. 'They won't go to hell, even if you and

I do. They have dedicated their lives to their country and their people.'

No one said anything.

Unni Nair felt anger and sorrow rising simultaneously within him. He felt breathless. And frightened, too. Until two days ago, he had had the right to abuse everyone associated with the freedom movement, call them names. The policemen and the goondas had encouraged him in this. But the uprising had changed the situation. The policemen were in hiding now and the goondas had disappeared, no one knew where. Achu had not been seen for two days.

The rebels were looking for Achu. Pappan and two other young men had come to Unni Nair's shop in the morning in search of him.

'I don't care where you're hiding, Achu,' Pappan had shouted. 'Nothing will save you. I'll not sleep until I've plucked out your eyes.'

Unni Nair knew that Pappan meant what he said. He would stop at nothing. After all, he was the one who had stabbed the Commissar.

Kunhanan and Kunjakkan finished their drinks and went out. Kunjakkan hobbled away, ladder on shoulder and oil tin in hand. Kunhanan walked down the Rue de la Gare. The doors of the houses were open and people had begun to move about the streets again, but with bewilderment, fear and anxiety in their eyes.

Vasutty's heart sank. Naturally, he had felt very happy when Mayyazhi won freedom. He had walked home with a sense of contentment. But what he had seen when he arrived there perturbed him deeply.

There was no one on the veranda. The front door was closed. Vasutty pushed it open.

Seated on the mat, Soumini and Purushu were laughing over something. They were startled to see him. Kallu Amma was seated on the kitchen step. All three seemed upset when he entered.

'What the hell are you doing here?' Vasutty shouted at Purushu, unable to control his anger.

He understood everything now. He was seeing, with his own eyes, what he had heard about Soumini when he was in exile outside Mayyazhi.

'You've come, son?'

Kallu Amma scrambled up. A new piece of cloth, with its unbleached colour still fresh, covered her sagging breasts. The big ear-studs, which had been pawned years ago to Kunhimmoosa Haji, were back on her ears. Soumini wore a cotton saree that looked fairly new.

'You're not pleased to see me back, are you?'

He sat down on the bench that stood against the wall. The toddy tapper Pokkan Achan had died on that termite-ridden bench.

Purushu slunk out, looking as embarrassed as a thief caught red-handed.

Vasutty thought, what can I say to him? Purushu was probably not the only one who had shared the mat with his sister, there might have been others as well.

'Soumini, I never thought you'd do this ...'

She didn't raise her eyes.

'You're the sister of a person who sacrificed everything for Mayyazhi's freedom. And yet, you did this ...'

'Find fault with us if you want,' Kallu Amma said. 'The children were crying with hunger. We had no clothes to cover our shame. Where were you at that time? You turn up now, to accuse us.'

Vasutty listened in silence. Whose fault was it? He felt partly responsible. He should have made sure that his mother and the young children were fed and clothed properly.

He paced up and down the veranda. He heard Soumini crying inside. He felt disgusted with everything—himself, his family, even the tricolour flags fluttering under the blue skies.

He had a bath. They served him rice. He had not had a meal in his house for a long time, not since he had resigned from his government job.

When he finished, he wondered whether he should have eaten.

Layers of darkness gathered over Mayyazhi.

'Soumini,' he walked up to his sister. 'Let's forget what happened. But never do this again.'

As she stood there weeping, with her head bent, he said to his mother, 'Amma, I'll never make you suffer again.'

Surely, it wouldn't be futile, what he had done for Mayyazhi. Another two or three days and the white men would go. His duty to Mayyazhi would be discharged then and he could attend to the needs of his family.

Vasutty went to sleep with a sense of relief.

Big Sayiv's bungalow had a look of Noah's Ark during the deluge. All those who owed the white men allegiance—the policemen, the goondas, all of them—had sought shelter there.

The rebels and their sympathizers were crowded on the pier, in front of the bungalow.

Big Sayiv stood at the arched window, binoculars in hand, gazing out at the sea.

'Let's surround the bungalow,' said Pappan. He was impatient.

'Be careful,' Vasutty was cautious. 'They have not fired as yet, but they are armed.'

'No one is afraid of their guns, anymore.'

'What shall we do then?'

The wheels of the colonial government had stopped turning. Schools and offices remained closed. The tricolours were still fluttering over Mayyazhi.

Kanaran and Dasan decided to go to the bungalow and have a talk.

'They'll skin you alive,' warned Vasutty.

Dasan and Kanaran walked in through the unguarded gate. The wind had blown away even the footprints of the policemen.

An attendant took them inside.

Dasan found himself once more in Big Sayiv's white bungalow.

The sea breeze brought back memories.

L'Etat se rèjouit de ton succès.

The State is happy at your success.

Dèsormais l'Etat s'occupe de toi.

The State will look after you from now on.

Dasan smiled. Much time had passed. He was no longer the same Dasan. Like an ox pulling an overloaded cart, he was to bear the burden of Mayyazhi's destiny. His eye was still swollen, his wounds raw. His mind bled with the thought of his father.

The sound of heavy footsteps awoke him. Mayor Raman, turned out immaculately as usual in a coat and trousers, with a bow at his neck. Secrètaire Karunan followed, dressed as elegantly.

'Venez, Messieurs.'

Please come in, gentlemen.

They went up the carpeted stairs. Kanaran's heart beat fast. They could do anything, put him in prison, or kill him and throw his body into the sea that agitated below them.

Holding all their fears in check, they walked on, escorted by Mayor Raman and Secrètaire Karunan. A series of curtains parted to allow them in.

Big Sayiv stood with his back to them, looking out. The sea thudded below the glass windows. In the distance, the horizon shone clear. Big Sayiv had his binoculars in his hand.

'What do you want?' he asked, without turning around.

'Freedom,' said Dasan.

Big Sayiv still had his back to them. The sea beat against the shore below the glass windows.

'Freedom?'

'Yes.'

Big Sayiv pushed open the windows.

'Look, my friends ...'

He pointed to the sea. The silhouettes of battleships were etched against the horizon. They were moving towards Mayyazhi.

Kanaran and Dasan stood there as if nailed to the floor. An icy chill spread through their bodies. They seemed to have become deaf and dumb.

They had no idea how long they stood there. They woke up from their stupor to hear Mayor Raman and Secrètaire Karunan laughing loudly.

The curtains parted to let them out. They turned and walked out as if in a dream. They walked over the long driveway, which seemed to have no end, to the iron gate.

'Battleships!'

'Battleships are coming!'

People screamed, running frenziedly in all directions. The pier emptied in a minute. Only the leaders of the freedom movement were left behind.

The battleships sounded louder. The national flags which had fluttered bravely over Mayyazhi trembled. The people of Mayyazhi would be forced to their knees again and the chains of slavery slipped over their feet.

'Big Sayiv has the wireless. Kanaretta, we forgot that.'

Dasan lit a beedi, trying to keep himself under control. He tucked up his mundu. Kanaran shivered as if he had malaria.

Thousands of battleships seemed to be blowing their sirens in his ears. He squatted on the roadside in sheer despair.

'Let's go, Kanaretta.'

'Where?'

'Let's leave Mayyazhi again. We'll organize another rebellion to overthrow the battleships ...'

'I'm not coming. I'll stay here and die.'

Kanaran stretched out on the ground, his arms embracing the soil of Mayyazhi. He wept, his black, withered hands spread wide. He would never leave Mayyazhi. The battleships would never snatch Mayyazhi from him, not even if they came in thousands.

'Get up, Kanaretta.'

'No, I'm not coming.'

Kanaran's bony hands tightened over Mayyazhi. He lay against the soil that had borne him as if it were truly his mother. He fought for breath and tears, hot as blood, flowed from his eyes.

With a great effort, Dasan raised Kanaran from the ground, and led him away. The sun of freedom, which had blazed over Mayyazhi for six days, was burning itself out. The policemen and goondas were coming into their own again.

Both were silent as they reached the Rue de l'Eglise. Dasan tried not to stumble.

The battleships drew nearer and the sirens sounded shriller. The church bells rang out suddenly, signalling a calamity. Their sound spread ominously over Mayyazhi. People rushed eastwards through the Rue de l'Eglise towards the border of Mayyazhi. The shops shut down. There was confusion everywhere.

It was dangerous to stay longer. The soldiers in the battleships had come ashore. Dasan realized that he had to flee once again. He saw Pappan standing in front of the church, watching the great bells swing to and fro, releasing cascades of sound.

'Pappan!'

'I've been waiting for you.'

'Where's Vasutty?'

'He escaped.'

Suddenly, Dasan thought of his sick mother and Achamma and Girija. To whom could he entrust them? He felt dizzy.

'Pappan, get out of Mayyazhi quickly. Take Kanarettan with you.'
'And you?'
'You know Amma is ill. I have to go home.'

A group of armed policemen appeared in the distance at the Rue de la Résidence.

'How can I leave you here and go?'
'You must leave.'

It was no time to argue. Pappan hurried away.

Voices urging each other to flee echoed in Dasan's ears. And the sound of footsteps hurrying away.

The army, which had descended on Mayyazhi after crossing the sea, could do anything to them. It could burn the people of Mayyazhi to ashes for having revolted. Blood would flow.

'Kurambi Amma, they are going to drop bombs on us,' Unni Nair shouted, running away with a bundle on his back.

Kunjakkan, Kunhanan and their families were close behind him. They were carrying whatever they had been able to grab, in bundles or boxes.

Kurambi Amma stood stupefied on the veranda. The church bells continued to unleash a deafening clamour.

People ran out from their baths, dripping wet, their clothes wrapped hastily around them. The sick and dying stumbled out of the hospitals. People streamed over the bridge on the Mayyazhi river. Screaming children. Old people who tottered and staggered along. The weak and the ill, slung over the shoulders of the younger ones. Wealth and possessions had been left behind in this wild flight. Fearing death and destruction, a great exodus had begun.

Smoke from the battleships mushroomed over Mayyazhi.

Dasan reached the courtyard of his house. He had decided to take all his people with him, he did not know where. Somewhere out of Mayyazhi was all he knew.

'Let's go, Amma.' He helped her sit up. Girija watched, crying.

'Will the white army drop bombs on us?'

'We have no time to talk. Let's go.'

'Where, Etta?'

'Where everyone else is going.'

'No, they won't drop bombs,' Kurambi Amma consoled herself. 'The white men are kind.'

Kurambi Amma adored the white men even at this moment, when their battleships had landed in Mayyazhi.

Dasan walked to the street, supporting his mother. Girija and Kurambi Amma followed. The street was now empty. All their neighbours had gone.

Suddenly, Dasan saw Achu standing in front of him.

Was this going to be another ordeal by fire?

'Get out of my way. I'll kill you if you touch me.'

Achu laughed. 'Don't stay here any longer, Dasan. Run for your life. If you don't go, even I won't be able to save you.'

Dasan looked at him, bewildered.

'You don't believe me?'

Dasan noticed that Achu did not have his knife with him.

Achu said, 'Go now. I'll take care of your mother and sister.'

'How can I trust you?'

'You fool, I could hand you over to the army now if I wanted to. Or even kill you here and now.' Achu laughed again.

'Achu, I place my trust in you. If you betray me, God will never forgive you.'

Achu pushed Dasan forward and he stumbled away. As he walked on, his footsteps faltered, were disoriented, as if he had gone mad.

Dasan was confused. Was it all a bad dream? Battleships and fleeing people. And now Achu standing unarmed in front of him. Was it real? Had he gone mad?

'Amma, I'm going mad. Save me.'

The church bells crashed to a stop.

The army marched through the Rue de l'Eglise. The soldiers wore dark blue uniforms. Their skins were as pink as the chekki flowers blooming on the pier. The guns in their hands glittered in the bright sunlight.

The white army found no rebels, no rioters. The Mayyazhi that welcomed them was as deserted and silent as a burial ground. The armed soldiers marched through the empty streets, pulling down the national flags flying over the Mairie and the Palais de Justice.

The next day, they came into the streets unarmed. Coconut palms dipped and swayed like peacocks. Crow pheasants flew around, flapping their red wings. The goats grazed, bells around their necks. The soldiers entered the toddy shop that Unni Nair had abandoned. They drank his well-seasoned toddy. Drunk, they went around Mayyazhi, savouring its idyllic beauty.

Big Sayiv issued a proclamation. The army would not harm his subjects. They had come to protect them from the rioters. Only the rioters would be punished. Big Sayiv requested his subjects to return to Mayyazhi.

But no one came back.

The battleships still lay at anchor on the wharf and the army wandered around the streets.

A few days passed.

It was a bright day. The streets remained deserted and the houses abandoned. Famished cows searched desperately for food. Fowl died of starvation and the few that survived were eaten by jackals. While the sun rose over the Mayyazhi river and the drunken soldiers basked outdoors, Antony appeared on the bridge in the distance. He came in dragging his swollen legs that were afflicted by elephantiasis. He was the first to obey Big Sayiv's summons and come back to his motherland. Wild with joy, the drunken soldiers welcomed him. They hugged him as he stepped on the soil of Mayyazhi. Others followed. Kunjakkan hobbled in, bundle on shoulder, along with the carpenter. Old men and women followed, leaning on their sticks, and children clutching their parents' hands.

In a few days, all those who had fled were back home.

They gave the soldiers tender coconuts to drink and made payasam for them with milk and sugar. The streets became alive again and wine flowed in abundance.

Now, it was time for the army to go back. The people of Mayyazhi flocked to the seashore to see them off. The anchors were raised. The battleships moved away slowly and disappeared into the horizon.

24

Bandman Kanari's daughter, not yet sixteen, was pregnant.

'How can that be? She's not married,' said Kurambi Amma to Achu, helping herself to a pinch of snuff from the ivory box.

'This is the Kali Yugam, isn't it? Anything can happen.' Achu was seated beside Kurambi Amma on the grass mat that he had bought at the Thira festival in Andalur.

'Give me a pinch too.' Kurambi Amma handed Achu the ivory box. He had started to take snuff of late. Actually, Kurambi Amma had taught him to do so. A new bond had now grown between them.

'Who do you think it is?'

'The Brigadier, who else?'

'Isn't the mother enough? Why does he want the daughter as well?'

Kurambi Amma's huge earrings moved as she laughed aloud. Achu's face turned as red as a hibiscus. His face always reddened when he laughed.

'If I ask you something, Achu, will you tell me?'

'Of course. Who would I tell things to except you?'

'Does the Brigadier have a woman and children in Pondicherry?'

'Oh yes,' said Achu. 'Her name is Alamelu. And four children—Kamatchi, Chinnammu, Arikesavan and Madanagopalan.'

'Nani and her daughter are really lucky.'

Nani and Devi had moved in with Chettiappa. Kanari lived alone in his hut. But he was much happier than he used to be. Chettiappa sent him money every morning for the day's liquor. What more did he want? He had stopped going to work. He spent all day in Unni Nair's toddy shop. In the evening, he came home and played his trumpet. Mayyazhi still heard the relentless strains of his trumpet music till dawn broke.

David Sayiv was not like Chettiappa. Although he had a son by Kunhichirutha and had built her a house, she was never seen in his company. He never visited her in the house he built her. The relationship between them existed only at night. At dusk, she took her bath in the pond, changed into a fresh mundu, combed her hair and tucked jasmine into it, applied kohl to her eyes, and went to David Sayiv's bungalow. Although she was no longer young, her skin still had the colour of beaten gold.

Kurambi Amma often said, 'Kunhichirutha will always look sixteen.'

Achu and Kurambi Amma chatted, breathing the shared ecstasy of snuff, until the sun went down.

Girija came to the door. Running her fingers over the door, her head bent, she said, 'There's no rice for the evening meal.'

'What else do you need?'

'Amma wants a little turpentine.'

Achu got up, took his sheathed knife from the windowsill and went out. It was he who looked after affairs in Damu Writer's house now. They would have had to beg if not for him. They might even have died of starvation.

AFTER HAVING SPENT TWO years in jail in Pondicherry, Damu Writer came back in the simmering heat of an afternoon. He looked even more thin and emaciated. His face had a pale, jaundiced look and handcuffs had left scars on both his wrists.

His hair had been cut close to his head.

People stopped him on the way to ask him the news but he would not speak to anyone. He hurried home, covering his head with the towel that lay on his shoulder to shield himself from the sun.

He had no idea of what had happened in his house and in Mayyazhi. Surprising as it was, he did not want to know either. He felt hatred and resentment against everyone, even against himself.

'Come and have a drink,' Unni Nair invited him. Damu Writer had come from Pondicherry, he was bound to have some news.

Damu Writer hesitated, then went in. Unni Nair brought him a bottle of tender toddy and served him puzhukku on a banana leaf.

'They must have beaten you up ...'

Damu Writer grunted. Seated with his head bent, he swallowed a mouthful. Kunhanan and Policeman Kannan, who were having a drink, moved closer.

'Your son has been sentenced to twelve years. Did you know that?'

Damu Writer was startled, but tried to look calm.

'Is he in jail?'

'No, he escaped before the battleships came in.'

What ships? Whose ships? Damu Writer swallowed another mouthful. He didn't touch the puzhukku.

'He's a clever boy, your son. But why did he provoke the white men? They've given him twelve years now. Not one or two, but twelve. That's what you get if you play games with Big Sayiv and the white men.'

Damu Writer listened in silence.

'They're brave all right. They took the Mairie and the police station. But they ran for their lives as soon as the battleships arrived. Cowards!'

Damu Writer put his glass down. He had had enough.

'Tell your son to ask the white men to forgive him. The white men are merciful.'

'Unni Nair,' Damu Writer turned on him suddenly, 'don't say a word to me about Dasan. He's no longer my son.'

His face darkened. His eyes narrowed. He walked away. Perspiring in the heat of the afternoon sun, his thin hair seemed pasted to his scalp.

'What a fate! Someone knifed the red-eyed Sayiv and the poor deed writer went to jail. There's no law or justice in Mayyazhi anymore.'

Kunhanan's remark was not addressed to anyone in particular. Damu Writer had not been the only one to go to jail. Many other people involved in the rebellion had gone as well. It was the price they had paid for the red-eyed Sayiv's blood.

Damu Writer stumbled on. All he wanted was to pitch into bed. If only he could get home faster ...

The first person he saw when he entered the courtyard was Achu, seated on the writer's easy chair and smoking, his legs stretched along the foot rests. Damu Writer's heart blazed. Kurambi Amma was seated on the floor near him leaning against the wall and inhaling snuff.

Achu sprang up when he saw the deed writer, threw his half-smoked cigarette away and helped him into the veranda.

Damu Writer felt uneasy in Achu's presence. He waited, breathing heavily.

It hurt Kurambi Amma to look at her son. At first glance, he looked older than her. She gazed at him.

'Girija, bring your father some tea.'

Achu helped Damu Writer into the easy chair. Girija wiped her eyes and went to the kitchen. She was relieved that her father had returned. Without her father or brother in the house, she had been frightened and had spent many sleepless nights. She was tired of their dependence on Achu.

She sobbed with sheer relief as she made tea. Her wet cheeks reflected the flames. Her days seemed to be made up now of fire and tears and she often asked herself where it would all end.

Everything had started with Dasan, so he would have to end it all for them as well. Until Dasan was free, they would never stop shedding tears and Dasan would be free only when Mayyazhi became free. Would that day of salvation ever arrive? Girija did not understand politics. She had wanted her Ettan to explain things to her, but she had never been able to get him to do so.

She took two glasses of tea to the veranda.

Achu was pacing up and down. Damu Writer lay in his chair. Kowsu stood by him, crying softly.

'Did they beat you a lot?'

'Hmm ...'

'Did you fall ill in jail?'

'That's my fate.'

Kowsu could not bear to look at her husband's shrunken face, covered with stubble and mosquito bites.

Girija gave her father and Achu tea. Damu Writer felt better with the steaming tea inside him. He suddenly realized that it was tea with milk and sugar. What a luxury! He had not expected to find even gruel water at home.

'How are you managing, Kowsu?'

No one answered. Achu continued to pace up and down. The silence grew heavy.

So much had happened since Damu Writer left. Mayyazhi's destiny had been rewritten. The white army had marched into Mayyazhi. And yet, the flowering bushes in the yard grew as thick as ever, and the asoka tree on the south had bloomed as usual.

'Did you see Ettan at the railway station?' Girija asked her father. Dasan was often seen at the station, which was outside the border, and people who came by one of the trains sometimes brought Kowsu news of him.

Damu Writer looked at his daughter. At her full breasts and shapely hips. She looked like a grown woman who had borne children.

'You didn't see Ettan?'

'I don't want to hear his name,' screamed Damu Writer. Girija looked at her mother, shocked.

'Don't be so harsh with him.'

'I don't want to hear a word from any of you about him, Kowsu.'

'He's your son, after all,' said Achu.

It wasn't only Damu Writer who had changed, Achu had changed as well, and Damu Writer had noticed it. Achu seemed less hot-tempered and insolent than he used to be.

'Achu stays with us,' said Kurambi Amma. Damu Writer frowned. But he realized that Achu had the right to stay wherever he wanted in Mayyazhi, since he was now its uncrowned king.

Two or three days passed. Achu was extremely polite to Damu Writer. One day, he even took him to Unni Nair's toddy shop for a drink.

'Achu, I don't mind your staying with us. But you know there's a grown up girl in the house ...'

'I know, Writer.'

Kurambi Amma intervened, 'You've no idea what happened here, Damu. A riot took place and the army came in. There was not a man in our house at the time. It was Achu here who looked after your wife and daughter.' She was really annoyed with her son. They had been so helpless, anyone could have done anything to them. Achu himself could have done what he liked. Instead, he had taken care of them and kept the fire in their hearth alive.

'Oh yes,' she went on, 'We have a man in the family—you. And another one, educated and all that. But what's the use? There's only Achu here to buy me three quarter anna's worth of snuff when I need it.'

Kurambi Amma felt desperate whenever her snuffbox started to become empty. She wanted a full box to keep under her pillow at night. She still spent her nights blowing her nose and inhaling snuff. Time had gone by, but even now, when the municipal lamps went out and Mayyazhi became silent and dark, she would hear Leslie Sayiv call out from the street, 'Kurambi, Kurambi, can I have a pinch of snuff?'

Every night, before she fell asleep, she wept for Leslie Sayiv.

Achu asked Damu Writer while they were eating one night, 'Writer, do you mind my staying here?'

The question distressed Damu Writer. How could he ask him to leave? He owed Achu even the food he was eating.

'Tell me if you have any objection and I'll leave.'

'What objection could I have, Achu?' Damu Writer did not look up from his plate. Achu knew he had won and was secretly happy.

Achu usually got up early morning, had an oil bath and drank his gruel with coconut scraped into it. After this, he would take his knife from the window-sill and go out. He and Damu Writer would have lunch together and walk to Unni Nair's toddy shop for a drink in the evenings.

Kurambi Amma was happy when she saw them to gether. Only Kowsu felt sad. She wondered whether her husband had forgotten Dasan.

'Did you see my son, Kunhanan?'

Kunhanan went to the Vadagara market every Tuesday and came back by the local train at two-thirty. Kowsu would be waiting for him.

'Yes, I did.'

'Is he all right?'

Kunhanan never answered that. One day, he said he wanted to see Damu Writer.

'I saw your son.'

Damu Writer pretended that he had not heard and sat down in his chair. He did not even look at Kunhanan.

'He wants you to meet him at the railway station. He has something to tell you.'

Damu Writer turned his face away.

Kunhanan was annoyed by his indifference.

Damu Writer did not go and see Dasan. Kowsu had been trying to persuade him to do so from the time he came back, but he had not agreed. Once, she had decided to go to him herself.

Damu Writer had said. 'Go if you want to, but don't ever come back.'

Achu had tried to advise him, 'After all, he's your son. You don't understand a mother's feelings.'

'Achu, don't meddle in our affairs. After all, this is my house.'

'Am I an outsider then? Tell me, Writer, have I no rights here?'

Damu Writer did not answer.

Finally, Kowsu did not go to see her son.

The cinema came to Mayyazhi. It was as important an event as the arrival of Big Sayiv's car on the wharf long ago. The cinema owner came from the south. He had come to Mayyazhi not only to make money, but also to enjoy the French wines that flowed in Mayyazhi.

A huge tent was put up in the maidan. Streamers fluttered everywhere. There were posters of N.S. Krishnan and T.A. Madhuram on the walls of the shops. The crier went through the streets with his drum accompanied by a boy with publicity placards. They distributed bright red notices to everyone.

Kurambi Amma had never seen a film. She had often watched Nani go with Brigadier Chettiappa to Narangapuram, a nearby town, to see a film and longed to go to one herself.

'Damu, will you take me to the cinema, son?'

'You're ready to be buried and all you can think of is the cinema.'

Disappointed, she turned to Achu, 'Will you take me, Achu?'

'Of course.'

He smiled and pulled out a handful of red cinema tickets from his pocket.

'What's the time, Girija?' Kurambi Amma couldn't contain her impatience on the day they were going.

'Just two o'clock.'

'Oh God, four hours more to go.'

Girija filled a big plate with live coals and ironed her saree and blouse with it. She had a bath, combed her wet air and tucked flowers into it.

It was like a festival in Mayyazhi that day. Crowds poured into the maidan. Brigadier Chettiappa, Nani and Devi were amongst the first to arrive. Chettiappa wore a kasavu mundu as usual and Nani and Devi wore new silk sarees.

Kunhichirutha also arrived, covered with jewellery, with David Sayiv's son in her arms.

Unni Nair closed down his shop earlier than usual and was there with Kunhanan.

At five-thirty the generator was turned on. The people of Mayyazhi were thrilled to hear its ear-splitting roar. Kurambi Amma was astonished. Achu explained, 'That's the machine that makes the electric current, Kurambi Amma.'

'Do they have electric lights here, Achu?'

'Yes, Kurambi Amma.'

Achu held Kurambi Amma's hand and cleared a way for Girija through the crowds. They entered the cinema hall, brightly lit by electric bulbs.

And that was how Girija and Kurambi Amma saw a film for the first time in their lives.

After dinner that night, Achu and Damu Writer sat in the veranda, talking of village affairs. Achu smoked a beedi, looking thoughtful. He was very quiet. The municipal lamps had started to burn lower.

'Damu Writer,' Achu threw the stub of his beedi into the courtyard and sat up straight. 'I've been wanting to tell you something.'

'Tell me.'

Damu Writer was half-asleep on his easy chair.

'People are spreading rumours ...'

'About what?'

'Girija and me.'

'You can't shut people's mouths.' Damu Writer grunted.

'Then let's go ahead with it.'

Damu Writer sank back in his chair. He had known that this was coming. And had even wondered what he would say in reply.

Achu swallowed his saliva. By the dim light coming from the kerosene lamp, Damu Writer could make out how tense he was.

'Girija is my only daughter, Achu. I want to marry her into a good family. You have no home, no family. You're a goonda ...'

Achu was silent. He walked up and down the veranda a couple of times. Then he stood in front of Damu Writer.

'If I find myself a decent job, if I conduct myself with dignity and self-respect, will you give me your daughter?'

'Hmm ...'

Lost in thought, the writer nodded. The municipal lamps had burnt out. The liquid darkness of a moonless night lay over Mayyazhi.

25

The Mayyazhi river, which had its source in the Kuttiyadi Mala, flowed past the Kanaka Mala into Mayyazhi.

Seated on its banks, outside Mayyazhi, Dasan thought: How long it is since I walked on the soil of my Mayyazhi ... over the pier, scattered with red gulmohur flowers, or in the Rue de l'Eglise, under the shadow of the cross, or on the bridge where I used to stand so often, watching the passionate mingling of the river with the sea. They were all so far away now. It seemed to him that Mayyazhi was no longer on this earth, but on some distant star.

He had not seen Velliyan Rock, where souls hovered between births, for a long time. In the old days, when he used to sit on the seashore, looking westwards, he had felt untouched by worldly problems. Thoughts of Mayyazhi's freedom, or of his father or Chandrika, had never disturbed him at those moments. He had never considered life a burden. Velliyan Rock, a silvery island, its outline blurred by the distance, had given him peace.

But Velliyan Rock was far away now ...

'What are you thinking about, Dasetta?' Chandrika threw pebbles into the river. The water nearly came up to their feet. It must be high tide.

'You're lucky, Chandrika. You have nothing to worry about.'

'I worry about you ...'

She stretched her legs out on the white sand. He looked at the anklets on her wet feet.

'It frightens me when you worry about me.'

'But you're my only worry.' She pulled her braid over her shoulder and caressed it.

He knew she worried about him. She had told him that she lived only for him and that frightened him.

He longed for her when she was not with him. But when they were together, he wanted to be alone.

He was unemployed. He had been sentenced to twelve years' imprisonment. His father hated him.

'Do you know what I am?'

'You're Dasettan,' she said.

He could not say anything to that. She had become part of his existence. He could never be free of her now.

The night before, he had gone to bed at three o'clock, but had not been able to sleep. He slept very little these days. He would lie flat on his mat, smoking beedi after beedi. Pappan, who lay next to him, always fell asleep the moment his head touched the pillow.

But even if he didn't sleep a wink at night, Dasan would get up early morning. It had become a habit with him to wait by the river for the seven o'clock local train that came from Kozhikode.

'Can you give me a beedi?' Porter Kunhanan was on his way to the station in his faded khaki shirt. He drew a beedi out from behind his ear and gave it to Dasan. 'The train will be here any moment. I'll get going.'

In the morning, Dasan had noticed a new shirt on the clothesline, a blue one with long sleeves. He had taken it down and looked at it.

'Pappan had that tailored. Can't you get one like it?' Cheeru, who was sprinkling cowdung over the courtyard, had asked.

She knew Dasan did not have enough clothes.

Dasan had put on Pappan's shirt. It was the first time he was wearing a full-sleeve shirt.

Every time Pappan had something tailored, Vasutty would scold him, 'There you are, decking yourself out like a bridegroom while we walk around with our heads on fire!'

Kanaran would add, 'New clothes are not everything. You should have a bath and clean your teeth as well.'

Pappan's hair was always matted and his teeth were as black as tamarind seeds.

Dasan walked over the fields, planted with root crops. He bought a packet of Sadhu beedis from Vappu's shop. Vappu jotted it down on the wall against his account. Dasan had been buying beedis for days now and had not paid a paisa. The longest account on the wall was his. It must have reached a sizeable amount.

I'll clear my debts one day, Vappu, to you and to everyone else, he said to himself.

The signal was down. Dasan began to walk faster. Chandrika would be in the train, on her way to her college in Thalassery. She would smile at him. Her hair would be blowing over her cheeks in the breeze from the Mayyazhi river. Long after the train had gone past, her face would stay in his mind.

The local train went by, swaying and jolting like a bullock cart, spitting out smoke. But he did not see Chandrika.

Maybe she was not going to class today. Was it a holiday? He had lost count of time. He didn't even know what day of the week it was.

There had been other college students in the train. So it was not a holiday.

He turned back and saw her walking along the railway line, holding her books against her breast.

'I missed the train, Dasetta ...'

She pushed back her hair. The breeze blowing across the river held the fragrance of the fields.

'A new shirt?'

'Not mine, it's Pappan's.'

She thought the shirt suited him. If only he would cut his hair and trim his beard ...

'I'm not going to class today.'

Her anklets tinkled as she walked. The tide had receded and they could see the bank of the river clearly. Crabs crawled by on their red legs, in search of prey. In the distance, Kanaka Mala shone, bright sunshine caught between its dark folds.

They sat down on the sand and leaned back against a coconut tree, their legs stretched out. The shrivelled river flowed beneath them. They began to perspire as the sun climbed higher in the sky. He realized that her sweat had a salty tang. The stubble on his chin scratched her tender skin.

'Shall I put on your anklets?'

She took off the silver anklets that snaked around her legs and put them on his hairy legs. They often did this for fun. The sun grew hotter. Tired and perspiring, he yawned.

'Want to sleep, Dasetta?'

He put his head on her shoulder, where her wet blouse clung to her skin, and dozed; he didn't know how long.

'I didn't miss my train,' she said while going back. 'I came late on purpose.'

Soon, this became a habit.

He was worried. What they were doing was wrong. How could he justify it? He lay drenched in her salty perspiration which was more intoxicating than arrack.

26

Everyone in Mayyazhi was surprised at the change in Achu. It was more than a decade since he had arrived in Mayyazhi. He had spent his days currying favour with the whites and the half-French, or fist fighting in the toddy shops. He had never done a day's work. He had always relied on his knife to get himself whatever he needed.

But now, he was hardly seen in the toddy shops.

'I haven't seen him for two whole days,' exclaimed Unni Nair. 'He must have given up toddy, now that he's staying with Damu Writer.'

It was after he moved in with Damu Writer that Achu had changed so much. He had protected Damu Writer's family when the French army came to Mayyazhi. Now, he and Damu Writer went for long walks in the evening. Achu bought rice and fish for Damu Writer's family. Everyone had seen him take Kurambi Amma and Girija to the cinema the first day it came to Mayyazhi.

'A miracle,' said Kunjakkan.

'No, no,' said Kunhanan. 'I can see what it's all about.'

'And what's that?'

'You'll soon see. You'll see what Achu has in mind.'

Like Kunhanan, Unni Nair and many others had made their own guess.

Unni Nair's toddy shop was quiet without Achu. And the people of Mayyazhi began to realize that they no longer needed to be afraid of him.

One morning, Achu woke up early, shaved, had a bath and put on clean clothes. For the first time in his life, he combed his hair.

'Your knife,' Kurambi Amma reminded him as he was leaving. Achu's face grew grim. He looked at his knife which was lying on the window-sill. Then he went off to the Revenue Office in the Rue de la Rèsidence without taking it.

It seemed as if a miracle had happened, turning the animal in him into a human being.

He had come out without his knife. But he was not unarmed. The thought of Girija was a weapon sharper than his knife, one that gave him greater self-confidence.

Achu arrived at the Revenue Office exactly on time and took his seat behind the table. There were many thick ledgers on the table. He worked hard. And began a new life as the clerk Achu.

In the evening, he went to Unni Nair's toddy shop. Everyone stood up as usual when he came in but he ignored all of them and sat by himself in a corner.

'Just a bottle of tender toddy. Nothing else.'

Unni Nair brought him the bottle and a glass. Everyone gazed at the new Achu, with his neatly combed hair parted in the middle and his fresh white mundu and shirt. Seated quietly, he sipped the toddy. It was not a sight they were used to.

'We haven't seen you for days.'

'Hmm.'

'Are you planning to give up toddy?'

Achu didn't reply. He was trying to finish the bottle as quickly as possible. But Unni Nair persisted, 'At this rate, will you give up eating by the time you get married?'

Achu smiled A few people laughed. Unni Nair would have never dared to talk to him like that in the old days, nor would anyone have dared to laugh.

Achu placed two quarter-anna coins on the table as he went out. Unni Nair looked at them in disbelief. Achu had never paid for his drinks.

Achu's heart was heavy. He had a job now. Would Damu Writer keep his word? Would Girija agree? The questions tormented him night and day.

Did Girija know what was in his mind? Although many occasions had come his way, he had never declared his feelings for her. She used to avoid him in the beginning, but now she came to him unhesitatingly to tell him that there was not enough rice for the evening meal. It was not only provisions that he bought. He bought Girija kohl for lining her eyes. And coloured glass bangles for both her hands at the Jagannath temple festival.

But he could never talk to her when they were alone with each other, he was not sure why. His throat would feel choked and he would grow tongue-tied. However, if Kurambi Amma was with them, he would tease Girija and tell her stories that made her laugh.

He could never bring himself to tell her what was in his heart. What if he told her, one day? He was afraid. He was a clerk now at the Revenue Office and earned a decent salary. But the past clung to him like a burden and he could not forget what he had been. Sometimes, he felt that even if Damu Writer consented, Girija would not. What would he do then? He did not know. Perhaps he would go back to his past. Then he would not need anyone's permission to make Girija his, not even hers.

He arrived home exhausted. Girija was placing a lighted wick near the tulasi plant in the courtyard. She had had her evening bath and water still dripped from her wet hair.

'You're home early,' she smiled and rubbed the oil on her fingertips into her hair.

Achu couldn't speak. He swallowed his saliva and sat down on the veranda. Children could be heard chanting their evening prayers from all the houses nearby.

Achu prayed silently, God, give Girija to me. Otherwise, I'll have to break Damu Writer's bones, or set fire to his house. Don't make me do that! Achu's face grew red and his eyes narrowed.

The municipal lamps that Kunjakkan had lit burned out. Damu Writer lay in his easy chair, smoking. His health had improved and he no longer had asthma. But he was not happy. How could Dasan's father ever be happy?

Achu went up to Damu Writer. 'I have a job now. You said that ...'

'You don't have to remind me, Achu. I'm a man of my word.'

A terrible weight seemed to lift from Achu's heart. He asked, 'Will Girija agree?'

'Don't worry. I know how to make my daughter obey me.'

Achu slept peacefully that night but Damu Writer did not. Lying near Kowsu, he turned and tossed. He knew he would have to tell her now. He had hidden it from her all this time. Not deliberately, but because he knew her nature.

Kowsu felt as if someone had dealt her a blow on the head. When she found her voice at last, she sobbed, 'I'll never agree, even if you kill me.'

'I'm not asking you for permission.'

'She's my daughter as well. You can't go ahead without my permission.'

'I cared for you all so much. What did I get in return? I had to go to jail in my old age! I no longer need anyone's advice or permission. I'll do exactly what I want.'

'Remember, Achu once kicked you in the street. He's made so many people suffer. You can't forget all that.'

Kowsu's voice trembled. Neither spoke for a while. When Kowsu was able to breathe freely again, she continued, weeping: 'Girija will never agree.'

'I don't need her permission.'

Meanwhile, the sun rose on another day and crows flew over the river to the seashore.

Girija shut herself up in her room. She would not eat or sleep. She opened the door only after Kowsu knocked for hours. She seemed to have grown much thinner in a day and her eyes were sunk in their sockets.

'Don't make things difficult for me, Girija.'

'Tell my father to kill me.'

She lay in her mother's arms and sobbed.

Tears flowed unceasingly in Dasan's house. The whole of Mayyazhi wept for Girija. Would the merciful Mother of Mayyazhi save her? Would the deities of the Meethalambalam shrine open their eyes to bless her?

27

Dasan paced up and down his room like a caged wildcat. The ends of his thick moustache quivered with anger. He walked faster and faster. Finally, tired and at his wit's end, he sank down on his mat, his head on his knees.

'I'll never allow it,' he raged. Kanaran, who was with him, could do nothing to comfort him.

'I'll never allow it.'

'What can you do? You're not even permitted to set foot in Mayyazhi.'

'So long as I'm alive, I'll never allow it.'

He had defied hurricanes with courage, but his legs trembled now.

If only he could get to Mayyazhi ... He would fall at his father's feet and beg him, 'Please don't give my sister to that goonda.'

He knew that Achu was staying in his house but he had assumed that he had forced his way in and that his father had not been able to protest. After all, the man was the uncrowned king of Mayyazhi.

But things had become clear now. The Achu who had appeared before him at the time when the battleships anchored in Mayyazhi had been a new person. If only he had guessed that Achu had had a motive when he offered to take care of Dasan's family ...

If he had known, Dasan would have killed his mother and sister. Or surrendered to the army. Or committed suicide. But he had not known, or suspected Achu. He had not been alert. He had failed the greatest test of his life. And it had taken him two and a half years to understand this.

A young woman, the wife of a Chettiar, used to go to Mayyazhi every day to sell buttermilk. It was she who brought him news from home.

'Did you see Amma?'

'Yes. She does nothing but think of you and weep.' The sun had turned the woman's face the colour of burnt clay.

'Did she say anything?'

'She said you must eat properly and take care of yourself.'

She always said that. Kunhanan always brought back the same message from her. Poor Amma!

Sometimes, he had a great longing to see her. He wanted to comfort her, to tell her he took good care of himself, even if it was not true. But he had been exiled from his home.

He knew his mother wanted to come and see him, but his father would never allow it. She would have come if she could, even from her deathbed.

He didn't hate his father. After all, he had turned his father's dreams to ashes. And had him sent to jail in his old age. How could he find fault with him? He could only hate himself.

If only there were someone he could find fault with. If only he could shift the responsibility for his grief on to someone else's shoulders. But he couldn't. He knew that his agony was rooted in himself and that he had to endure it.

The buttermilk woman asked, 'Want some buttermilk?' They had walked to the banks of the river. Ferries from the south moved slowly over the river to Mayyazhi.

'I don't have any money.'

'Pay me later.' She poured the buttermilk that was left in the pot into his cupped hands. The cool, slightly sour buttermilk moistened his parched throat.

'Why don't you cut your hair?' she asked.

'I don't have money for a haircut.'

'And your moustache? Don't you have enough money to trim it?'

A smile flashed on her lips, red with betel. She was right, not only his hair but his moustache had grown too long.

He bought a quarter anna's worth of beedis. There were three. He lit one and walked back. Kanaran and Vasutty would be waiting for him. Discussions, arguments, arguments, discussions ... Where was this going to end?

The buttermilk woman looked very upset when she came next day.

'Who told you?' He did not want to believe her, but he had to. Even though he found it difficult.

'Everyone says so.'

He couldn't bear to talk to her any longer. He hurried away. He had to know the truth.

Kanaran and Vasutty were in the house. The freedom fighters used it as their office. It was always crowded with people associated with the movement.

Their faces had the same expression as the buttermilk woman's.

'You've heard?' asked Vasutty.

Dasan felt cramps moving up his legs.

'Is it true, Kanaretta?' If only he would say it was not true ...

'It's true, son.'

He felt as if he was paralysed.

'Look, man, this concerns all of us.' Vasutty's voice seemed to come from far away. 'It's a disgrace to the movement if the white man's paid goonda marries your sister.'

'How can the deed writer allow such a thing?' Kanaran sat with his head bent.

Dasan had sent a note to his father some time ago requesting him to come and see him if he had the least affection left for his son. Nanutty, who took the note, had returned, his face pale.

'He wouldn't take it.'

The deed writer had shouted, 'If you bring me any more letters from that good-for-nothing, I'll break every bone in your body.'

So I've become a good-for-nothing, thought Dasan. What has happened to my father? To the love in his heart?

Dasan knew that his father had changed after he came out of jail. He had sent his father many messages asking him to come and see him, but he had not come. Dasan had tried to justify this. After all, he had been sent to jail for a crime his son had committed. And that son had been sentenced for treason. He had every reason to be afraid of being sent to jail again.

One more letter was sent to Damu Writer. This time, it was Kanaran who wrote it. He begged Damu Writer not to decide on Girija's marriage without first discussing it with Dasan.

'What did the deed writer say?' They were all waiting for the messenger's return from Mayyazhi.

'He said he could look after his own affairs. He doesn't want other people to meddle in them.'

They kept silent. Damu Writer's strange behaviour astonished them.

That night, Dasan stayed with Kanaran. He could not sleep at all. He lay on the grass mat, his eyes wide open. He heard the midnight train clatter past, making the earth tremble. When the bells pealed from the church in faraway Mayyazhi for morning service, he was still awake.

But he had made up his mind. He would creep into Mayyazhi at night. He would try to reason with his father, fall at his feet and implore him if need be. Fate had placed his father against him. But he was still his father. How could he not have affection for his son?

'I'm going home today,' he said to Kanaran when he woke up. At first, Kanaran did not comprehend. When he did, he was shocked.

'It's suicidal.'

The thought of Dasan in Mayyazhi, with the police and goondas prowling around, made him go hot and cold with fear.

'Do you think your father will listen to you?' asked Vasutty. 'I think it's futile to try. You won't achieve anything.'

The deed writer was like a wounded animal, no one would be able to control him.

But Pappan said, 'Go ahead Dasan. If you can't persuade your father, kill that Achu and pull out his entrails.' Fire blazed in his eyes.

Vasutty cautioned Dasan not to fall into the hands of the police. Kanaran was still seated silently with his head bent. He could not face the thought of Dasan in Mayyazhi.

Vivre dangèreusement ...

Live dangerously.

Pappan thought of Andrè Gide's words.

Kanaran pleaded with him not to go. He thought sadly, if only there were no tension, no conflicts ... no sorrow, no pain ...

Dasan decided to go to Mayyazhi that night.

Policeman Kannan was on duty at the eastern border. He was a sympathizer. Kanaran was relieved. At least, he would not harm Dasan.

Nomads who had come to Mayyazhi for liquor had pitched their tents near the railway station. Though it was past midnight, there was still light and noise in the tents. Parrots screeched and dogs whined. The nomads chattered in strange dialects.

The long road stretched past Assu's shop, with rice fields on one side and coconut groves on the other. All they could hear was the sound of their own footfalls. There was pale moonlight.

Pappan and Vasutty stopped when they saw the policeman at the bamboo barrier laid across the road. They could not go any further.

Dasan stopped too. The three of them stood there in the darkness. They could hear their own hearts beating. Silence lay heavily over the rice fields. Not even a night bird chirped. The noise and lights of the nomads' encampment were far behind.

'Keep this with you.' Pappan took out a knife from his pocket. Dasan recognized the weapon which had wounded the red-eyed Sayiv.

'Pappan, I'll never have the courage to stab anyone.' He paused. 'But give it to me anyway. I can kill myself with it if necessary.'

Dasan took the knife. Its blade gleamed in the darkness like Death's teeth.

'Go now.' Vasutty placed his hand on Dasan's shoulder.

'I'll stay awake until you come back,' Pappan said.

Dasan tucked up his lungi and entered the coconut grove. He walked forward hiding himself in the long shadows of the coconut trees. In a little while, he saw the cross over the church in Mayyazhi, stretching its arms against the night sky. His eyes on the cross, he asked himself, will I return safely?

Vasutty and Pappan watched until he was out of sight, then walked back silently.

Only the pale, soundless night remained.

28

Dasan was back again in Mayyazhi, on the soil that had borne and nurtured him. Suddenly, he felt happy. He forgot the danger hovering over him. If he was caught, he would have to serve twelve years in jail. It was possible that he would never get out of jail. He walked contentedly through the moonlight refusing to think of all that.

Having come out from the coconut grove, he entered a narrow lane. It was dark, but the risk was greater here because he could not move under cover. He would know nothing until a prowling policeman flashed a torch in his face.

In the distance, the Rue de la Gare lay as still as a dead python between the rice fields.

He could see Meethalambalam. The deities would be walking about now. He thought of the legends that Achamma had told him as a child. Of how Kunjakkan's great-grandfather had stolen a bunch of bananas and gone lame. The steps leading to the temple glowed in the pale moonlight. Was Gulikan, clad in tender palm leaves, seated on them? Was the sound Dasan heard the tinkle of his heavy anklets?

He suddenly thought of the silver anklets on Chandrika's feet.

He had told her he was going to Mayyazhi, although Kanaran had advised him not to. One of the many enemies of the freedom movement could turn informer. Then it would be the police that welcomed him to Mayyazhi.

In spite of this, he had told her ...

'Don't go, Dasetta.'

She began to cry. He had felt then that he should not have told her. But that would have been wrong as well. If he was caught, she would not see him for twelve years. Perhaps never.

'Don't cry like a child. If I don't go, Achan will give Girija to Achu. And her life will be ruined. Don't you understand?'

'Will you come back tonight?'

'I will, Chandrika,' he promised. She wiped her eyes with the end of her saree.

'I won't go to college tomorrow. I'll wait for you.'

They often used this deserted spot on the banks of the river, covered with white sand and young coconut trees, as a meeting place.

He knew that she would be awake now, thinking of him anxiously.

He crept through the coconut grove behind Unni Nair's toddy shop, keeping to the shadow of the palms. He had not met anyone so far. All Mayyazhi was asleep. Let them sleep, he thought. Dasan, who is not destined to rest, will find his way home.

The Rue de la Gare stretched before him and he could see the Rue de l'Eglise beyond. As he hurried through streets fraught with danger, he saw the cross on the church clearly. Shadows moved in the Rue de l'Eglise. Were they policemen?

The municipal lamps that Kunjakkan had lit had burned out. Pale moonlight lay like mist over the trees and the tiled roofs of houses. He saw his house in the distance. His heart began to beat very fast. He would be face to face with his father in a few minutes. What would Achan's reaction be? He was going to see all of them after two years: Achan, Amma, Girija, Achamma. A secret joy filled his heart. I forgot to buy a half anna's worth of snuff for Achamma, he thought with regret. It would have made her so happy.

There was a light upstairs. The veranda was dark. The trees cast unmoving shadows over the courtyard. He saw the flowering asoka tree glimmering in the pale light. And the jasmine and rose plants that Girija had nurtured with love.

He climbed into the veranda. Whom should he call out to? Should he knock on the door? He hesitated a moment. They would all be asleep. Except perhaps Girija.

There was a white cat curled up on the earthen floor. Whose cat could it be? They had never had cats and dogs here.

It would be better to see Girija first. He could ask her for news. He could see his father after that.

He walked along the veranda taking care not to disturb the cat. In the moonlight, he could make out a policeman in the Rue du Cimetière.

'Girija,' he called softly, standing near the window. Its shutters were open.

She moved in bed.

'It's me, Ettan ...'

She sat up, alarmed. Her sari and hair had come undone.

'Open the door.'

Suddenly, he felt exhausted. He had crept over two miles under cover of the shadows and darkness. He had jumped over a canal, broken a fence. His body stung as if thorns were pricking him all over.

'Open the door,' he repeated.

She gathered her dishevelled hair, tucked in her sari and came to open the door.

'Shall I light a lamp?'

'No.'

He could still see the policeman standing under the lamp-post. He closed the door, bolted it and hurried to her room. He sat down on the cot. He could just make out Girija's face in the light that fell through the window.

'Have you agreed to this?'

He saw tears trickling down her cheeks. What could he say to comfort her?

'You were crying when I came?'

She didn't answer. In the half dark, her face became clearer. Her eyes were full of the accumulated sleeplessness of many nights, of tears.

'Tell me, have you said yes?'

'No,' she said without raising her face. 'I won't give in, even if they kill me.'

Her determination comforted him. He would need her support when he spoke to his father.

'I knew that you wouldn't consent.'

After all, who knew her better than he did?

'Is Achan angry with me?'

She refused to meet his eyes.

'Does he hate me?'

'He's changed a lot since he returned from jail. We don't mention your name. It makes him mad.'

He had known this, but it hurt him to hear her say it. Once, his had been the only name heard here. They had talked of him incessantly.

A heavy silence pervaded the room for a while. Dasan took out a beedi and lighted a match, covering the flame with his hand. He inhaled deeply.

'Are you hungry? Shall I bring some rice?'

'Is there any?'

'There is.'

They used to have gruel every night. Evidently, they had rice now and enough was left over even after everyone had eaten. Although he had become a good-for-nothing, there was prosperity and plenty in his house.

He suddenly remembered that he had not seen Achu in the veranda, in the place where he used to sleep.

'Doesn't Achu sleep here now?'

'Yes, he sleeps inside.'

Why should Achu sleep outside anymore? He was the master of the house now. And would soon be his brother-in-law.

He heard her sobbing in the darkness. He drew her to him and stroked her hair.

'Let me come away with you, Etta.'

'Where can I take you, Girija?'

He had no place of his own. The freedom movement had gathered momentum. Life was precarious. Those who were fighting for freedom could be arrested or shot at any moment. How could he take Girija to that chaotic world? How could he shoulder another person's burden when his own existence was threatened?

'Have courage, Girija. I'll save you.'

He would plead with his father ...

'Will Achan listen to you, Etta?'

'He will.'

'I won't, you scoundrel.'

Damu Writer's voice and the red glow of an oil lamp entered the room together.

'The time when I listened to you is over.'

Girija scrambled up, terrified. Damu Writer stood in the room, clutching his mundu, an oil lamp in his hand.

They faced each other, father and son. All Mayyazhi was asleep. Only the midnight rooster crowed feebly. Give me courage, Dasan prayed. Give me courage to fight for my sister.

Trying to be as calm and controlled as he could, Dasan said, 'Sit down, Achan. I want to talk to you ...'

'Don't talk to me about anything.'

His eyes blazed like a devil's. The lamp in his hand shook.

'You know who Achu is.'

'I do.'

'Achu is a rowdy ...'

'So are you. You set fire to the Mairie. You started the riots ...'

Was this his father? He couldn't believe his ears. Was he a goonda like Achu? Was the uprising of an awakened people mere hooliganism?

'Achu is a rowdy, but he has never sent me to jail. You did. You had the police beat me up.' Damu Writer's voice rose higher. 'Achu cares about us. He protected your mother and sister when the white army came. Where were you then?'

Is this really my father, thought Dasan.

'Don't pretend to be so ignorant, Achan. If I have become what I am, it is for the sake of my country. The tears my family shed are for the country as well. You should feel proud of us.'

'Enough of your speechmaking.'

'Soon all our problems will be over.'

'I have no problems.'

'Don't you see Girija's tears? Tell me, Acha, why are you giving her to Achu?'

Damu Writer had a ready answer for that. To have peace for the rest of his days. To die happy. Achu was strong and fearless. The family would be safe in his care.

'Now get out!' Damu Writer said. The lamp in his hand shook violently. He panted like an animal.

'I'll go.' Dasan got up. 'Let me see my mother before I leave.'

Damu Writer barred his way. 'She's not your mother. I'm not your father either.'

He placed the lamp on the window-sill and pointed to the door.

Was this the end? Was it for this that I came to Mayyazhi risking my life?

Nails seemed to pierce Dasan's heart.

The lamp on the window shone bright in the surrounding darkness. The policeman's red cap could be seen in the Rue du Cimetière. Damu Writer made no attempt to move the lamp from the window.

'Etta, please don't go ...' Girija pleaded.

'Keep quiet.' Damu Writer raised his hand to hit her. Dasan unbolted the door,

'Listen, Acha, it is better to give Girija to that scavenger, elephant-legged Antony than to Achu.'

'Get out, you scoundrel!' Damu Writer screamed, pushing Dasan towards the door.

The entire household woke up. Kowsu and Achu rushed up. Kurambi Amma slithered down from the loft.

Dasan stepped into the yard. Behind him, Damu Writer closed the door. Dasan heard a policeman's whistle nearby.

It was pitch dark. The moon had set. Dasan could hardly walk. Tears burned and blinded his eyes. He stumbled into the street, groping his way. He heard the sound of approaching boots. Lathis were raised in the dark ...

He fell down.

29

There was a pale glow over Mayyazhi. The sky was overcast. Rain clouds brooded over the Kanaka Mala.

Pappan sat outside porter Kunhanan's hut, his eyes swollen with sleep. A storm was blowing through his mind. He would not drink the jaggery coffee or the gruel that Cheeru brought him.

He knew now that Dasan would not come back from Mayyazhi.

There was a lamp on the mat near him. *The Communist Manifesto*, which had always brought him solace in moments of suffering, lay under his pillow. He used to read it whenever he could not sleep, and it would calm him. Marxism-Leninism had always slaked his hunger and thirst, even satisfied his carnal desire.

'Workers of the world, unite. All you can lose are your chains.' The first time he read these lines, he had felt ecstatic.

The sacred text had no more power to calm his agitated mind.

He thought of Dasan incessantly. Last night, as he walked home, he had shuddered with an intuition that Dasan would not come back. The midnight wind blowing over the Mayyazhi river had muttered: 'Dasan won't come back'.

Maybe he would never see Dasan again. Twelve years was a long time. Anything could happen. Would Dasan survive such a long sentence? The police would beat him up, break his limbs ... Pappan felt unbearably anguished.

'Pappan, be a bourgeois in the feudal age or a proletarian in the bourgeois age, but never stop being a human being.' Pappan remembered Dasan's words. They had been seated on the pier, under the Republic Memorial.

Harvested rice fields lay as far as the eye could see. The jaundiced river flowed sluggishly farther down. He saw the morning train go by, the one in which Chandrika usually went to college.

All those who worked for the freedom movement knew about Chandrika and Dasan.

Kanaran used to say, 'Chandrika and Dasan will be married when Mayyazhi is free.'

Chandrika appeared in the distance. She walked towards the deserted rice field. Coconut palms wove dense shadows on the river bank.

Maybe Chandrika didn't yet know about Dasan's arrest. She would not have come to the river bank if she did. She waited for Dasan in vain, not realising that he would never come back.

Kanaka Mala vanished behind the clouds. The sky began to descend. The wind blowing across the river was cold and wet.

He could see Chandrika, a shadow standing on the bank of the pale Mayyazhi river. How long would she wait for Dasan? Someone would have to tell her that he would not return. Destiny had placed that burden on Pappan's shoulders.

He got up, pulled on his shirt and went out. The lane was still full of water from the rains.

How could he tell Chandrika? How could he meet her eyes?

As he climbed out of the fields, the first raindrop fell on his hair. The wind was stronger now. The palm trees had begun to moan.

The sand was white here. Pappan remembered the two pairs of footprints he used to see on the sand, a small one and a big one, side by side. Dasan's and Chandrika's.

Chandrika didn't look back, even though she heard him behind her. Her hair blew in the breeze, the hair Dasan's fingers used to run through.

'Chandrika ...' he said. She didn't answer. He knew she was crying.

'Please don't cry ...' he said, mustering his courage. He swallowed hard. Was she crying because Dasan was late? What if she knew that he would never come?

'Chandrika ...' Pappan called again. Wiping her tears with her finger tips, she turned her face towards him. He saw tear stains on the cheeks that had taken on the pallor of the river.

'You didn't go to college?'

'No.' She shook her head.

It began to drizzle. Pappan watched raindrops spatter the river's surface. Beyond the river, the Kanaka Mala seemed agitated. Was there a hurricane blowing?

'I came to tell you something.'

She did not look up.

'Promise you won't cry.'

She did not answer.

'Dasan,' he swallowed hard again. 'Dasan didn't come back yesterday.'

'The police have taken him away, haven't they?' Chandrika smiled through her tears. 'I know, Pappan.'

He felt very foolish.

'Please leave me alone, Pappan.'

He had done his duty. There was nothing more he could say.

It began to rain heavily. Pappan walked back. The rain continued and the rice fields were flooded. Even at noon Pappan saw Chandrika in the distance, still standing on the river bank.

CHANDRIKA HELD HER UNCLE'S hand and climbed the steps to her house.

Leela could hardly bear to look at her daughter. She was drenched. The end of her sari trailed in the rain water on the ground. Her hair had come undone.

'Where were you all this time?'

Chandrika went in without answering. Leela followed.

'Where are your books?'

Chandrika couldn't remember where she had left them.

Her uncle took off his wet shirt. 'She was sitting by the river. In the rain ...' He dried his hair with a towel. 'She wouldn't come when I called her. She gave me such trouble, I don't know how I managed to drag the wretched girl back.'

Leela was not sure whether she felt angry or sad.

She dried Chandrika's long hair and rubbed powdered pepper into her scalp so that she would not catch a cold. She made her sit in a chair and covered her with a blanket.

'Dasettan ...' she sobbed silently. Her chin trembled as if she had a fever.

'He went into it with his eyes open.' Leela was upset. She had feared this would happen to Dasan.

In the incessant rain, the river grew muddy and turbulent. Water flooded the rice fields. Was this the deluge?

Next day, the newspapers carried the news of Dasan's arrest, with his photograph. It was a picture taken in his student days at Pondicherry. He had spiky hair and a thick moustache. And his eyes had the hardness of stone.

Kowsu almost lost consciousness. Girija found one more reason to cry.

Dasan was sent to jail to undergo imprisonment for twelve years. He had to withdraw from the yajna he had initiated long before it drew to a close.

30

Girija's marriage took place without any fanfare. She was Damu Writer's only daughter and he had certainly wanted to conduct the ceremony as elegantly as he could.

'She's all I have to give away. It's her destiny to go with a husband like this.'

However much he tried to justify it, Damu Writer could not bear to think of Achu marrying his daughter. His heart rebelled against it.

What sort of wedding was this, lamented Kurambi Amma, with no pandal, no nadaswaram, and no invitees. She had dreamed of Girija's wedding long before the child had grown up. She liked Achu and was happy that he was going to marry her. But what kind of a wedding was this?

'Damu, at least let's have a pandal in front of the house.'

'We're in no situation to celebrate a marriage, with Dasan in jail and his mother lying ill ...'

Kowsu would not eat, would not have a bath. Since the night Dasan left, she had refused to get up from bed. As for Girija, she was always crying. Was this a house of celebration or a house of mourning?

Huddled against the pillar in the veranda, Kurambi Amma inhaled a pinch of snuff. She liked to look at the brighter side of things. She wanted everyone in Mayyazhi to be happy, like the white men and women who walked hand in hand under the flowering gulmohar trees, breathing in the sea breeze. Or like the elegant white men in trousers who drove horse carriages and smiled and waved their hats as they passed by. She wanted life to be an eternal Quatorze Juillet, with coloured lights, music and crowds.

She sensed that something had gone wrong with the world. Young men were being sent to jail. Mothers and sisters shed tears all the time. More and more armed policemen filled the streets.

She closed her eyes, thinking about the bad times ahead.

Achu took a house near the cemetery on rent. He hired carpenter Raman to make him a cot, a table and chair. He bought pots and pans from the blacksmith. Errand boys went in and out of the house, carrying things. The house was ready long before the wedding day.

While going to the office after lunch one day, Achu announced, 'I won't be back this evening.'

Damu Writer was seated on the veranda.

'My house is ready. I thought I would move in today.'

He had found shelter in Damu Writer's house when he was homeless, when he had wandered around like a wild animal. And he had been transformed into a civilized human being. But now he had a place of his own.

Damu watched Achu pack his clothes and his shaving set in a gunny bag which advertised Pattanam-scented areca nut, manufactured in Madurai. The knife, which had once been Achu's most valued possession, was not in the bag. It had lain unused for days on the window-sill. Its blade had grown rusty. Then one day it had disappeared. Achu had thrown it secretly into the Mayyazhi river.

'I'm leaving.' He picked up his bag and walked away. The Writer and Kurambi Amma watched until he was out of sight. Achu even walked in a different way now. He no longer swung his knife threateningly as he walked. He talked, he moved, more gently. He kept to himself. He had given up his old companions.

'Have you forgotten me, mon copain?' Policeman Andru stopped him on the street. But Achu only smiled. They had been close friends for many years. They had quarrelled and fought with each other, drunk together and gone together to women.

The day after he moved, Achu took Kurambi Amma to see his house. She wore a kasavu mundu for the occasion and tucked her ivory snuffbox into its folds at the waist. They could easily have walked the distance, but Achu brought a horse carriage for her. Kurambi Amma was delighted.

Emotion choked her. She had watched people go by in carriages, but had been in one herself only once.

That was in Leslie Sayiv's time. Gaston came to fetch her when Missie fell ill. It had been years and years ago. Leslie Sayiv lay under the earth now. And Missie had followed him.

She asked Achu to stop the carriage in front of Brigadier Chettiappa's house.

'Are you there, Nani?'

'Where are you going, Kurambi Amma?' Nani and Devi came out.

'To Achu's house,' she said proudly. 'You know Kuttiappa's place? That's the one he's taken.'

'Come in and have some tea,' said Nani.

Achu used to come and see Chettiappa often in the old days. It was a long time now since he had come.

'Not now,' Achu excused himself. 'I'll come when the Brigadier is at home.'

Kurambi Amma made Achu stop at many houses on the way so that she could pop out her head proudly and talk to the people inside. It was an unforgettable day for her. She had always worshipped those who rode through the Mayyazhi streets in their own horse carriages and dreamt of going around in one herself.

After that, Kurambi Amma visited Achu's house at least every other day. She lay on the big rosewood cot that Carpenter Raman had made. She had never lain on a cot before. Even when Kelu Achan was alive, they had slept on the floor on a mat.

She told Achu that she would stay with him after he was married. Achu was happy. Kurambi Amma counted the days to the wedding on her fingers. The wheel of time moved steadily forward and brought her to it at last.

Girija no longer spoke to anyone. She sat still all the time, lost in thought. On the day of the wedding, the women came to give her a bath with scented soap and wrapped her in a kasavu saree. They wore jasmines into her freshly washed hair. They touched up her face with talcum powder and outlined her eyes with kohl over and over again because her tears kept washing all of it away.

There were no invitees. Five people went with Girija and Achu to the Mairie. Lawyer Nanu and Nathan, who were witnesses, were among them. They signed in the register and went to Achu's house. He had arranged for a small tea party there.

'It's true I don't belong to Mayyazhi. But I've made a few friends and I would like to give them at least a cup of tea,' Achu had said to Damu Writer. Damu had not wanted any kind of celebration, but could hardly object to this. It was Achu's business, after all.

The invitees came to Achu's house in their cars and horse carriages.

'Fèlicitations, nos vives fèlicitations.' They shook hands with Achu.

The party went on quite late. By the time it was over, the old, well-worn burial stones and crosses in the cemetery had come to life in the bright moonlight. The toddy shops had shut down. As usual, Kurambi Amma had begun to hear the hoofbeats of Leslie Sayiv's horse, now long dead. When the last guest left, Achu bolted the front door with trembling hands.

The day he had waited for had arrived at last. His legs trembled as he went to the bedroom. He had not seen Girija after they had returned from the Mairie. There had been so many people. But he carried her face in the mirror of his mind. He longed for the fragrance of the talcum powder on her tearstained face. He wanted to wipe away her tears.

The bedroom was dark. He paused on the threshold.

'Girija ...' he called out softly.

He had the right to go in. He could do anything he wanted now. Instead, he kept calling out to her. He was not sure his voice was audible.

'Are you angry with me?' He still stood outside the room. He had watched her crying and promised himself—I'll dry your tears with my love. I'll burn the past. I'll conquer you with my love ...

He waited. The minutes ticked by. Then he went in. There was no fragrance of talcum powder or jasmine in the room. There was only the smell of the varnish on the doors and windows.

He lit a match. The cot was empty.

He shouted her name. He lit all the lamps, one by one, took one in his hand and went out.

He heard her sobbing under the parijatham tree, now shorn of its flowers.

'Girija, please come.'

He saw her clearly in the glow of the lamp. Her blouse was wet with tears. The jasmine flowers she had worn in her hair were scattered over the ground.

'Don't be foolish. What if the neighbours see us here now?'
'I won't come.'

She refused to look at him. He stood quietly for a while, then turned on her suddenly. The man who had taken so many of Mayyazhi's daughters by force lifted her in his strong arms as if she were a child. He rushed into the house like a whirlwind. The doors slammed shut behind them ...

As the bells chimed at dawn from the church of the Mother of Mayyazhi, peals of laughter and the tinkle of glass bangles could be heard behind the closed door.

Girija came out in the morning, her virginity taken, her face no longer stained with tears. Her cheeks were flushed. She smiled.

The man named Achu had put an end to her agony.

31

Dasan's absence affected Kanaran very deeply. Although he was the leader of the freedom movement, Dasan had been its voice. He knew the white man's history and psychology better than any of them. For many days after Dasan's arrest, Kanaran went without food or sleep. He was like a one-legged man who had lost the stick he used for support.

'They've only given him twelve years, Kanarettan. They haven't killed him. Let's be happy for that,' said Vasutty. Pappan was silent.

'It's my fault. I let him go into Mayyazhi.'

'What's the use of saying that?'

'That father of his is the guilty one, he just handed over his son to the police.' Pappan's face grew red with anger.

Kanaran tried to console himself. 'What's the use of finding fault with anyone now? What is destined to happen must happen.'

Kanaran believed in God and in destiny. Even during the busiest days of the freedom struggle, he used to go to the temple, and he always abstained from fish at the time of the Mandala Pooja.

For a few more days, Kanaran was sunk in inertia. But he could not go on like that forever. He had to act, his duties claimed him. Mayyazhi's pitiful cries began to echo in his ears once more. He pushed all his sad thoughts behind him and moved on towards his goal.

At the boundary, the number of freedom fighters dressed in khadar had multiplied. They wore white khadar caps now. They were reincarnations of the angels who had spread the message of peace in Gandhi's time.

One day, Janardanan, who worked secretly for the movement in Mayyazhi, brought some news: 'It looks as if Secrètaire Karunan might join us.'

Many government officers in Mayyazhi had resigned from their posts and joined the movement by this time. Abdulla, who was in Public Works, Kesavan, a teacher at the Cours Complémentaire, and Lakshmi, a teacher at Labourdonnais College, were among them. And now Karunan, who was the sentinel of the white regime, had heard the call of history.

Kanaran had written Karunan many letters asking him to consider the demands of the times. You cannot go on being the white man's middleman much longer, he had told him. They will have to leave one day. The day they leave, we'll punish you. Try to avoid this. If you join us now, we will forgive the cruelty and injustice you showed to the people of Mayyazhi.

At first, Secrètaire Karunan used to crumple up the letters and throw them away. Then he began to read them. He sat on the veranda of his mansion for a long time one day, with Kanaran's letters on his lap, lost in agonising thoughts. He realized that the throne he was seated on was unstable. The ground under his feet had begun to tremble.

He read Kanaran's letters all over once again. Sweat broke out on his dark, chubby face. His skin, puffy with wine, grew pale. The hand holding the letter began to shake.

History roared in Secrètaire Karunan's ears.

'Why aren't you asleep?' Soumini, his wife, asked. He refused to go in. He would either spend the night in his easy chair or pace up and down, his hands joined behind him, until the municipal lamps that Kunjakkan had lit went out.

'I'm not sleepy, Soumini.'

Soumini did not question him further. She did not really understand why he was so worried. He had administered the affairs of Mayyazhi for decades. She knew little of what was taking place. She spent the greater part of her days sleeping and the rest in the pooja room. She was a gentle woman with compassionate eyes, excessively fat.

It was past midnight now. The street beyond the whitewashed outer wall was deserted. People were afraid to go out at night now in Mayyazhi. The policemen caught anyone who looked suspicious. Until now, the people of Mayyazhi had led a leisurely life, a wine-drenched existence. But now conflict and turmoil had entered their lives.

Secrètaire Karunan remembered the days when, resplendent in a coat and hat, he had ridden in a horse carriage; he thought of the visits to Big Sayiv's bungalow, the walks on the beach with Soumini. All that was drawing to a close.

None of the government officers or white men dared to go on walks now. These were uncertain times. Danger lurked around every corner.

Karunan realized that times were changing. Why grieve over the past, he thought, when he was sure the old days would never come back? Let me change with the times.

And so he finally replied to Kanaran.

'Janardanan, you must go to Mayyazhi and meet Karunan.'

'Can we trust the Secrètaire?' asked Vasutty. He could not help being afraid. How could they be sure that Karunan would not hand him over to the police?

But Janardanan had no qualms. 'They can't do anything to us. They know their days are numbered.'

He walked to Secrètaire Karunan's house fearlessly.

They sat face to face in the office room upstairs. A large framed portrait of Big Sayiv adorned the wall.

Karunan looked like an overgrown child with his chubby face and striped pants. In a few minutes, Janardanan was convinced that the Secrètaire had no intention of trapping him. He began to talk more freely. He described the progress of the freedom movement, smoking beedi after beedi.

'No one can stop us now, not even God,' he said defiantly. 'You must join us, Monsieur. That'll paralyse the government.'

Karunan shifted in his chair. 'I'll give you as much money as you want. Don't ask me to do anything else just now.'

'We don't need the money. We need you, Monsieur.'

'It's difficult. You know who I am.'

'I do. That's why we insist that you join us.'

Karunan stood up and began to walk up and down. His bloated body moved aimlessly among the furniture. He could see Big Sayiv's face clearly in his mind. He had served the white man faithfully for nearly three decades. Would Big Sayiv be able to bear it if he went over to Kanaran now?

He shrank into himself like a dog that had bitten its master, and continued to pace up and down. He felt his legs were wearing out. His face was bathed in perspiration. He felt short of breath.

Janardanan watched Karunan's lips move and his expression change. He waited.

Finally, Secrètaire Karunan came up to Janardanan. 'Go and tell Kanaran that I'll do anything he wants.'

'Merci, Monsieur.'

Janardanan ran down the carpeted stairs, rushed out of the bungalow and past the gate.

'Wasn't that Kuttiachan's son? Why did he come at such a late hour?' Soumini came out. Karunan didn't answer. He lit a Gauloise. He smoked rarely and only when he felt restless. Of late, he had been smoking a great deal.

A few days passed.

'Soumini, take the children and go to Kannur. It's dangerous to stay here. Come back when it is calm.'

'Why, what's happening here?'

'Lots of things.'

'What about you then?'

'I'll come if I get leave from work. You and the children had better go at once.'

Soumini left the same day with the children.

People were leaving Mayyazhi every day, those who worked for the government as well as those who did not. Policemen patrolled the boundary to prevent them leaving. For most people, crossing the boundary was an ordeal by fire. They could easily become targets for the bullets of the French police.

In the morning, Secrètaire Karunan went to work as usual in Big Sayiv's mansion. He had lunch with the white men. When he came out of the Secrètariat in the evening, he wiped his eyes furtively with a handkerchief. He turned and looked at Big Sayiv's bungalow atop the hill for the last time, at the sea crashing below it and the river flowing by. He looked at the Secretariat, lying in the bungalow's shadow, the place where he had reigned for years ... Adieu! he whispered to the wind.

He went home, sat alone in the empty house and opened a bottle of wine. The bottle was empty by the time Janardanan arrived.

He climbed into the car with Janardanan, his head bent. The driver dropped them near the boundary and returned. Karunan walked forward, gasping for breath.

Karunan saw Kanaran's bony figure in the pale darkness beyond the boundary.

'Thank you, Karunan.'

Kanaran smiled as Karunan came up to him. He embraced Karunan, then drew back hastily. Karunan's body was icy cold. He swayed, then fell back. His hairnet fell off.

Kanaran knelt down by Karunan. He had stopped breathing. Kanaran realized that Karunan's lifeless feet lay on the other side of the border. On French soil.

32

The twenty-seventh of April 1954. A group of freedom fighters challenged the soldiers who were brandishing guns and tried to liberate Cherukallai, which was part of Mayyazhi. The army opened fire. Comrades Achuthan and Anandan became martyrs.

Kunhanan, who was going to the Vadagara shandy on the early morning train, had to come back. Kurambi Amma had woken up early that morning and was seated on the veranda inhaling her first pinch of snuff for the day when Kunhanan came that way. Her eyesight was failing. And she had become much less alert.

'Kurambi, I'm Kunhanan.'

'I can't see too well, Kunhanan. Where are you going so early in the morning?'

'I was going to Vadagara but they would not let me cross the border. Kanaran's people stopped me.'

'What for, Kunhanan?'

'They said it was a demonstration for freedom. You can't lead a normal life these days.'

'Who is doing all this?'

'Your Dasan and his friends. They're the ones who started the trouble.'

Kurambi Amma was upset. She knew Dasan was in jail. No one had had news of him. The police would not allow anyone to visit him in jail. She often thought of Dasan until her heart was ready to break, and then she would cry.

Kunhanan took off the towel around his head, wiped his face and went his way. She could see his fat money bag in his pocket through the thin mull of his sleeveless shirt.

Kurambi Amma was aware that dreadful things were happening in Mayyazhi. The police and the goondas had entered the house, broken things, put Damu in jail. Battleships had arrived. And now Dasan was in jail.

Something had gone wrong somewhere. Times were changing. Kurambi Amma did not mind that. But she hated the thought that all this violence was aimed at driving the white men away from Mayyazhi. She could not believe that it was the white men who had put Dasan in jail.

'Why was he sent to jail?'

'Dasan is the white man's enemy.'

'Listen, Unni Nair, don't talk ill of my Dasan.' Kurambi Amma spoke in a warning voice. She could not bear them to speak ill of Dasan. But they did, all the time. Especially Unni Nair and Kunhanan. They kept accusing Dasan of being the white man's enemy. She found it hard to believe. Old age had affected her mind. A shadow obscured the greater part of the past. Her memories were confused.

It was not only Kunhanan who was turned back that day. Bullock carts bound for Thalassery were stopped on the bridge by the freedom fighters. They came back, one by one. Next day, the freedom fighters stopped the goods train coming from Karaikkal with rice.

It became difficult to enter or leave Mayyazhi. Buses and other vehicles going from Kozhikode and Vadagara to Thalassery were prevented from passing through Mayyazhi and were forced to bypass the town. The freedom fighters laid new roads for this purpose.

As the siege continued, Mayyazhi became as isolated as an island. The roads were deserted. Rice, sugar and oil grew scarce since the freedom fighters had sealed the boundary.

Shops closed down.

'They say there's only enough rice for four days more. What will the white men do? Everyone will rush to them demanding rice. Do you think they'll let us die of starvation?'

'Maybe we'll starve. Or survive on roots and leaves. What'll the white men do, Janardanan?' Vasutty laughed. 'We've trapped them.'

'Maybe ten days at the most now. In ten days, Kanarettan, Mayyazhi will be ours.'

The number of the freedom fighters increased steadily. The movement started by Kanaran and Kunhanandan Master had grown into a massive agitation. Big groups of teachers and government officers fled from Mayyazhi to join the agitation.

As expected, in a week's time there was not a grain of rice left in Mayyazhi. There were no medicines for the sick in the hospitals. Schools were forced to close down because there were no teachers. The government machinery was paralysed.

The municipal lamps were no longer lighted because there was no oil. Soldiers could be heard pacing through the town all night. The people of Mayyazhi sat behind closed doors, deprived of food and light. The streets through which wine had once flowed happily became dark and gloomy.

Vasutty and Pappan called out to the people of Mayyazhi through the loudspeaker that had been installed at the boundary: 'The people's revolution has started. Children of Mayyazhi, wake up!'

The tension increased over the bridge which formed the western boundary. Freedom fighters crowded over it screaming slogans. The soldiers faced them, guns extended. Beneath all of them, the Mayyazhi river flowed quietly into the sea.

'Kanarettan, give me a flag.'

'What for?'

'Give it to me.'

Pappan snatched a national flag from someone's hand. He shouted slogans with fury. It seemed as if he was fully a man only now. He rushed to the bridge, waving the flag, with a crowd of demonstrators following him. They pushed into Mayyazhi from all directions.

'They've taken Cherukallai, and the bridge.' Unni Nair gasped for breath. He had closed his shop early.

Achu felt an icy chill run through his spine.

The streets were empty. The soldiers were moving in large numbers towards the border.

'What is it, Achu Etta?' Girija came out, with fear in her eyes. She had a bit of green tamarind in her hand, which she loved to eat, as pregnant women do.

'It seems Cherukallai has been taken and the bridge as well, Girija. I'm going out for a while.'

'Oh no, please.'

'Let me find out what is going on. I'll be right back, Girija.'

He tucked up his mundu and stepped into the street. Girija watched him go with fear, trying not to throw up.

He came back in half an hour.

'They're a hundred yards inside Mayyazhi. They're crowding in on the south as well, just beyond the toll gate.'

'I'm scared, Achu Etta.'

'Why?'

'What if they harm you?'

Girija placed her head on his shoulder. Her head was spinning.

'Go and lie down, Girija.'

She stumbled into the house, holding on to the wall for support.

Achu stayed on the veranda, his heart beating faster and faster. He remembered the children he had once chased like dogs through the school compound, the streets and the library. They had all grown up now. And become strong. They had taken Cherukallai and Palloor. Mayyazhi could fall now, at any moment. They were streaming in, with the certainty of freedom burning in their eyes. He heard the echo of their footsteps everywhere.

'Achu, son ...'

He was startled. It was Damu Writer. He stood in the courtyard, supporting Kowsu. Kurambi Amma hobbled in behind them.

'They've entered Mayyazhi: Kanaran, Vasutty, everyone. They say that all those who remained loyal to the white men are going to be punished. I sided with them, Achu ...'

The deed writer's ageing eyes were full of fear.

Achu did not say anything. Damu Writer had delivered Dasan into the hands of the police. They would never let him off lightly. Achu knew Pappan and Vasutty. He was afraid. He was even more guilty than Damu Writer. He would have to look out for himself first.

'You protected me and my family in our hour of danger. You must save me now, son.'

Damu Writer was in tears.

'My time is up too. But come in, all the same.'

Damu Writer and his family came into the house.

Achu looked at the cross on the steeple of the church.

'Bharat Mata ki jai!'

The shout came from somewhere near. The crowds were closing in. The church bells pealed loudly, announcing the impending calamity.

THE FOURTEENTH OF JULY 1954.

Kanaran and his companions marched into Mayyazhi leading hundreds of unarmed freedom fighters. Sympathizers who had been in hiding came out to join them. They moved in procession towards Big Sayiv's bungalow. The national flag went up everywhere. Slogans echoed through the air.

They reached the bungalow. The pier resounded with cries of victory. The sea and the river seemed to take part in the slogan shouting.

Big Sayiv came slowly to the balcony. He looked steadily at the children of Mayyazhi massed in front of him screaming for freedom. Freedom! They had once worshipped him as if he were God. His beloved subjects ...

Big Sayiv came slowly down the stairs.

He recognized Kanaran in spite of his emaciated frame, the long hair and beard. He looked into his sunken eyes. Big Sayiv's right hand rested on Kanaran's shoulder.

'Mahè ... c'est á vous.' Mayyazhi is yours.

Kanaran burst into tears.

The sun of freedom rose over Mayyazhi. And the inviolable laws of nature, which create the gale over the sea and the floods on the land, continued to take their course.

33

The ship's whistle echoed over the wharf. The ship that had come to take the white men away from Mayyazhi.

They were going. They had forfeited their rights over Mayyazhi's destiny.

'We're going as well.'

'Where?'

Unni Nair had no answer to Pappan's question. All he knew was that he was going with the white men—if need be, to the ends of the earth.

'Don't be too sure the white men will go away, just like that. They'll come back, with ships and cannons. Wait and see,' warned Kunhanan, unaware of the decrees of history.

'The white men won't come back.' Just as the water of the Mayyazhi river which had flowed into the sea for ages would never flow back again ...

'We'll see.'

Unni Nair, Kunjakkan and Kunhanan were amongst those who prepared to go to an unknown destination. In all, they were about a hundred in number.

Kunjakkan and Kunhanan were the first to arrive on the wharf. Kunjakkan had abandoned the oil tin and ladder that he had carried on his shoulder for over five decades. Kunhanan had closed his shop permanently. They stood on the seashore, awaiting their turn, their eyes fixed on the ship that lay at sea, emitting smoke.

People arrived, singly and in groups.

'Aren't you coming, Achu?' Unni Nair called out as he passed Achu's house, a bundle on his shoulder. But Achu was not to be seen. No one answered, so Unni Nair went on his way. Like Kunhanan, he too had shut down his shop.

Carpenter Raman was ready to go. He said goodbye to his wife, 'I'll go to France and build a house there. Then I'll come and get you and the children.'

'Don't forget me and the children.' The carpenter's wife wiped her eyes.

Raman followed Unni Nair. He too had a bundle, but he had abandoned the chisel that had carved cots for so many people in Mayyazhi, including Achu.

Achu watched through the bars of the window. He had lost all peace of mind ever since Kanaran and his followers entered Mayyazhi. He kept thinking of all the cruel acts he had performed. He realized that his hour had come. Pappan or Vasutty could turn up any moment and demand their revenge.

Achu broke into a sweat. Every time he heard a footstep, he started in fear. But no one came for him, even by the evening. He began to feel a sense of relief.

Damu Writer was as worried as Achu. He had not slept at all the previous night.

'Why are you so anxious? You've not done anyone any harm.'

'It's true, I've never harmed anyone deliberately. And still, they put me behind the bars and tortured me, didn't they?'

'That was when the white men were here. They're going now.'

Damu Writer knew that the white men were leaving and would never come back. But was this a good thing or a bad thing? He was not sure.

The freedom fighters had won. And it was he who had made the greatest sacrifice. His family had been destroyed. He had lost his only son.

Damu Writer turned to the cross on the steeple. 'Mother, I have just one prayer. Please don't try me anymore. Let my family be safe.'

Achu's eyes went to the cross too. He prayed silently. When the ship now anchored on the wharf moved away, a new era would begin. May it be one of peace and happiness. Not just for him. May all Mayyazhi know the meaning of peace.

Kurambi Amma stumbled towards them, holding on to the wall for support. 'Unni Nair and the carpenter have gone. Let's go, Achu.'

'Where can we go?'

'Let's go with Big Sayiv.'

'The white men are going to their country. This is our country.'

Kurambi Amma looked at Achu in despair. How could Big Sayiv belong to one country and the people of Mayyazhi to another?

'Will the white men come back, son?'

Everything would be all right if they came back. She would wait, counting the days, until they returned and restored Mayyazhi's lost glory.

Achu did not answer her question. He had been asking himself the same thing: would the white men ever come back?

Kurambi Amma stared at Achu for a while. Then she sat down on the bench in the veranda. She closed her eyes and pondered. 'They'll come, they're sure to come back,' she said to herself.

Brigadier Chettiappa put on his coat and trousers, wore all his medals, and got ready to leave. He generally dressed like this only on festival days like Quatorze Juillet and Christmas. His big tin trunk was packed.

'Don't cry, Nani.' She stood on the threshold, crying. Devi was just behind her, whimpering as well. Chettiappa's children waited, clinging to their mothers' mundus. 'I'll come back.'

He took out his handkerchief and wiped his thick neck. Chettiappa knew that he was telling a lie. He would never have to set foot on the soil of Mayyazhi again.

The more he tried to console Nani and Devi, the harder they cried. The children began to cry as well. Chettiappa did not linger. Pushing his women aside, he walked out. Sanku from the police station followed with the heavy trunk on his head.

David Sayiv was outside Kunhichirutha's house, saying goodbye. 'I'll come back. I'll come and take you and the children to France.'

'My children have no one but you.'

'I'll come,' repeated David Sayiv, careful not to look at Kunhichirutha's face, giving all his attention to the ship's whistle in the distance. He waved his hand and went down to the road, wiping the beads of sweat from his forehead. David Sayiv's tall, slightly stooped figure disappeared. Kunhichirutha gathered the children to her and wept bitterly.

The ship's whistle sounded from time to time. People kept moving through the Rue de l'Eglise and the Rue du Gouvernement towards the wharf. More and more people gathered on the shore to say goodbye. They stood silently in the blazing sun, waiting for Big Sayiv.

Big Sayiv came out on the balcony of his bungalow for the last time. He looked at the cross on the steeple, at the Rue de la Rèsidence, scattered with blood-red gulmohar flowers, at the bridge over the Mayyazhi river and at the green hills in the distance ...

His eyes wandered over Mayyazhi for the last time ...

The whites and the half-French moved slowly in procession to the wharf. The sea breeze blew steadily, proclaiming the message of history.

Big Sayiv's blue eyes hovered over each of his subjects, standing in rows on the seashore.

'Adieu, my children!'

He raised his right hand slowly. Kurambi Amma, who stood in the crowd holding Achu's hand, broke into sobs. The ship's anchor was raised.

All Mayyazhi wept as the ship moved away. Their tears moistened the burning sand. The ship disappeared gradually into the vastness of the sea, beyond the horizon until it could no longer be seen.

34

THE DOORS OF THE JAIL WERE OPENED WIDE. DASAN CAME OUT. AFTER many years, the sun's rays touched his sunken eyes. The ground on which he stood was still wet with the previous day's rain.

He waited in front of the jail, not sure where to go. Achan, Amma, Chandrika, Achamma, Girija ... their faces swam before his eyes as if they were part of a film.

None of them had been allowed to come and see him in jail. Achan and Girija may not have come. Achan would not have permitted Amma to come. But Chandrika, could she not have come, even if no one else did?

He noticed the national flag fluttering on the flagpole on top of Big Sayiv's hill. So freedom had dawned at last.

He walked slowly, through the Rue de la Rèsidence, the Rue de l'Eglise, the Rue de la Gare, and the Rue de la Prison. Until he reached a gravel-covered lane that had only one lamp-post on it. He could see his house clearly, but he stood rooted to the ground. His feet refused to move.

'Get out.' He remembered his father's voice as if it came from another world. And his father's image, pointing to the street.

He turned quickly and walked away. It was years since he had walked like this. The six-foot cell in the prison had become his entire universe.

No one recognized him, he had changed so much during his sojourn in jail.

He retraced his steps, renewing his bond with the Mayyazhi he had once known. This was where Vaisravanan Chettiar had come disguised as a serpent and overcome Kunhimanikkam. And this was where St. Sebastian had come riding his white horse, to do battle with Vasoori Amma when she spread the seeds of smallpox through Mayyazhi. This was where Kunjakkan's great-grandfather had fallen and broken his leg when the Gulikan, clad in a dry grass skirt, had come out to punish him for stealing. And this was the spot where Malayan Uthaman had broken his neck under the weight of the great headgear balanced on his head, writhed in agony and died. Emily used to walk along this street every morning supporting Bear Sayiv who had drunk himself senseless. And here, in this worm-eaten house, Gaston Sayiv had played music all through the night.

Dasan did not know where to go. His heart felt empty, like that of a mountain climber when he stands on the summit of a peak. A terrifying exhaustion, like that experienced at the end of the act of love, swept over his nerves.

He finally reached the seashore. It was quiet and deserted. The grey sea stretched endlessly before him. He saw Velliyan Kallu gleaming in the starlight in the distance. The resting place for souls between death and rebirth. Souls still fluttered over it in the form of dragonflies.

THE UNFINISHED BUILDING THAT once belonged to Abutty Mapilla of Penang became a meeting place for Dasan and

Chandrika. Soon after its floor had been laid and the walls had come up halfway, Abutty Mapilla had died of brain haemorrhage. Plants thrived in the shade of the unplastered walls. Touch-me-nots and wild screwpine covered the floor in all the rooms. Crow pheasants had built nests in the corners where the walls met.

Dasan had needed a refuge where he could lay his burden down. Chandrika had become the Velliyan Kallu in his life. He could find repose in her, flutter within her like a carefree dragonfly. Savouring the warmth and scent of her body, he tried to forget everything else. But once he came out of the unfinished house, everything would dissolve into the question: where shall I go now?

When he had worked for the movement from outside he had slept wherever he wanted. How could he do that now?

He stayed with Leela for a few days.

'You've wandered around long enough,' Leela said to him. 'Damu Writer is your father, after all. A father does not have to ask forgiveness of his son.'

'I know,' he said with deliberate harshness, 'I don't need advice from anyone.' Leela was upset. He didn't go to her house for a few days after that.

Pappan said to him, 'Come home with me.'

'There's no place I can call home,' Dasan answered. 'That's my destiny.'

He hated and despised himself when he slept in Pappan's or Chandrika's house. Why not make some money, he thought, and rent a small place? Even a room? No, not yet. He had to plan the future. He had to chalk out a set of rules for a new existence.

He could hardly think, his mind was so confused. He took to wandering around, smoking incessantly. Sometimes, when he had the money, he drank a couple of drams of arrack.

Achu came to him many times, to try and persuade him to forget what had happened and go back home. But Dasan would not think of it.

He found it difficult to think of Achu as part of the family. He was still the old Achu to Dasan. The Achu who had raped toddy tapper Kumaran's daughter. The Achu who had knocked out Vasutty's tooth. Achu could not be freed from his past after all.

He visited Achu's house once, to see Girija and the children. Achu was not at home.

Girija had grown almost unrecognisable. She had put on weight, looked much fairer. She seemed confused when she saw him. She stood half-hidden behind the door.

'Are you happy Girija?'

She nodded to say yes.

'How many children do you have?'

'Two.' Two boys, plump and healthy, like Achu.

She stayed behind the door and he waited in the veranda. Silence filled the space between them. Did they have nothing to say to each other? Did she have nothing to tell him, this sister who had been so dear to him, who had lain in his arms and wept on that night of destruction when he had crept stealthily into Mayyazhi?

He felt as if his own soul had grown unfamiliar to him.

'I'll be going, then.'

She tried to say something but could not. He never went there again.

Kanaran was now the head of the government council. He lived in the house that Big Sayiv had stayed in. Soon after he took charge, he sent for Dasan.

Dasan went straight from the arrack shop, knowing that his breath would smell of alcohol. There were many people waiting outside the house to see Kanaran. Dasan did not have to wait. He stopped short as he parted the curtains and stepped into the room.

Kanaran was seated on the chair that Big Sayiv used to sit on. Big Sayiv, whom the people of Mayyazhi had considered an avatar of God. Kanaran wore a freshly washed and ironed khadar cap on his head.

The pictures of Napoleon and Jeanne d'Arc had disappeared from the walls, to be replaced by those of Gandhi and Nehru. Below the bungalow, waves thudded on the shore.

'What has happened to you, my son?'

'Why did you send for me?'

'I can't bear to see you roam around like this, wasting your time. Where would you like to work? In the Mairie? The Secretariat? Tell me.'

The words that Big Sayiv had used to him once.

'I once refused the job you are offering me now. Can you give me anything better?'

'What do you want? Tell me.'

'Only your love and affection.'

Kanaran said, 'This bungalow is yours as well, Dasan. Stay here.'

Dasan wondered how was he going to live what remained of his life. His mind grew confused if he tried to think ...

35

It was nearly six months since the white men's ship had left Mayyazhi.

One day, Unni Nair, who had abandoned his home and his possessions in order to follow the white men, reappeared in Mayyazhi.

'Didn't you go to France?' asked the sexton, surprised. Unni Nair's grey beard and hair had grown very long. His eyes were sunk in their sockets. He hardly had the strength to walk.

Unni Nair did not answer the sexton's disturbing question.

Two days later, Kunjakkan stumbled out of the Mangalore Mail when it stopped at Mayyazhi. Kunhanan followed. They too looked emaciated and unkempt. Kunhanan supported Kunjakkan as they walked into Mayyazhi.

Carpenter Raman returned as well in a few days, looking as if he was back from a long journey. He had grown weak from starvation and from having walked miles.

Many of those who had gone away in the ship came back in the days that followed.

When the ship had rounded Colombo and anchored in Pondicherry, Unni Nair and many like him had been forced to disembark. Black and white Sayivs from Pondicherry had been taken on board.

'So what if we didn't go to France? We went on a ship, didn't we? And we saw Colombo.' Carpenter Raman sounded satisfied.

Unni Nair did not venture out for days. When he eventually did, the sexton asked again, 'Didn't you go to France?'

'Don't make fun of me, I'll certainly go to France.'

'When, Unni Nair?'

'You'll see.' Hurt, Unni Nair walked off in a huff.

After a few days, he opened his shop again. Kunjakkan went back to lighting the municipal lamps in the evening, and Carpenter Raman took up his chisel.

'We'll go. Another ship will come and take us,' said Unni Nair. He and many others in Mayyazhi believed that another ship would really come.

'Will the white men come back, Unni Nair?' Kurambi Amma asked, straining her eyes, layered with cataracts, to look at him.

'Of course they will.' Unni Nair answered confidently.

She took a pinch of snuff from her ivory snuffbox and inhaled, her eyes half-closed.

The rocks on the river bank were still warm with the sun. The clear river flowed beneath the iron bridge into the sea. Kanaka Mala could be seen in the distance, glistening in evening sunshine.

Dasan and Pappan were seated on the rock. The bridge rattled as a train hurtled over it.

'The train makes me restless. If only I could go away to some place where no one knows me.'

Now that Mayyazhi had achieved freedom, the fire of rebellion in Pappan had died down. His eyes no longer blazed. Sometimes, he would gaze at his left arm, where he had been shot, and feel sad that he no longer had a battle to fight.

'Don't go away, Pappan.'

'I've nothing to do here.'

Pappan needed to find a new field of action, ignite another fire of rebellion.

'You can go back to college and finish your studies.'

'I've forgotten everything I studied. I only know how to organize demonstrations and be kicked by policemen.'

Pappan had grown lazy. He slept for hours. Or wandered around with Dasan. Sometimes, Vasutty went with them.

Many of those who had lost their jobs when they joined the freedom movement had been given back their posts. Vasutty had refused to accept his, saying that he was not yet ready. Everyone was surprised, since he had constantly lamented the loss of his old job.

Vasutty said to Pappan, 'I'm going to astonish all of you. Wait and see.'

Vasutty stopped wandering around with Dasan and Pappan. He began to keep to himself. Sometimes, he spent time with Kanaran. Often he was not seen outside for days.

Before Mayyazhi joined the Indian Union legally, its people were given the 'option', the right to choose the citizenship they wanted—French or Indian. Caught between two destinies, many of them were confused, unable to take a decision.

Nani called out to Unni Nair as he walked through the Rue du Cimetière, 'What's the meaning of 'option', Unni Nair?' Unni Nair had already found out what the term meant and was thinking about it seriously.

'It means that you can become a white woman if you want.'

'How can I, Unni Nair? I'm black. They have a skin as red as the gulmohar flowers on the pier.'

'It doesn't mean that your skin will grow white,' Unni Nair explained. 'It means that you're taking French citizenship.'

He had to explain the term citizenship. But Nani still did not understand. At last, when she realized what it meant, Nani wanted to know: 'Do we gain anything by it, Unni Nair?'

'Imagine asking that!'

Unni Nair came up to the veranda, wiped the bench with his towel and sat down. Nani, her daughter Devi, and their children had been in despair ever since Chettiappa left. They had no food to eat, no clothes to wear. The jewels that Chettiappa had had made for Nani had begun to disappear one by one.

'Those who take the 'option' will not have to starve, ever. The white men will send them money from France. Those who want to go to France will be able to go. Those who worked for the Government will make a fortune.' Unni Nair enumerated the benefits that French citizenship would confer.

Nani's heart began to beat joyfully when she realized that she would be able to go to France. There had been no news from Chettiappa since he had sailed. If she and Devi and the five children could somehow get to France, they would be saved.

'Can everyone take the option, Unni Nair?'

'Why not?'

'Will you take it?'

Unni Nair laughed as if it was a foolish question. As he was leaving, he said to her again, persuasively, 'You and Devi had better take the option. You have your children to feed. Do it at least for them. Don't let them starve.'

Nani thought it over. So did many others in Mayyazhi.

Unni Nair said to all of them: 'Those who want to go to France can go. People who have no work will be given jobs and money. Why should you hesitate folks?'

Corporal Kittu, who was in the army, came home from Indo-China at that time. All of Mayyazhi watched him smoke expensive cigarettes and spend money lavishly.

'France is heaven.' Kittu dressed up every evening and went for a walk. 'There are women in plenty for those who want them. And wine.'

The hungry, half-starved people of Mayyazhi listened to him open-mouthed. Jobs for the unemployed. High salaries. And if they took the option, money would come for them every month from France even if they did not choose to go there.

'I, my wife and my children are going to become white people.' Carpenter Raman announced his decision in the toddy shop. Unni Nair had already opted for French citizenship. He said to the regulars in the toddy shop, 'You'd better look out for another toddy shop now. I'm going to France.'

'We're coming too, with you,' said Kunjakkan and Kunhanan.

Policeman Kannan, who was seated in the corner having a drink, was amused.

'You closed down your toddy shop and went away in the ship. What happened?'

'Another ship will come and we'll go in it. Wait and see,' said Unni Nair confidently.

Corporal Kittu, out on his evening walk, stood in front of Nani's house. He took off his hat, gazed at it and said: 'Why do you hesitate, Nani, Devi? Unni Nair and Kunhanan have already taken the option and become French.'

'Will we be able to go to France?'

'Just take it. You'll both be in France with your children in ten days. With Chettiappa.'

The Corporal came in and sat down.

'Did you see the children's father in France?' Nani's and Devi's eyes widened with expectation.

'See him? We meet every day. Chettiappa and I go to the beach in Paris every evening.'

'How is his health? Does he have anyone to cook for him?'

'Alamelu and the children are with him.'

Nani's blood boiled. So did Devi's.

The Corporal talked to them about the wonders of France until it was dusk. Actually, he had never seen France. He had fought in Indo-China for a year and had been sent home when he was wounded in the arm. As he left, he repeated, 'Don't waste your time. Take the option. You can sail the day you opt.'

Nani and Devi took the option to become French and so did Kunhichirutha.

Pappan and Janardanan warned all of them: 'None of you will be able to go to France. Only government employees win benefit from French citizenship.'

No one listened to them. More people took French citizenship in the days that followed. Some took it because they were greedy for money. Others were inspired by a great nostalgic love for royalty. Some, like Kunhichirutha and Nani, took it in the hope of recovering their lost Sayivs who were now in France.

EVERYONE WAS ASTONISHED TO learn that Vasutty had taken French citizenship.

Kanaran's head spun. Unni Nair, however, was delighted. 'He's seen reason at last.'

Unni Nair hated Vasutty, Dasan and Kanaran. He cursed them all the time. When Kanaran had moved to Big Sayiv's bungalow, Unni Nair had been furious. Vasutty had redeemed himself now.

'There's a man for you,' said Unni Nair happily.

Vasutty became Mayyazhi's favourite topic of discussion. Achu came back from work one day and woke up Damu Writer who was dozing in his easy chair:

'Did you know Vasutty has taken the option? He's French now.'

'Who told you?' Damu Writer did not believe him. 'Why did he rebel against the white men then?'

Achu could not answer that. Vasutty had given up his job to join the freedom movement. And reduced his family to starvation.

'If he had done this earlier, his poor father would not have died starving.'

There had not been even gruel water in the house to wet load-bearer Pokkan's parched throat when he was dying.

Damu Writer got up and started to pace up and down the veranda. 'So people are coming to their senses at last,' Damu Writer said to himself. 'Thank God Vasutty is not like my son.' He lay down in the easy chair and closed his eyes.

Vasutty stopped going out and refused to meet those who went to see him. Kanaran sent for him repeatedly but he did not go.

After a week, he went to Pappan's house. He knew he would find Dasan there.

Standing in the courtyard, he called out to Pappan. Pappan and Dasan came out. They looked at one another.

'I came to say goodbye,' said Vasutty. 'I'm going to Pondicherry tomorrow and sailing from there to France.'

Pappan and Dasan stared at him.

'What's come over you?'

Pappan was trembling. 'I won't let you go to France, Vasutty. I'll kill you first.'

Vasutty laughed. He wore clean, ironed clothes. His hair was oiled and parted neatly on the side.

'Tell me, Vasutty, why are you doing this?'

'I can do what I please, can't I? The struggle for freedom is over. Now, we have the freedom to do what we want.'

'What about your conscience? And the principles you had?'

'My old principles died with the freedom of Mayyazhi. I have new ones now.'

'Are principles like clothes that you can change when you want?'

'They have to change with the times. I never hated the white men. I asked them to leave Mayyazhi because history demanded it. They did not recognize that demand, so I had to demonstrate it to them with my actions. They've gone now. And they're not our enemies anymore. They're nothing to us. Taking French citizenship now is like taking British or American citizenship.' Vasutty cleared his throat. He wiped his neck and face with his handkerchief. 'There'll be one person who will understand why I am going to France: to put an end to my family's poverty. My father, who starved to death, his buttocks eaten by bedsores.'

There was silence.

'Adieu, my friends.'

Vasutty held out his hand. Neither Dasan nor Pappan moved. Vasutty stood with his hand extended for a while, then turned and went away.

Next day, he took the train for Pondicherry. He sailed for France a week later.

Soon after Vasutty left, Pappan also left Mayyazhi. He had no clear idea where he was going. He came to Dasan one day, a bag on his shoulder.

'I'm going away.'

'Where, Pappan?'

'I don't know. Somewhere far away.'

Pappan had been talking constantly of going away. He had taken to going to the station to watch the trains come and go.

Dasan accompanied Pappan to the railway station.

'I'll write. Say goodbye to Chandrika for me.'

Every day, trains passed through Mayyazhi at twelve-thirty and one. One came from the north and the other from the south. They were mail trains bound in different directions. They were always late. It was never certain which one would come first.

'I'll take the one that comes first,' said Pappan. 'I have no clear destination.'

They waited on the platform.

'Dasan, you must take a decision of some kind now. You can't go on like this.'

'I've made my decision.' There was a vacancy for a teacher's post at the Cours Complémentaire that he could easily get. He would find a place to live in near the Place d'Armes where the half-French crowded together in small tenements.

Pappan felt relieved.

They heard the train. One of the trains. Pappan kept his word and boarded the train that came first.

'Some day, I'll be back.'

He climbed in and waved as the train moved. Dasan watched until it disappeared from sight. Then he walked back slowly, wrapped in his solitude.

36

Once he became a pensioner, Bharathan said goodbye to the sea and the wharves and came home.

Leela, Chandrika, his old uncle, who could hardly hold himself upright, and many relatives were assembled on the veranda. He looked for Dasan amongst them. He had thought of him when he got down from the train. Now that Mayyazhi was free, surely Dasan would have come out of jail and be waiting to receive him.

'Doesn't Dasan come here?' he asked Leela as they sat down to eat. She shook her head. Chandrika stopped eating. Chandrika had grown very thin and her face looked smaller. Only her black hair was as dense as ever. Her pale eyes had no kohl in them.

Bharathan discussed his plans that evening with Leela. He wanted to build a big house and find Chandrika a good husband.

He met Dasan after a couple of days. 'Where do you live now?' he asked, as they walked through the Rule de l'Eglise, his arm over Dasan's shoulder.

'You think I have nowhere to stay?'

'Stay with me. It's better than being with strangers.'

'Let me think about it.' Dasan knew he could not stay with Bharathan. He visited Bharathan often though. Leela no longer talked to him as she used to. Her eyes followed him all the time as if she was afraid of him.

The plants in Abutty Mapilla's house grew thick and wild. Lying against the wall, Dasan stroked Chandrika's hair and said, 'Your mother doesn't like me anymore. But I like you more than ever.'

Chandrika laughed softly.

IT BEGAN TO RAIN incessantly. The sky descended to the level of the cross on the steeple. The red, muddied river flowed beneath a heavy screen of rain into the sea. One day, the river finally broke its bounds and flooded the land. The whole town was waterlogged. Boats plied along the Rue de la Gare. Only one lamp-post showed above the endless sheet of water. Hundreds of living creatures—scorpions, snakes, worms, frogs—clung to it as the water surged higher and higher. It looked like a little Noah's Ark.

Chandrika's house was surrounded by water. All day, Bharathan sat hunched over his table, perusing the blueprints for his new house. He had bought the land on which Abutty Mapilla's unfinished house stood. Bharathan could not bear to be parted from the blueprints. He pored over them for hours, marking, jotting, scoring out with a pencil. They lay on his bed even at night.

Sometimes, he went to the site with Dasan. 'This is our bedroom.' He would mark the place with his cane on the ground. 'There's a bathroom here, and here a small balcony, where we can sit and have a chat. Or a drink.'

Bharathan would shake with laughter. He had put on weight after he came home. His face was as red as a cashew fruit.

'Is Abutty Mapilla's house going to be demolished, Acha?' asked Chandrika.

'Of course, you foolish girl.'

'Don't do that, please.'

'All right, I won't.' Bharathan laughed. 'When you get married, you and your husband can stay in it. What do you think, Dasan?'

Dasan kept quiet. Kanaran had told him that he would receive his appointment order for the post of a teacher at the Cours Complémentaire in a week. After that, he would have to pluck up courage and talk to Bharathan about Chandrika.

Bharathan's workers began to pull down the unfinished structure. The crow pheasants flew away with piercing cries, beating their red wings. Their eggs fell down and broke, the walls were soon razed to the ground.

The sky grew heavier and the incessant rain turned into a flood. Darkness lay over the town. Only the menacing sound of raindrops splashing on the rising water would be heard.

It was past midnight, the hour that brought bad dreams to Mayyazhi.

Suddenly, the lights began to flicker alive in Bharathan's house. Bharathan was hurrying upstairs with a lamp in his hand, Leela behind him. Chandrika's room was bolted from inside. Bharathan banged on the door and called out. There was no answer. Leela muttered something indistinct. In the glow of the lamp, the veins on Bharathan's neck stood out. His eyes were narrowed.

'Chandrika, open the door or I'll break it down.' The lamp in Bharathan's hand shook.

The door opened. Dasan and Bharathan looked at each other. Chandrika stood behind Dasan, her hair dishevelled.

Blind with anger and pain, Bharathan could hardly breathe.

'How could you do this to me?' The words choked in his throat.

'It's not his fault, Achan,' Chandrika said. 'I asked him here.'

'Don't you dare talk to me.' Bharathan's voice rose above the wind and the rain. 'Come down, Dasan.'

Dasan followed him downstairs.

'Do you have anything to say to me?'

'Yes, I do. Ever since I began to grow up, I've not known peace of mind for a single day. The freedom of Mayyazhi dried everyone's tears except mine. I'll go mad without Chandrika, she's my only hope.'

'You want my daughter to share her bed with you so that you don't go mad?'

'It's the first time you've seen us together. That's why you're so upset. But it's not the first time we ...'

'Get out!' Bharathan pointed to the door. The lamp shook so much that it nearly fell from his hand. He unbolted the door.

Thick layers of darkness lay over the rice fields.

'Don't ever set foot here again.'

The door slammed shut. Dasan stepped into the darkness and was soaked through in a moment. He walked along the muddy road, shivering in the cold wind.

He walked to the Vignanaposhini Library, where he and his friends had once held so many discussions. The library which had shaped Dasan's destiny. It had introduced him to the literatures of the world. He had learnt his first lessons in history there.

Dasan asked for permission to sleep in the library. The young men who worked there knew his tragic story and held him in high esteem. The Vignanaposhini Library with its moth-eaten volumes of the French classics became Dasan's home.

37

Clouds drifted over the Mayyazhi river and blew away. The cross on the church steeple glittered in the clear sunlight. The water had drained out of the rice fields and roads. Birds flew in again over the quietened river.

'We can start work now,' Koran Maistry said to Bharathan.

'You must finish the work by the Thira festival. Can you do that, Maistry?'

'Yes. But I'll have to get workers from outside.'

Bharathan took out the blueprints which he kept locked up in the cupboard and gave them to Koran. Work was begun at once. A truckload of workers came from the east. Dust and sand filled the air.

Bharathan would call out to Chandrika when he went to the building site. 'Aren't you coming?'

'No,' Chandrika would shake her head.

'It's your bungalow,' Bharathan would say to her. 'I'm building it for you.'

'Why would I need a bungalow?' Chandrika would ask, wiping her eyes with the tip of her saree. She had not seen Dasan since he went away on the day of the flood. Bharathan would not allow her to go out alone.

The house was ready before the Thira festival. When the palm leaf screens were removed, it sprang like a marvel from the earth, excelling Leslie Sayiv's in elegance. Bharathan had designed it with the arches and decorative details he had observed in the beautiful houses in the countries he had visited.

'It's your house, Chandrika,' he said, his arm around her shoulder. 'How fortunate you are.'

Bharathan lay awake all night, thinking. He got up many times to light a cigarette. His eyelids ached, but he did not fall asleep until dawn. And he woke up almost at once. Leela was awake as well and gazing at the crystal lamp hanging from the ceiling. The sky was growing brighter.

Leela had not slept either. Every time she closed her eyes, she had seen Chandrika's tear-stained face.

'Chandrika won't agree to this, I'm sure of it,' she said.

'If she doesn't, we'll go ahead without her consent. We can't go on like this.'

'I'm tired of seeing her in tears.'

Exhausted with weeping, Chandrika had fallen into a heavy sleep. She did not know that a wealthy young man was coming that morning from Thalassery to see her and that her parents were planning to separate her from Dasan.

When she woke up, Leela had to force her to have a bath and change her clothes. Her heart lightened a little when she saw Chandrika's image in the mirror. She prayed silently, let her not cry, let her not have a tear-stained face. But the tears washed away the kohl she applied on Chandrika's eyes even before she took her hand away.

Chandrika recognized the young man, he had been at college with her. But she could not even manage a smile for him. He kept talking to her but she could not make out what he was saying, her mind was elsewhere. When the young man left, her parents asked her what she thought of him.

'I won't agree to this, even if you kill me.' Chandrika covered her face with her hands.

Bharathan lunged forward furiously, his face flushed.

'You evil creature, you were born to give us trouble!' He left the room, slamming the door. Next morning, he said to Leela, 'I'll see that the wedding takes place whether she consents to it or not. Or my name is not Bharathan.'

He began the preparations for the wedding. The date was decided. As he sat smoking cigarettes one morning, relief battling with a sense of foreboding, he heard a footstep in the courtyard.

Dasan. Perspiration was running down his sunburnt face. His shirt was buttoned in the wrong order. He was gasping for breath.

Bharathan rushed upstairs and bolted Chandrika's door from outside. He did not want her to see Dasan.

'Is it true, what I heard?' asked Dasan.

'Yes.'

'Has Chandrika consented?'

'Yes.' Bharathan did not look at Dasan's face.

'That's a lie. I want to see her.'

'You mustn't see her again. Go away.' Bharathan went to his chair and sat down, his head bent, covering his face with his hand.

'God will never forgive you.'

Bharathan heard Dasan's footsteps recede. He raised his head. Leela was beside him. They watched Dasan walk through the field in the hot sunshine, reeling like a drunken man.

Dasan's head spun with the lack of sleep. He gazed at Velliyan Kallu, glimmering in the distance. Sometimes, it disappeared from sight behind a rising wave and then took shape again. He saw souls hovering over it like dragonflies. Some of them, he knew, would take on human form and return to Mayyazhi to live another life.

He started, hearing footsteps and voices next to him. Bharathan and his neighbour Shanku. Dasan's heart turned over. Why was Bharathan here? Could he have changed his mind at the last moment?

'Where is Chandrika?' Bharathan's face looked like a madman's.

'Where is Chandrika?' he repeated. Dasan looked at them in turn, bewildered.

Shanku gripped Dasan's shoulder and shook it. 'Didn't she come to you? Where have you hidden her?'

'Dasan, tell me the truth. Have you seen Chandrika?'

'No.'

Desperate, Bharathan stared at Dasan.

'Where can we look for her now?' murmured Shanku.

Bharathan's bungalow was crowded with people. All of them turned to look at Dasan. No one spoke. Leela could be heard weeping inside.

Someone entered.

'What is it?'

'We looked in the church tank as well.'

'What about Assanar's well?'

'There's no tank or well left now to search in.'

She had gone with only the clothes she wore. No gold, no jewels. Those who had gone in search of her returned at dusk. Bharathan's bungalow turned into a house of mourning.

Dasan stayed in the courtyard, standing as still as stone. The breeze blowing from Velliyan Rock carried Chandrika's voice to him. 'When I grow up, Dasetta, will you marry me?'

He knew then where Chandrika was. No one would ever find her. Only he knew. That she was on Velliyan Rock where souls fluttered like dragonflies.

Much of the fortune that Bharathan had amassed on the sea was spent in trying to trace his daughter. But Chandrika was never seen again.

Only Dasan often heard her anklets tinkling in the gentle breeze that blew in from the sea in the mist-filled dawn.

TIME WENT BY. WITH every day, the features of free Mayyazhi changed. And the destiny of its people changed as well.

Kunhichirutha no longer waited for David Sayiv. She went to work in the new cloth mill and her life had a different purpose. Nani died waiting for Chettiappa to come back. Devi worked as a domestic servant, so that she could earn enough to bring up Chettiappa's children. Unni Nair and Kunhanan disappeared behind time's curtain.

The roads which used to be filled with potholes are now firm and tarred. The oil lamps that Kunjakkan used to light no longer shed their glow over Mayyazhi. Electric lights have taken their place.

Thirty years after he had closed his door on the outside world, Gaston Sayiv hobbled slowly out of his house with the aid of a stick and wandered through the streets of Mayyazhi like a ghost. His hair had grown completely white. He walked until he reached the calm sea. He did not want to go further, he knew he had reached his destination. The stick fell from his hand.

Leslie Sayiv's deserted house collapsed one day, succumbing to the violence of time, when a strong wind blew from the sea. With the arrival of the monsoon, it was reduced to a heap of rubble.

The drama that had unfolded on the banks of the Mayyazhi river was drawing to a close. Kurambi Amma, one of its main actors and spectators, waited, grey and wrinkled, for her end to come. Opening her unseeing eyes as Kowsu and Girija moistened her lips with water, she asked in a feeble voice,

'Has the ship arrived?'

'No,' said Girija.

The grip on the ivory snuffbox loosened. The precious box, a treasure house of legends and tales, fell on the ground and broke. The worn-out eyes closed slowly. Two teardrops glistened under the eyelids.

The bells from the Church of the Virgin tolled mournfully over Mayyazhi.

The next day, as the sun rose over the river, the funeral crows flew in from the east, across the Kanaka Mala. The church bells rang for morning service.

Damu Writer opened his eyes. He had been lying unconscious for two days. He looked at the faces around him. He found them difficult to recognize.

'Water ...' His discoloured lips moved. Girija lifted his head and Kowsu poured water slowly down his parched throat.

Damu's feet had turned icy cold. His eyes went around again, searching for someone. They finally rested on Achu.

'Dasan ...'

The cold crept up through his blue fingertips.

'I want to see him.'

Achu hurried out, praying, let Damu Writer be spared until Dasan comes. Breathless, he reached the seashore. He stopped, unable to move forward.

The place where Dasan used to sit was empty.

Across the water, Velliyan Rock could be seen like a large teardrop. Souls fluttered over it like dragonflies. One of them was Dasan.

About the Author and Translator

Maniyambath Mukundan (born 10 September 1942) worked as a cultural attaché at the Embassy of France in Delhi from 1961 to 2004, while concurrently working as an author. Many of his early works are set in Mahe (Mayyazhi), his homeland, which earned him the moniker 'Mayyazhiyude Kathakaaran' (Mayyazhi's storyteller). He is known to be one of the pioneers of modernity in Malayalam literature.

Mukundan has been awarded the Ezhuthachan Puraskaram, the highest literary honour given by the Government of Kerala, the Crossword Book Award twice, first in 1999 for *On the Banks of the Mayyazhi* and again in 2006 for *Kesavan's Lamentations*, the Sahitya Akademi award and N.V. Puraskaram for *Daivathinte Vikrithikal (God's Mischief)*, and the 2023 JCB Prize for Literature for *Delhi: A Soliloquy*. His stories and novels have been widely translated into various Indian languages, English and French, and four of his books have been adapted into award-winning films. He is also a recipient of the Chevalier des Arts et des Lettres of the Government of France.

Gita Krishnankutty has been translating works of Malayalam writers, including M.T. Vasudevan Nair, Lalithambika Anterjanam, Paul Zacharia, Anand and others into English for several decades. She has received the Katha Award for Translation twice, in 1993 and 2000, and also the Crossword Award in 1999 for *On the Banks of the Mayyazhi*. She lives in Chennai.

HarperCollins *Publishers* India

At HarperCollins India, we believe in telling the best stories and finding the widest readership for our books in every format possible. We started publishing in 1992; a great deal has changed since then, but what has remained constant is the passion with which our authors write their books, the love with which readers receive them, and the sheer joy and excitement that we as publishers feel in being a part of the publishing process.

Over the years, we've had the pleasure of publishing some of the finest writing from the subcontinent and around the world, including several award-winning titles and some of the biggest bestsellers in India's publishing history. But nothing has meant more to us than the fact that millions of people have read the books we published, and that somewhere, a book of ours might have made a difference.

As we look to the future, we go back to that one word— a word which has been a driving force for us all these years.

Read.